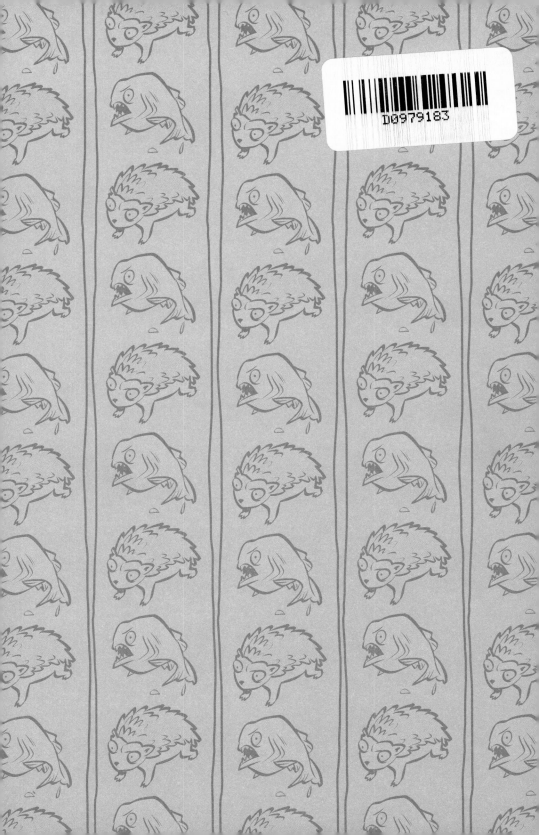

PLANTS VS. ZOMBIES

BULLY FOR YOU

Written by **PAUL TOBIN**
Art by **RON CHAN**
Colors by **MATTHEW J. RAINWATER**
Letters by **STEVE DUTRO**
Cover by **RON CHAN**

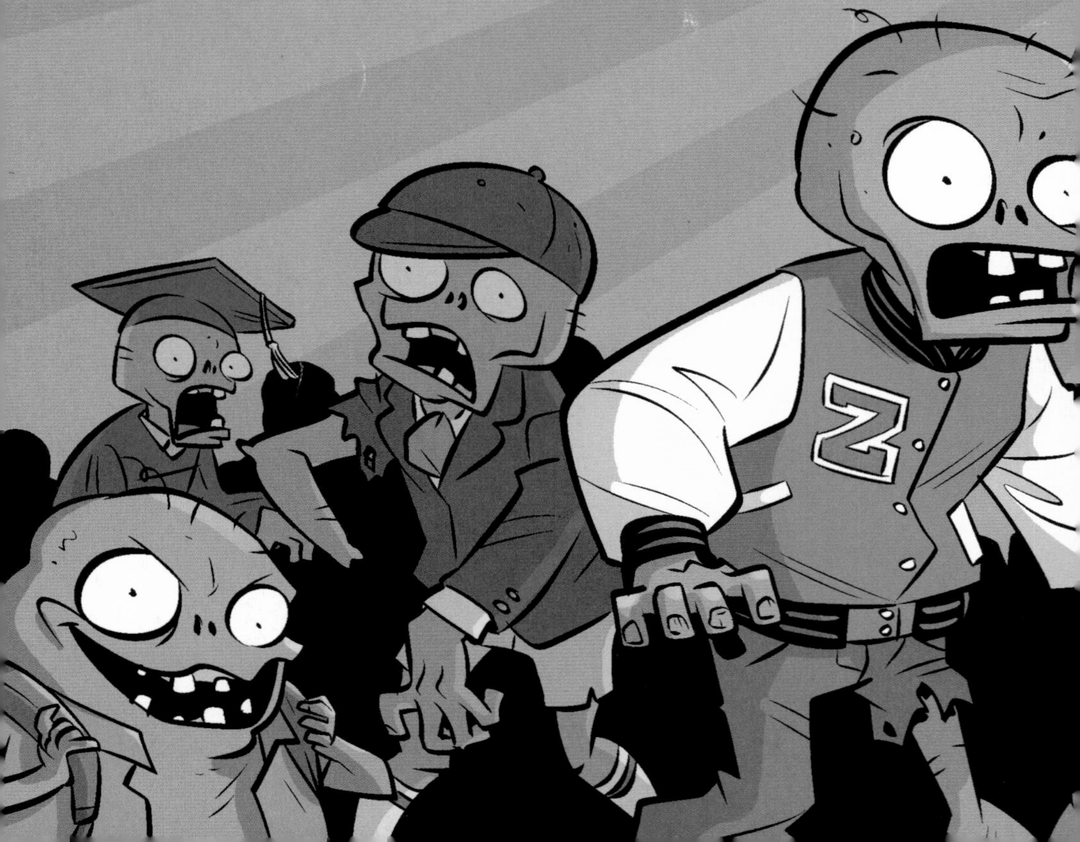

PLANTS VS. ZOMBIES

BULLY FOR YOU

DARK HORSE BOOKS

President and Publisher **MIKE RICHARDSON**
Editor **PHILIP R. SIMON**
Assistant Editor **ROXY POLK**
Designer **KAT LARSON**
Digital Production **CHRISTINA McKENZIE**

Special thanks to **LEIGH BEACH, GARY CLAY,
SHANA DOERR, A.J. RATHBUN, KRISTEN STAR,
JEREMY VANHOOZER,** and everyone at PopCap Games.

First edition: October 2015
ISBN 978-1-61655-889-5

10 9 8 7 6 5 4
Printed in Canada

DarkHorse.com | PopCap.com

▷ No plants were harmed in the making of this comic. Numerous zombies
with various zombie-focused collegiate majors, however, definitely were.

This volume collects the stories found in *Plants vs. Zombies: Bully for You* #1–#3 and the *Plants vs. Zombies* "The Curse
of the Flower-Bot" short story that appeared in *Free Comic Book Day 2015: All Ages*, originally published by Dark Horse
Comics in 2015. | Published by Dark Horse Books, a division of Dark Horse Comics LLC, 10956 SE Main Street, Milwaukie,
OR 97222 | International Licensing: (503) 905-2377 | To find a comics shop in your area, visit comicshoplocator.com |

NEIL HANKERSON Executive Vice President **TOM WEDDLE** Chief Financial Officer **RANDY STRADLEY** Vice President of Publishing
MICHAEL MARTENS Vice President of Book Trade Sales **SCOTT ALLIE** Editor in Chief **MATT PARKINSON** Vice President of
Marketing **DAVID SCROGGY** Vice President of Product Development **DALE LaFOUNTAIN** Vice President of Information Technology
DARLENE VOGEL Senior Director of Print, Design, and Production **KEN LIZZI** General Counsel **DAVEY ESTRADA** Editorial Director
CHRIS WARNER Senior Books Editor **CARY GRAZZINI** Director of Print and Development **LIA RIBACCHI** Art Director **CARA NIECE**

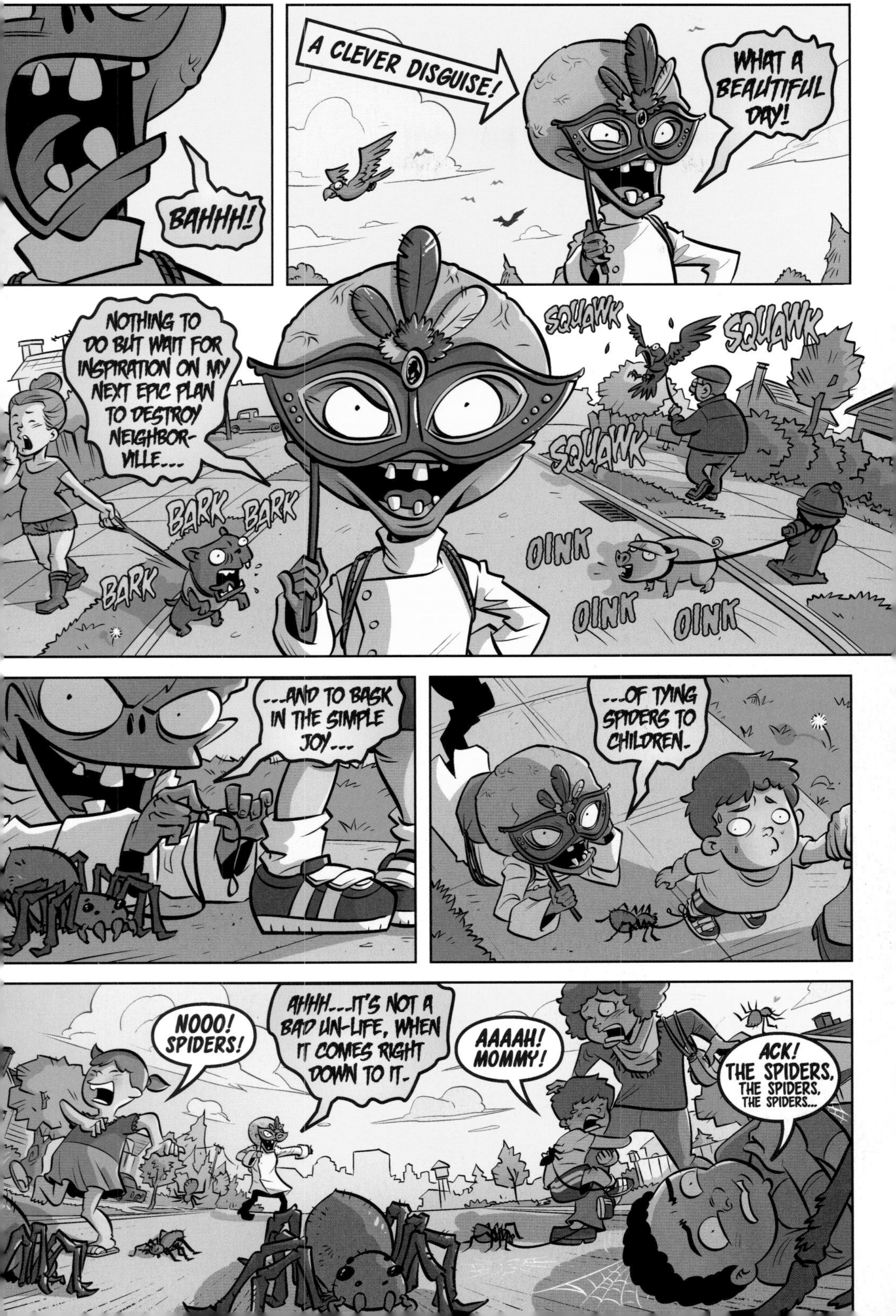
BAHHH!
A CLEVER DISGUISE!
WHAT A BEAUTIFUL DAY!
NOTHING TO DO BUT WAIT FOR INSPIRATION ON MY NEXT EPIC PLAN TO DESTROY NEIGHBOR-VILLE...
SQUAWK
SQUAWK
SQUAWK
BARK
BARK
BARK
OINK
OINK
OINK
...AND TO BASK IN THE SIMPLE JOY...
...OF TYING SPIDERS TO CHILDREN.
NOOO! SPIDERS!
AHHH...IT'S NOT A BAD UN-LIFE, WHEN IT COMES RIGHT DOWN TO IT.
AAAAH! MOMMY!
ACK! THE SPIDERS, THE SPIDERS, THE SPIDERS...

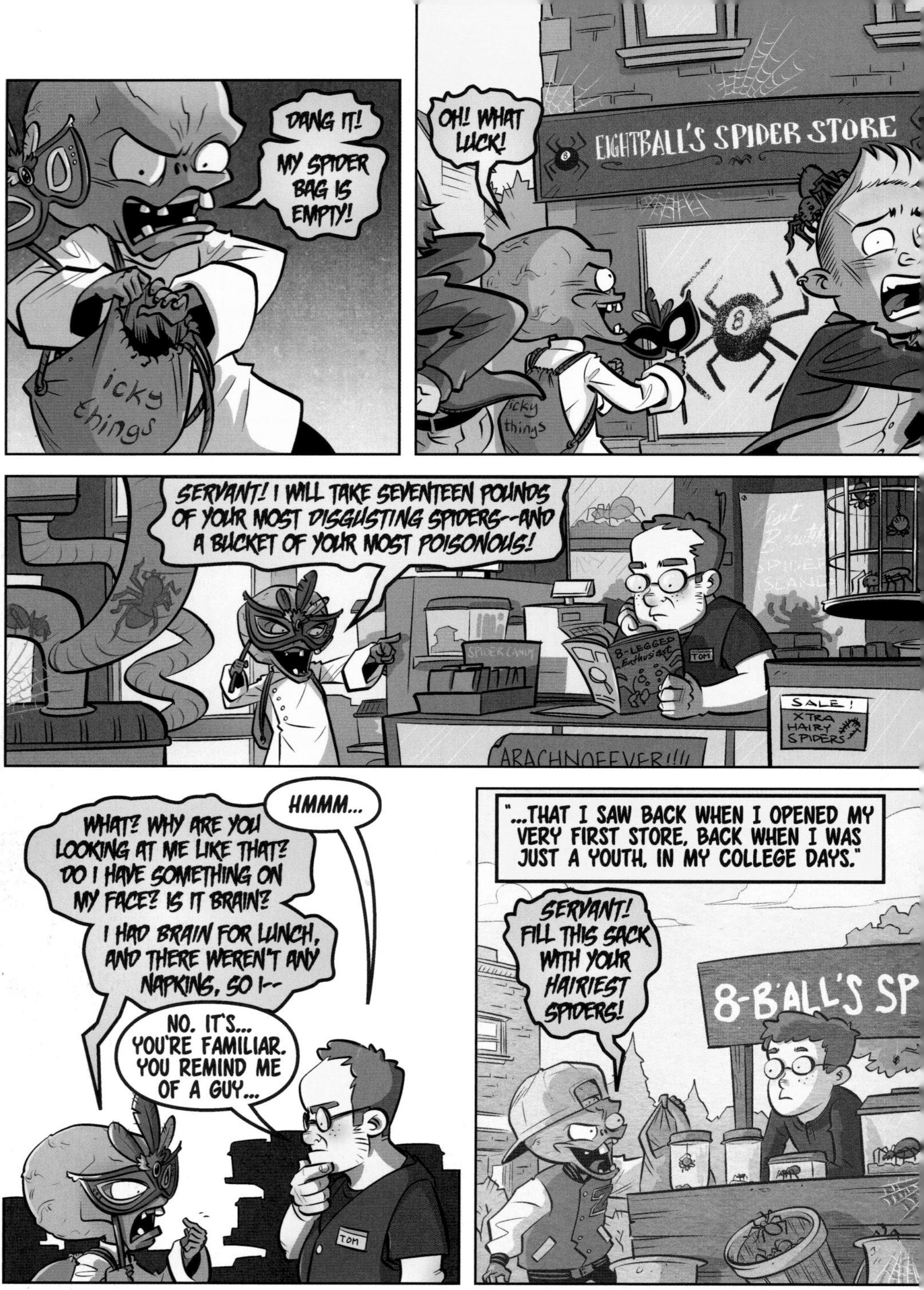
DANG IT!
MY SPIDER BAG IS EMPTY!
icky things
OH! WHAT LUCK!
EIGHTBALL'S SPIDER STORE
icky things
SERVANT! I WILL TAKE SEVENTEEN POUNDS OF YOUR MOST DISGUSTING SPIDERS--AND A BUCKET OF YOUR MOST POISONOUS!
SPIDER CANDY
8-LEGGED Enthusiast
TOM
SALE! XTRA HAIRY SPIDERS
ARACHNOFEVER!!!
HMMM...
WHAT? WHY ARE YOU LOOKING AT ME LIKE THAT? DO I HAVE SOMETHING ON MY FACE? IS IT BRAIN?
I HAD BRAIN FOR LUNCH, AND THERE WEREN'T ANY NAPKINS, SO I--
NO. IT'S... YOU'RE FAMILIAR. YOU REMIND ME OF A GUY...
TOM
"...THAT I SAW BACK WHEN I OPENED MY VERY FIRST STORE, BACK WHEN I WAS JUST A YOUTH, IN MY COLLEGE DAYS."
SERVANT! FILL THIS SACK WITH YOUR HAIRIEST SPIDERS!
8-B'ALL'S SP
AH, YES... COLLEGE DAYS.

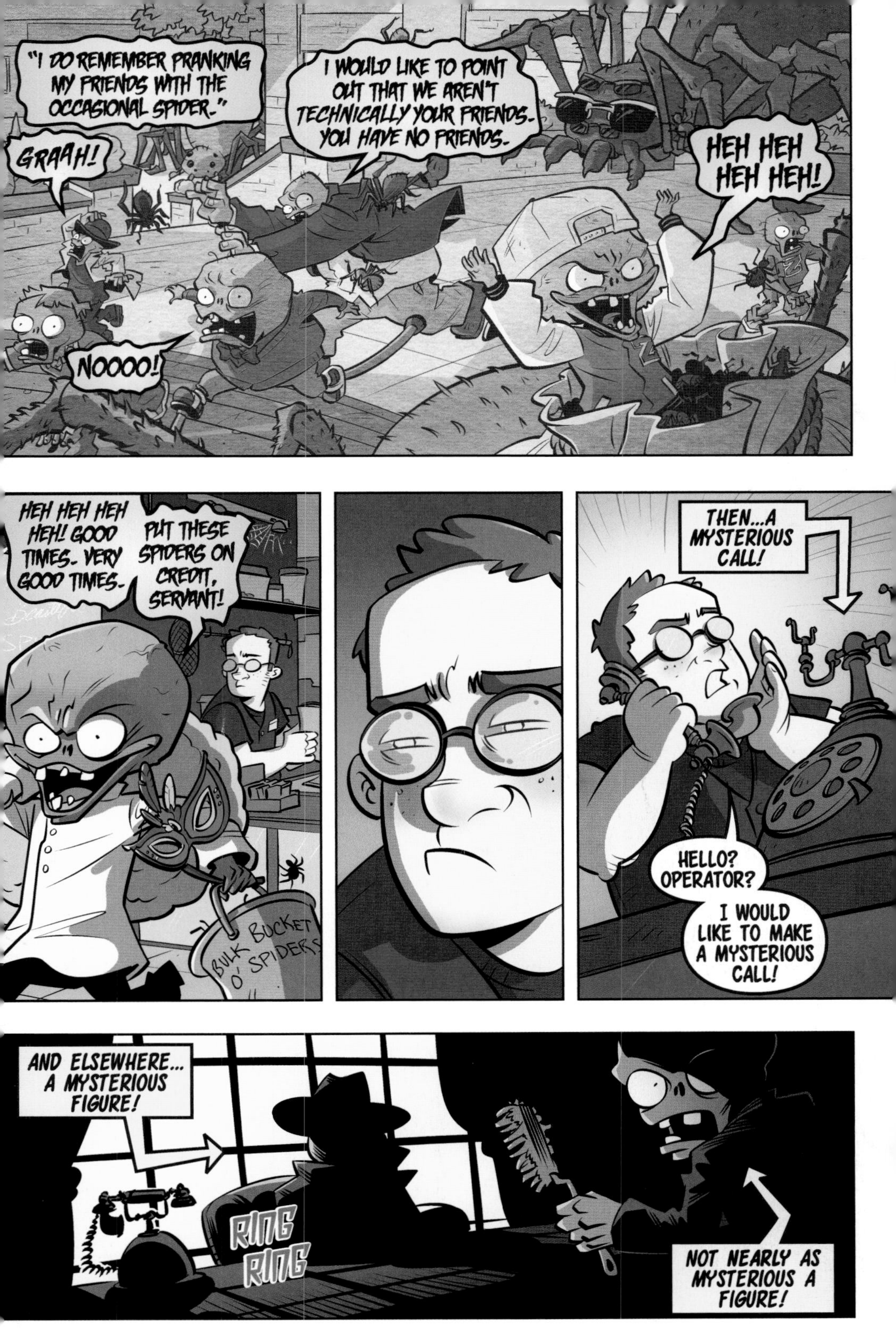
"I DO REMEMBER PRANKING MY FRIENDS WITH THE OCCASIONAL SPIDER."
I WOULD LIKE TO POINT OUT THAT WE AREN'T TECHNICALLY YOUR FRIENDS. YOU HAVE NO FRIENDS.
GRAAH!
HEH HEH HEH HEH!
NOOOO!
HEH HEH HEH HEH! GOOD TIMES. VERY GOOD TIMES.
PUT THESE SPIDERS ON CREDIT, SERVANT!
BULK BUCKET O' SPIDERS
THEN...A MYSTERIOUS CALL!
HELLO? OPERATOR?
I WOULD LIKE TO MAKE A MYSTERIOUS CALL!
AND ELSEWHERE... A MYSTERIOUS FIGURE!
RING RING
NOT NEARLY AS MYSTERIOUS A FIGURE!

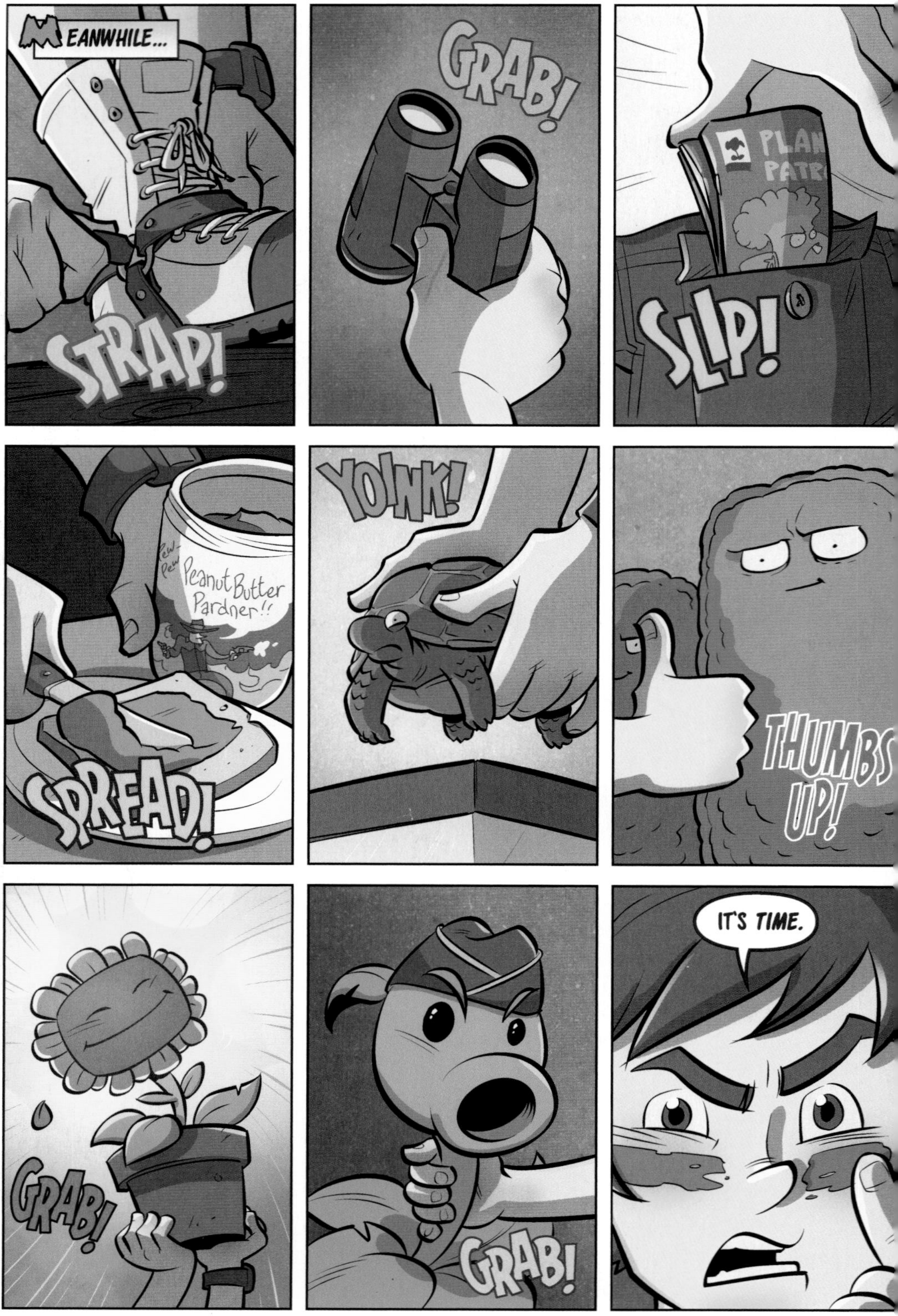
MEANWHILE...
STRAP!
GRAB!
PLAN
PATR
SLIP!
Pew-Pew
Peanut Butter Pardner!!
SPREAD!
YOINK!
THUMBS UP!
GRAB!
GRAB!
IT'S TIME.

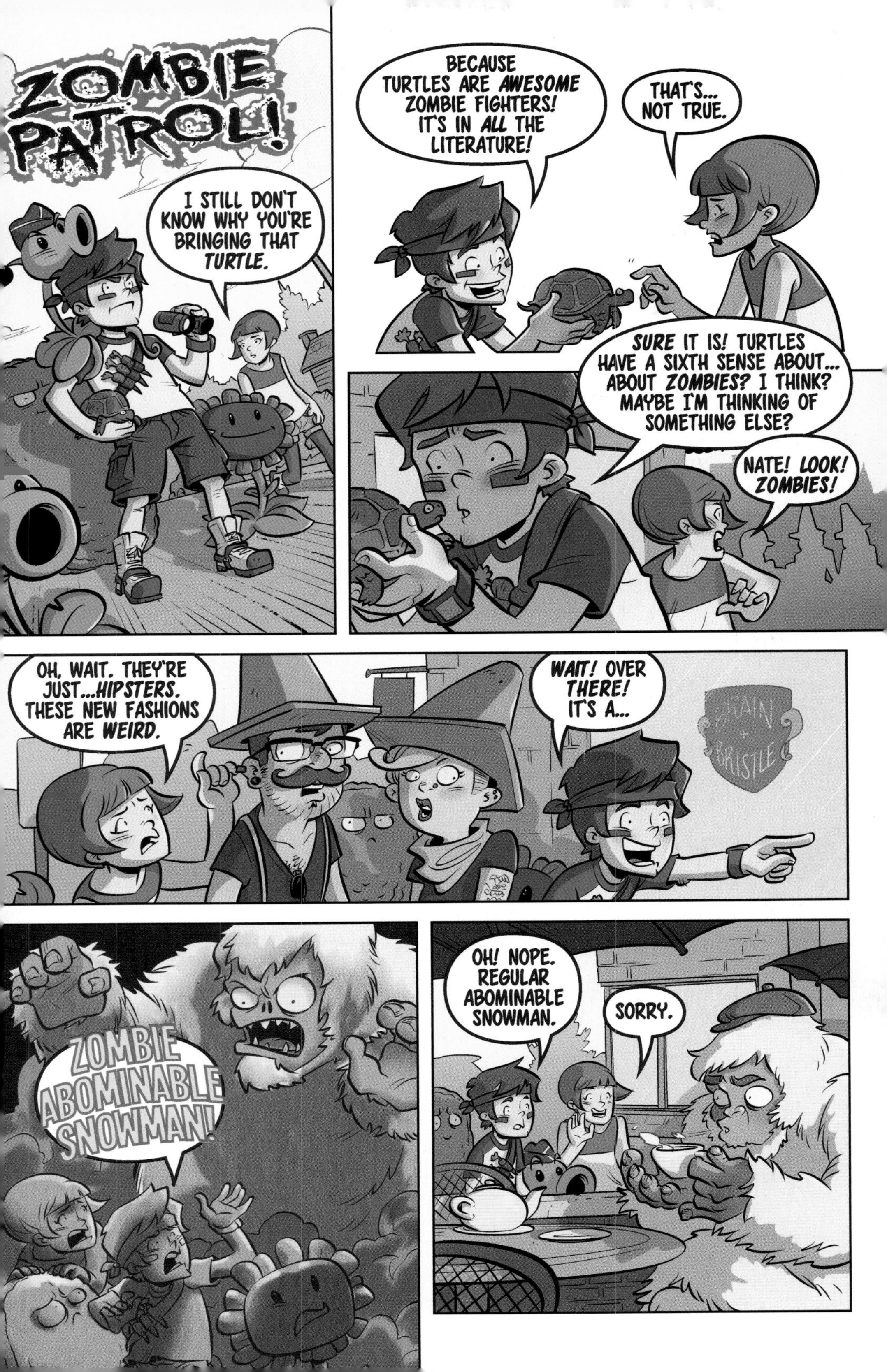
ZOMBIE PATROL!
I STILL DON'T KNOW WHY YOU'RE BRINGING THAT TURTLE.
BECAUSE TURTLES ARE AWESOME ZOMBIE FIGHTERS! IT'S IN ALL THE LITERATURE!
THAT'S... NOT TRUE.
SURE IT IS! TURTLES HAVE A SIXTH SENSE ABOUT... ABOUT ZOMBIES? I THINK? MAYBE I'M THINKING OF SOMETHING ELSE?
NATE! LOOK! ZOMBIES!
OH, WAIT. THEY'RE JUST...HIPSTERS. THESE NEW FASHIONS ARE WEIRD.
WAIT! OVER THERE! IT'S A...
BRAIN + BRISTLE
ZOMBIE ABOMINABLE SNOWMAN!
OH! NOPE. REGULAR ABOMINABLE SNOWMAN.
SORRY.

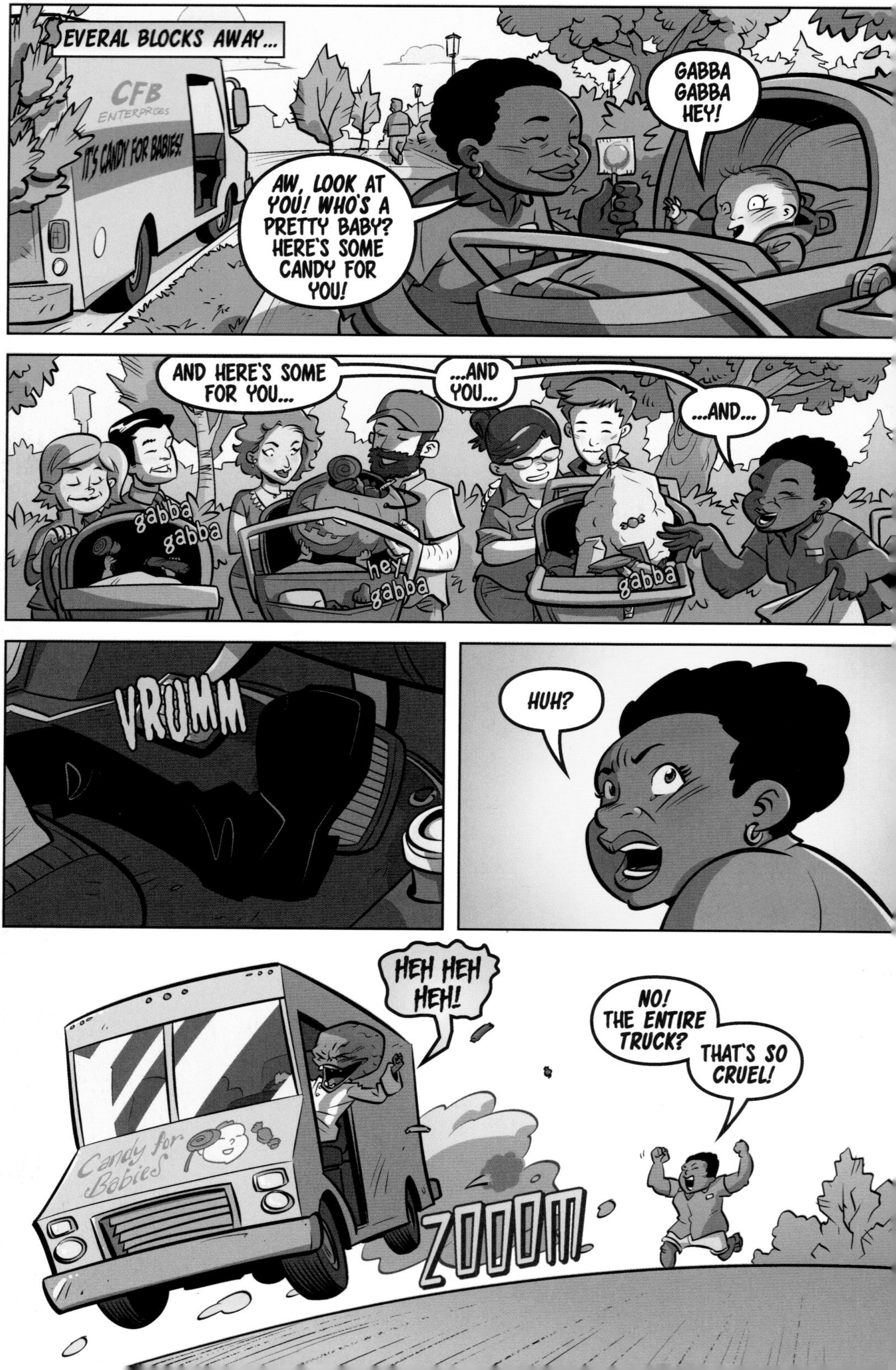
SEVERAL BLOCKS AWAY...
CFB ENTERPRISES
IT'S CANDY FOR BABIES!
AW, LOOK AT YOU! WHO'S A PRETTY BABY? HERE'S SOME CANDY FOR YOU!
GABBA GABBA HEY!
AND HERE'S SOME FOR YOU...
...AND YOU...
...AND...
gabba gabba
hey gabba
gabba
VROMM
HUH?
HEH HEH HEH!
Candy for Babies
ZOOOM
NO! THE ENTIRE TRUCK?
THAT'S SO CRUEL!

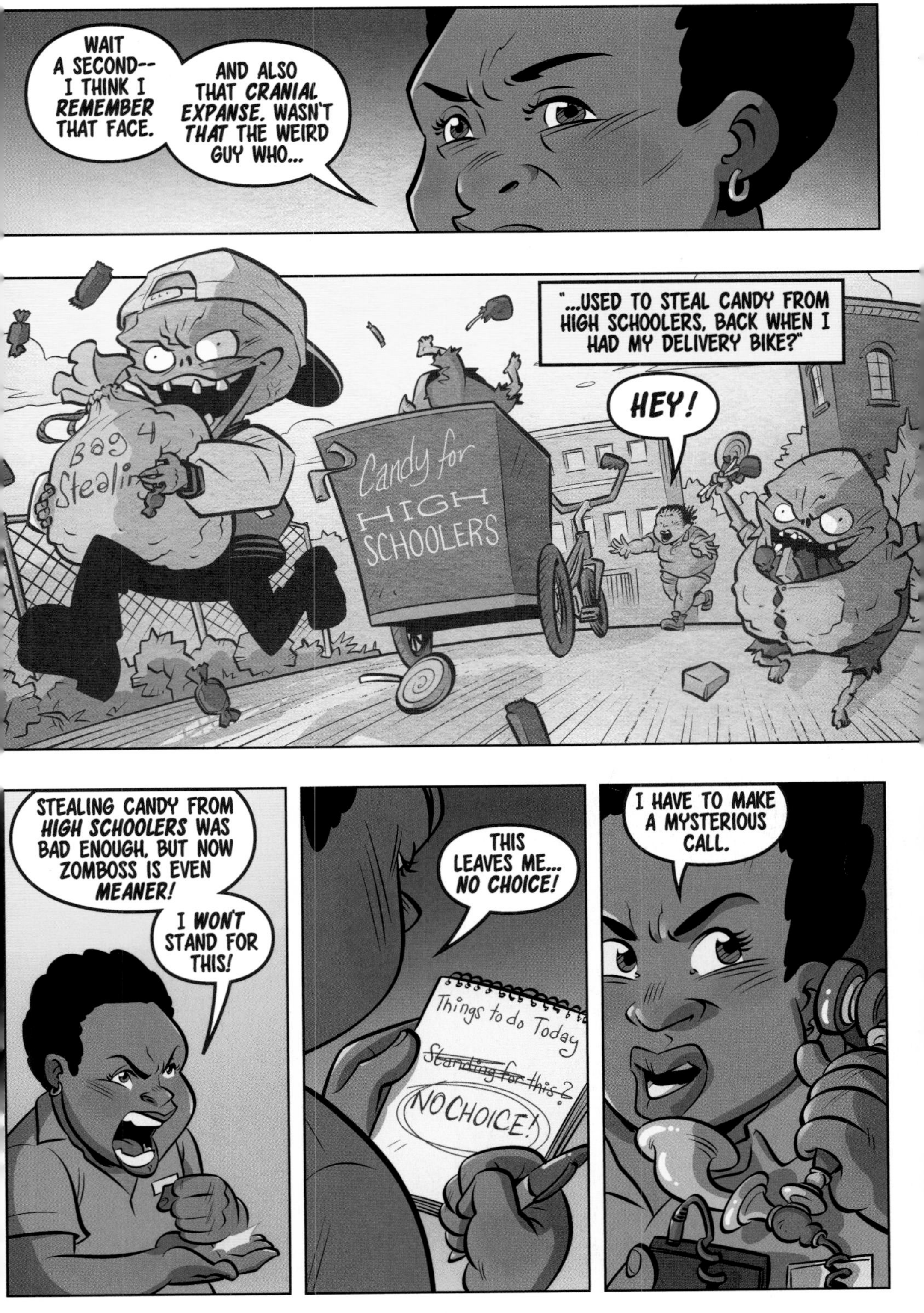
WAIT A SECOND-- I THINK I REMEMBER THAT FACE.
AND ALSO THAT CRANIAL EXPANSE. WASN'T THAT THE WEIRD GUY WHO...
"...USED TO STEAL CANDY FROM HIGH SCHOOLERS, BACK WHEN I HAD MY DELIVERY BIKE?"
HEY!
Bag 4 Stealin
Candy for HIGH SCHOOLERS
STEALING CANDY FROM HIGH SCHOOLERS WAS BAD ENOUGH, BUT NOW ZOMBOSS IS EVEN MEANER!
I WON'T STAND FOR THIS!
THIS LEAVES ME... NO CHOICE!
Things to do Today
Standing for this?
NO CHOICE!
I HAVE TO MAKE A MYSTERIOUS CALL.

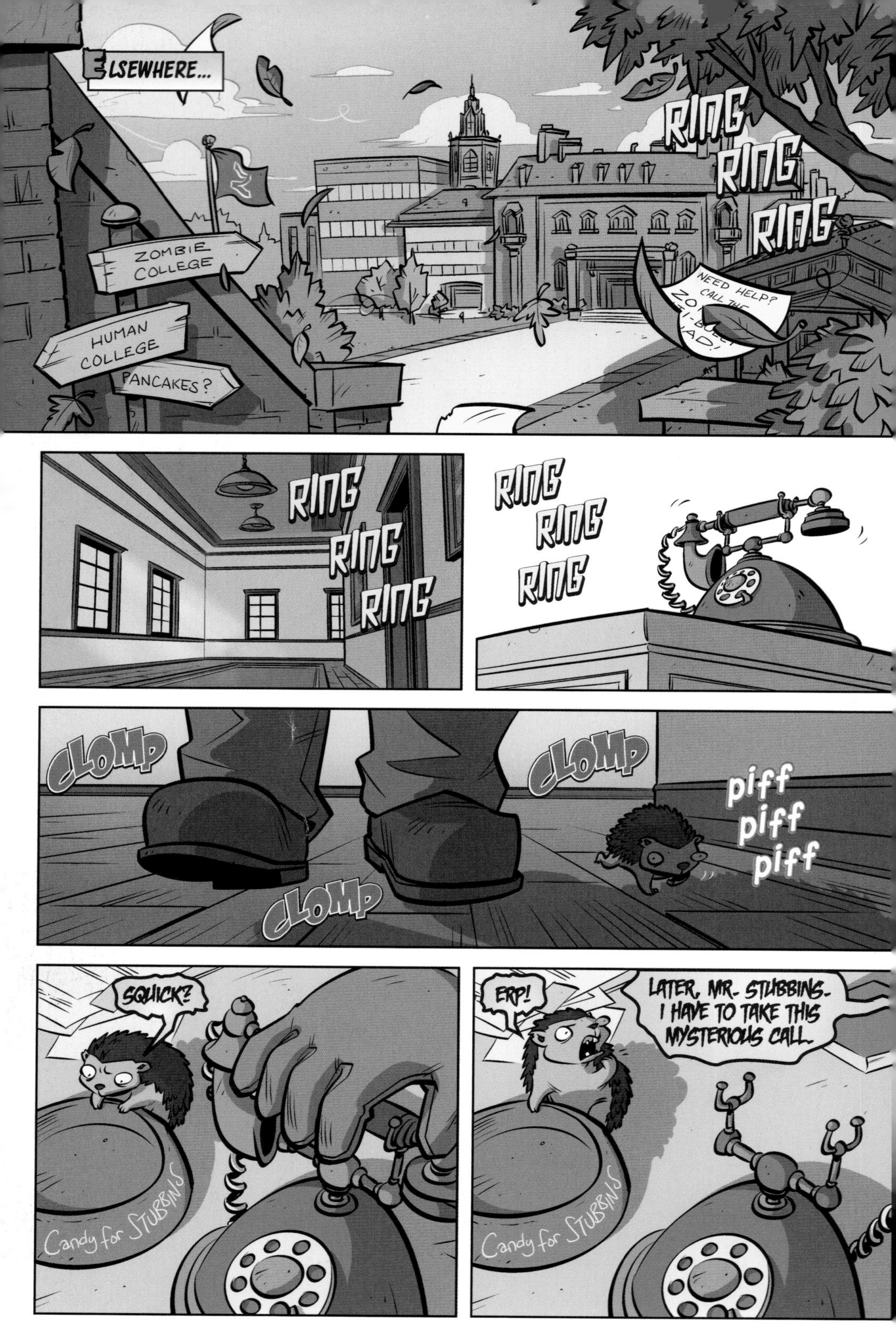
ELSEWHERE...
ZOMBIE COLLEGE
HUMAN COLLEGE
PANCAKES?
NEED HELP? CALL THE
RING RING RING
RING RING RING
RING RING RING
CLOMP
CLOMP
CLOMP
piff piff piff
SQUICK?
Candy for STUBBINS
ERP!
LATER, MR. STUBBINS. I HAVE TO TAKE THIS MYSTERIOUS CALL.
Candy for STUBBINS

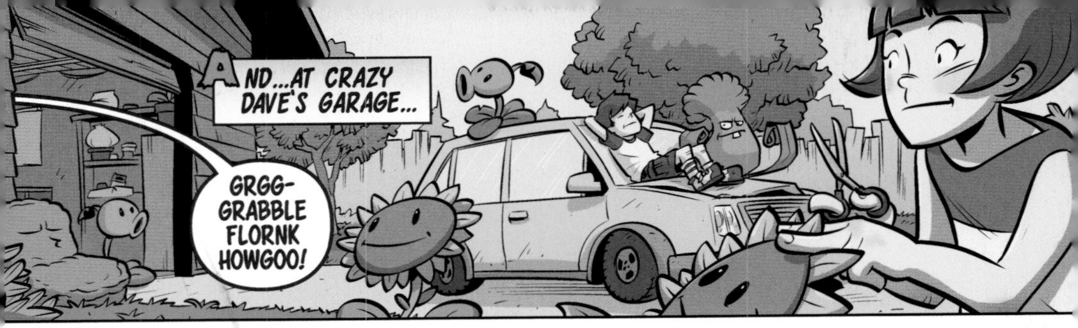
AND...AT CRAZY DAVE'S GARAGE...
GRGG-GRABBLE FLORNK HOWGOO!

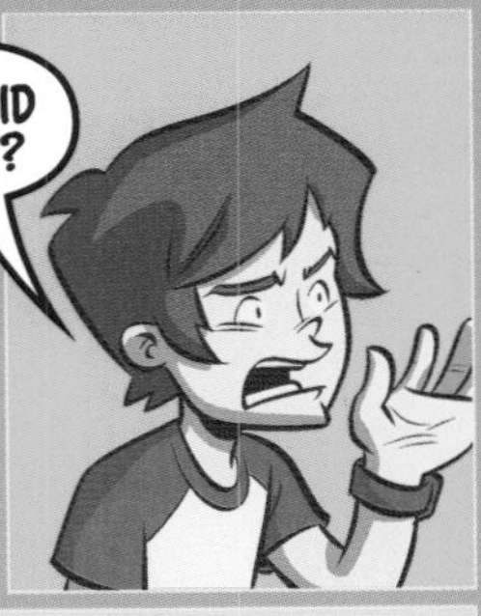
WHAT DID HE SAY?

NATE TIMELY

Eleven-Year-Old Adventurer

LIKES

Baseball. Pirates. Comic books. Bicycles. Lemonade.

DISLIKES

Rainstorms. Meals without pizza. Zomboss. Clowns.

ZOMBIES DEFEATED: 117
ZOMBIES RUN FROM: 32
FAVORITE PLANT: Peashooter
PERCENTAGE OF CRAZY DAVE'S WORDS UNDERSTOOD: 0%

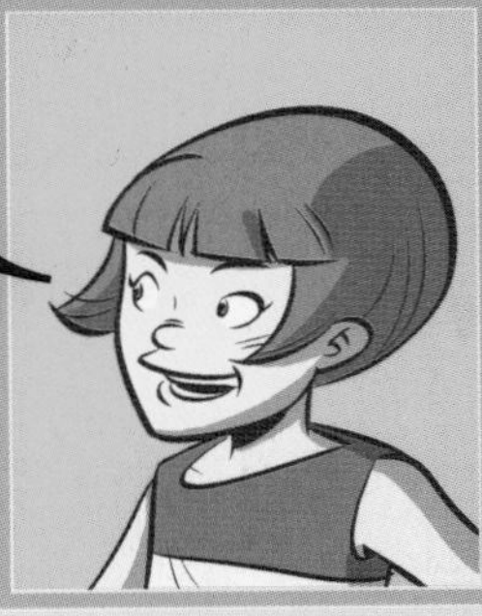
HE SAYS HE HAS A NEW INVENTION.

PATRICE BLAZING

Eleven-Year-Old Adventurer

LIKES

Soccer. Lemonade. Rainstorms. Leaping. Punching. Spaghetti.

DISLIKES

Zomboss. Being told what to do.

ZOMBIES DEFEATED: 117
ZOMBIES RUN FROM: 14
FAVORITE PLANT: Sunflower
PERCENTAGE OF CRAZY DAVE'S WORDS UNDERSTOOD: 84%

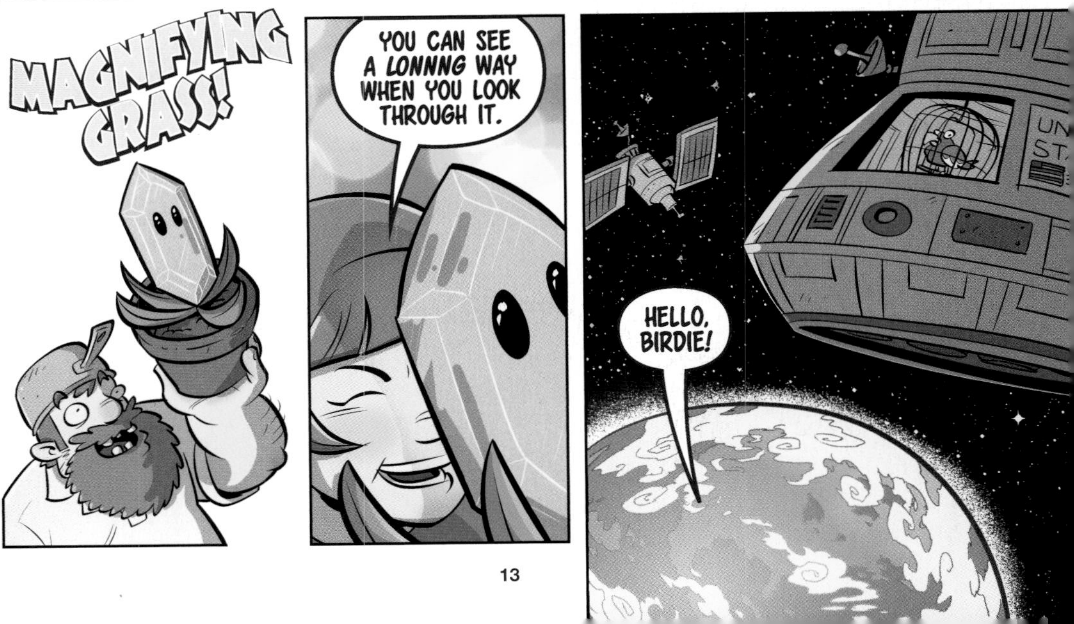
MAGNIFYING GRASS!
YOU CAN SEE A LONNNG WAY WHEN YOU LOOK THROUGH IT.
HELLO, BIRDIE!

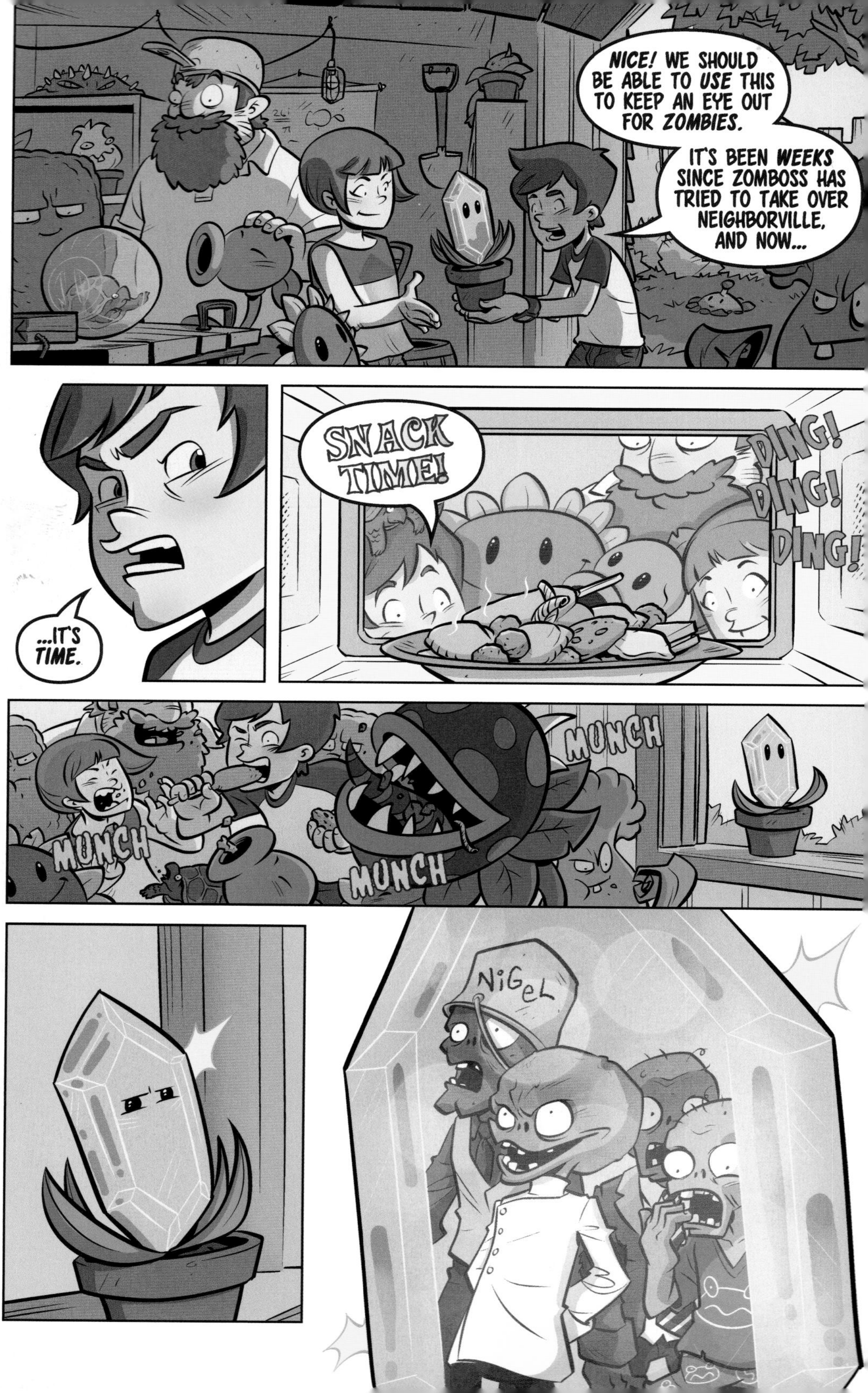
NICE! WE SHOULD BE ABLE TO USE THIS TO KEEP AN EYE OUT FOR ZOMBIES.
IT'S BEEN WEEKS SINCE ZOMBOSS HAS TRIED TO TAKE OVER NEIGHBORVILLE, AND NOW...
...IT'S TIME.
SNACK TIME!
DING! DING! DING!
MUNCH
MUNCH
MUNCH
NiGeL

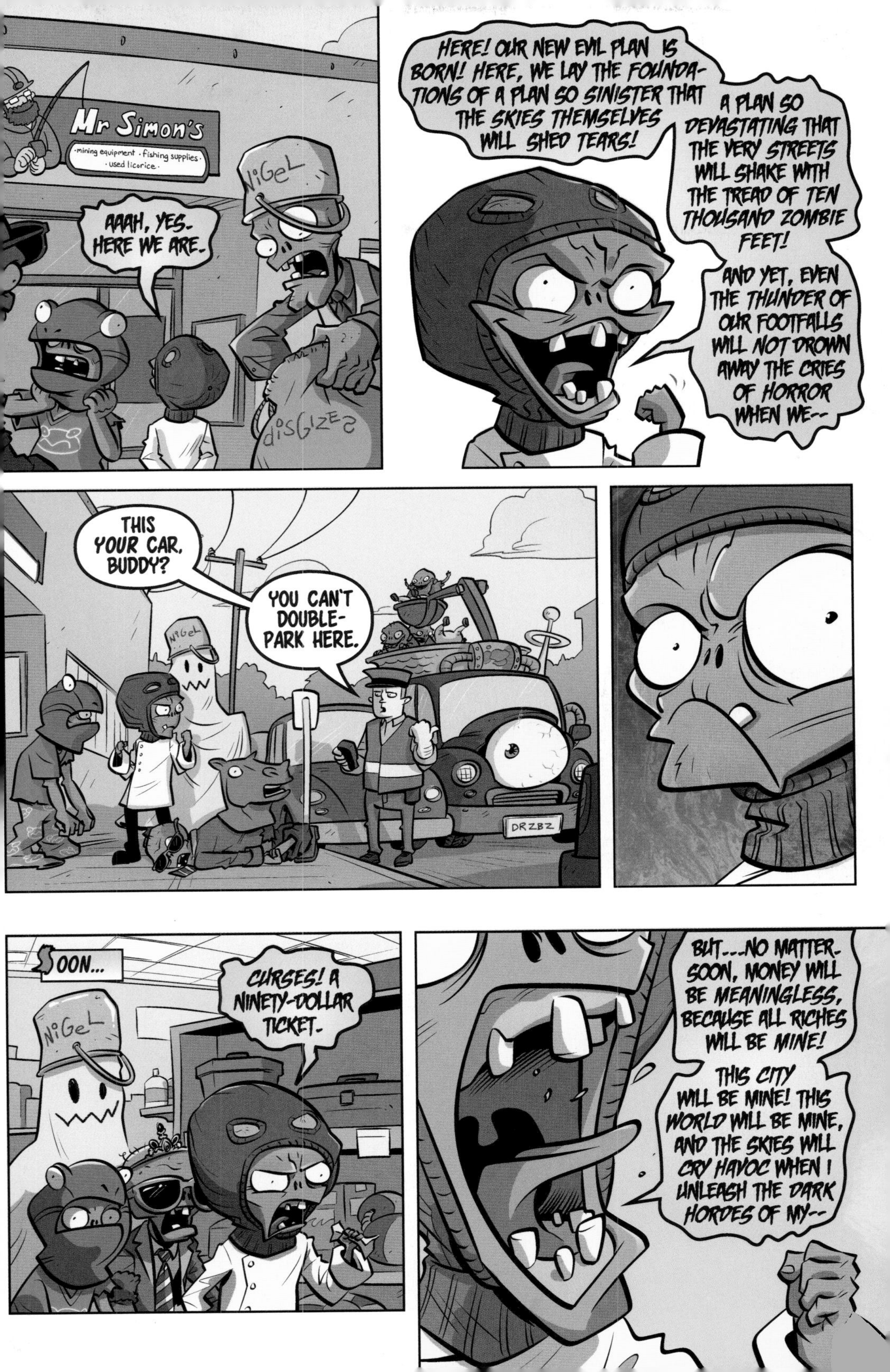
Mr Simon's
·mining equipment · fishing supplies · used licorice ·
NiGeL
AAAH, YES. HERE WE ARE.
disGIZeS
HERE! OUR NEW EVIL PLAN IS BORN! HERE, WE LAY THE FOUNDATIONS OF A PLAN SO SINISTER THAT THE SKIES THEMSELVES WILL SHED TEARS!
A PLAN SO DEVASTATING THAT THE VERY STREETS WILL SHAKE WITH THE TREAD OF TEN THOUSAND ZOMBIE FEET!
AND YET, EVEN THE THUNDER OF OUR FOOTFALLS WILL NOT DROWN AWAY THE CRIES OF HORROR WHEN WE--
THIS YOUR CAR, BUDDY?
YOU CAN'T DOUBLE-PARK HERE.
NiGeL
DRZBZ
SOON...
NiGeL
CURSES! A NINETY-DOLLAR TICKET.
BUT...NO MATTER. SOON, MONEY WILL BE MEANINGLESS, BECAUSE ALL RICHES WILL BE MINE!
THIS CITY WILL BE MINE! THIS WORLD WILL BE MINE, AND THE SKIES WILL CRY HAVOC WHEN I UNLEASH THE DARK HORDES OF MY--

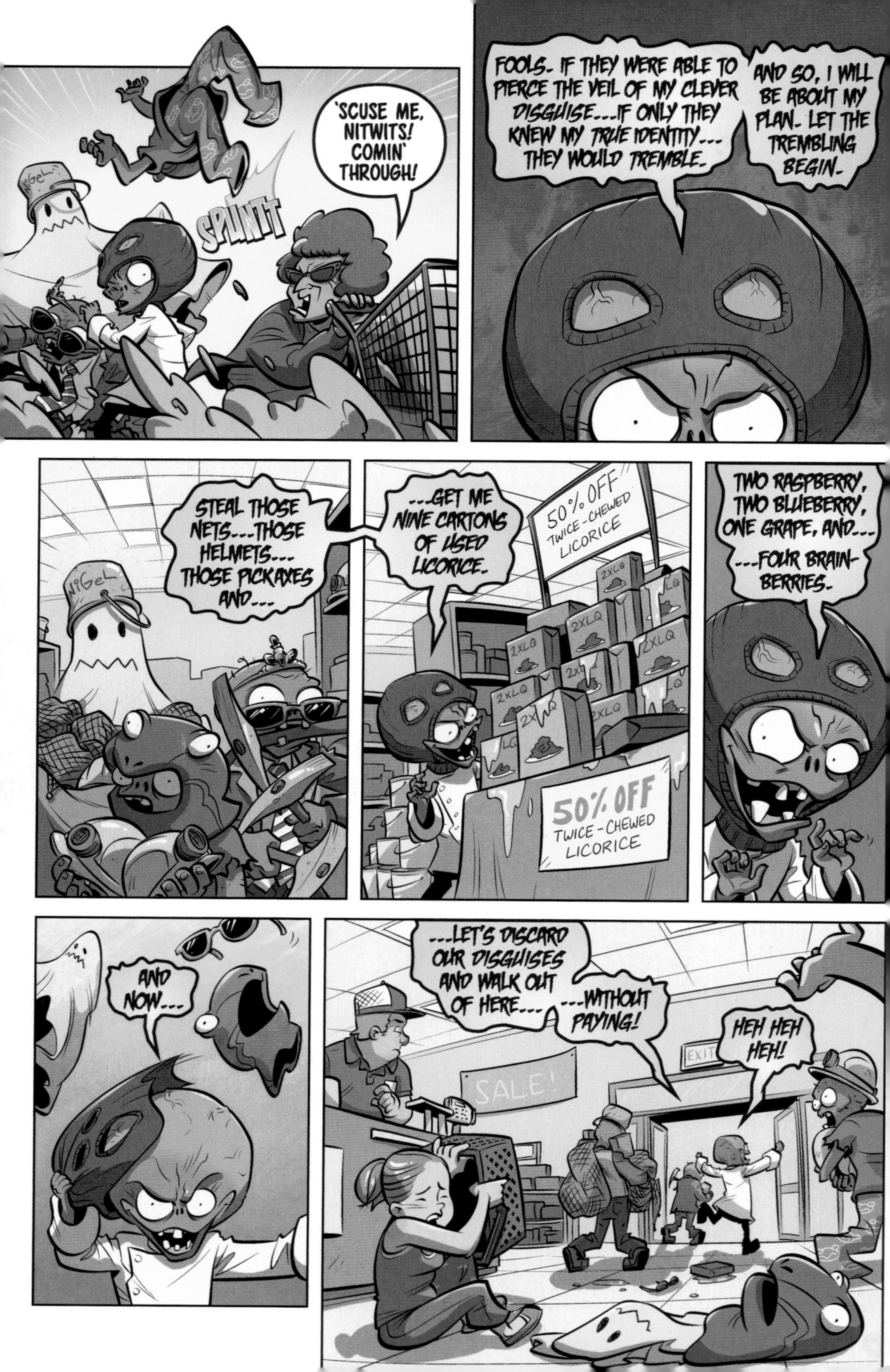
'SCUSE ME, NITWITS! COMIN' THROUGH!
SPLNTT
FOOLS. IF THEY WERE ABLE TO PIERCE THE VEIL OF MY CLEVER DISGUISE...IF ONLY THEY KNEW MY TRUE IDENTITY... THEY WOULD TREMBLE.
AND SO, I WILL BE ABOUT MY PLAN. LET THE TREMBLING BEGIN.
NiGeL
STEAL THOSE NETS...THOSE HELMETS... THOSE PICKAXES AND...
...GET ME NINE CARTONS OF USED LICORICE.
50% OFF TWICE-CHEWED LICORICE
2XLQ
50% OFF TWICE-CHEWED LICORICE
TWO RASPBERRY, TWO BLUEBERRY, ONE GRAPE, AND...
...FOUR BRAIN-BERRIES.
AND NOW...
...LET'S DISCARD OUR DISGUISES AND WALK OUT OF HERE...
...WITHOUT PAYING!
HEH HEH HEH!
EXIT
SALE!

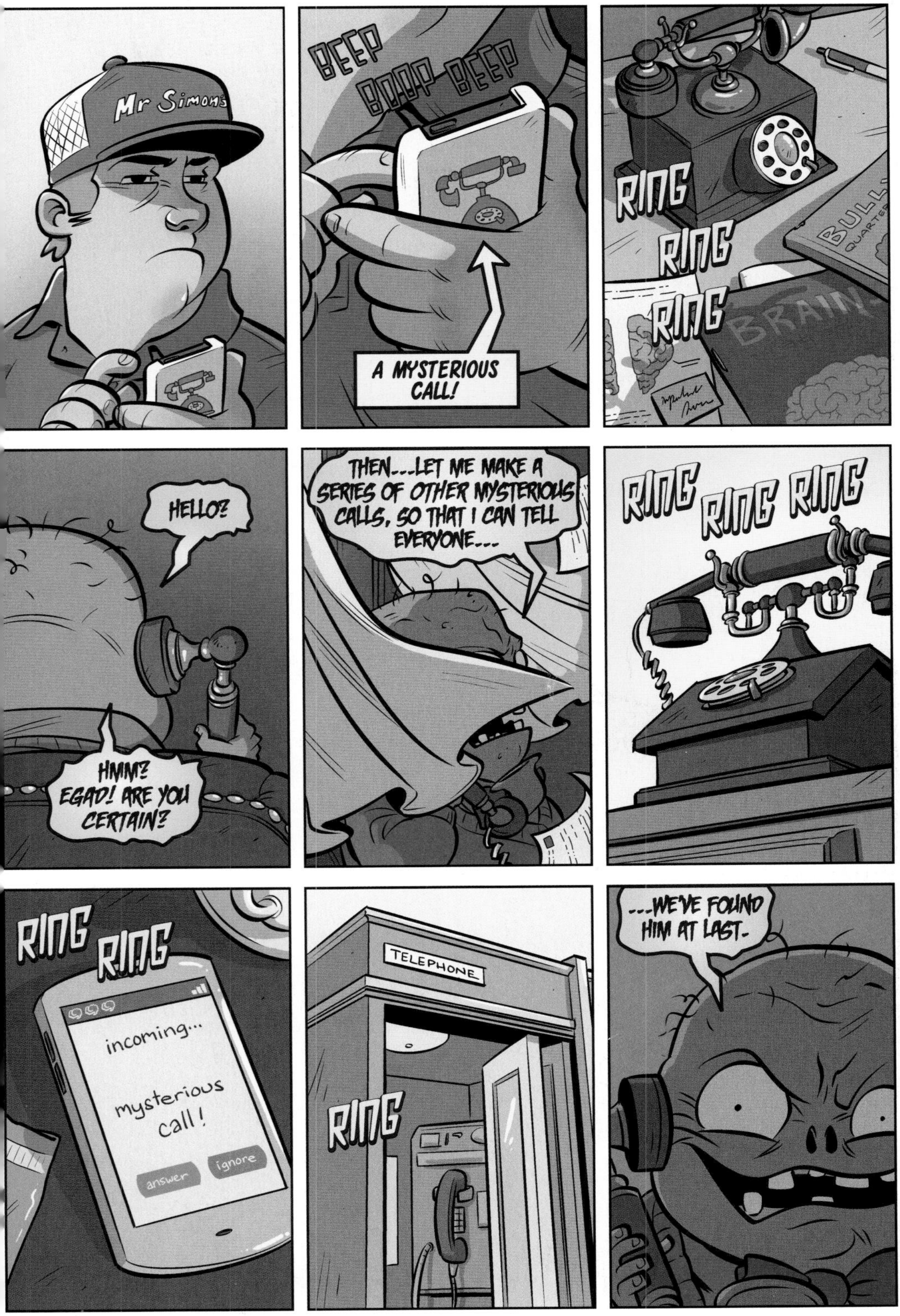
Mr Simon's
BEEP BOOP BEEP
A MYSTERIOUS CALL!
RING RING RING
BULLY QUARTER
BRAIN
HELLO?
HMM? EGAD! ARE YOU CERTAIN?
THEN...LET ME MAKE A SERIES OF OTHER MYSTERIOUS CALLS, SO THAT I CAN TELL EVERYONE...
RING RING RING
RING RING
incoming...
mysterious call!
answer
ignore
TELEPHONE
RING
...WE'VE FOUND HIM AT LAST.

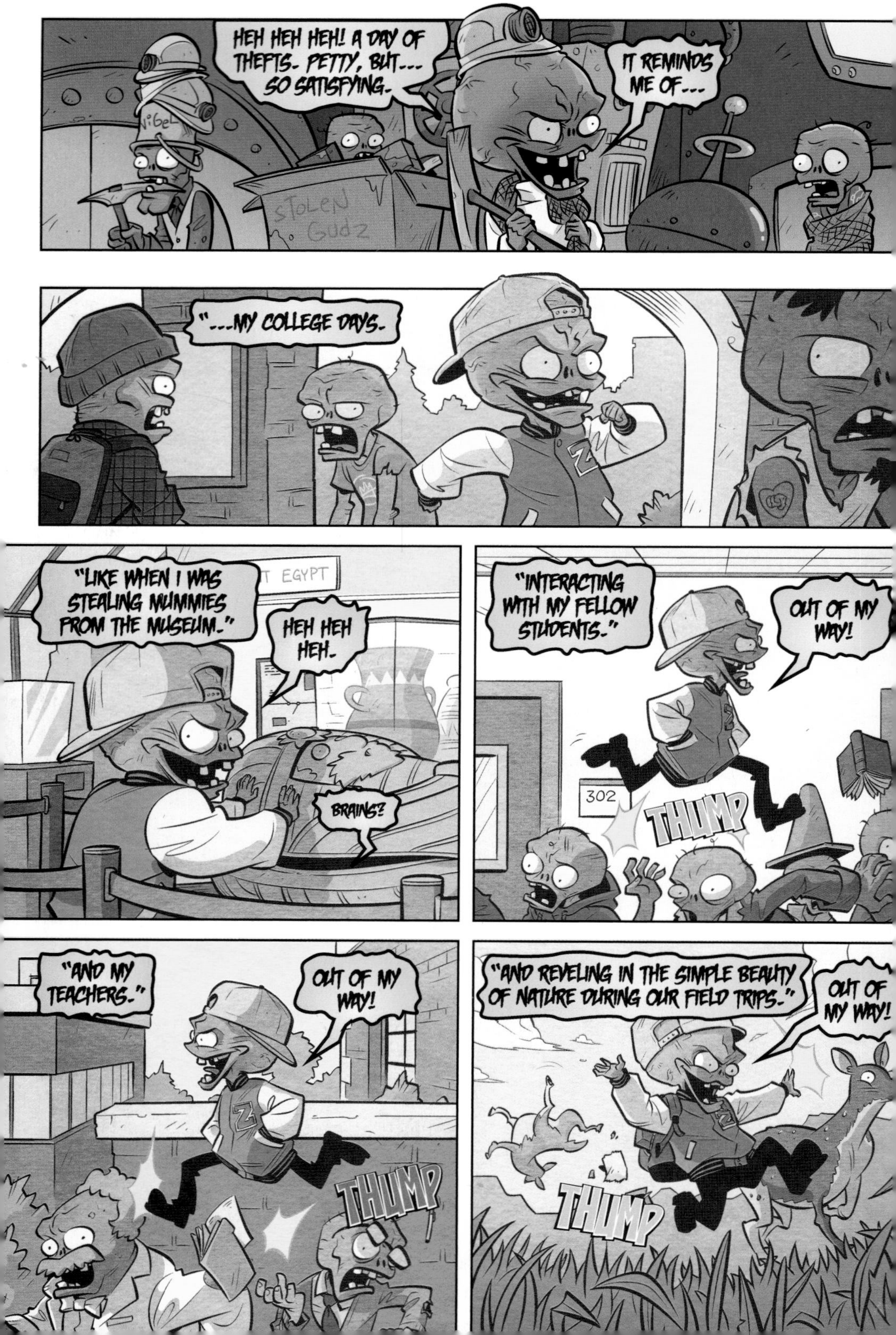
HEH HEH HEH! A DAY OF THEFTS. PETTY, BUT... SO SATISFYING.
IT REMINDS ME OF...
Nibel
STOLEN Gudz
"...MY COLLEGE DAYS.
"LIKE WHEN I WAS STEALING MUMMIES FROM THE MUSEUM."
T EGYPT
HEH HEH HEH.
BRAINS?
"INTERACTING WITH MY FELLOW STUDENTS."
OUT OF MY WAY!
302
THUMP
"AND MY TEACHERS."
OUT OF MY WAY!
THUMP
"AND REVELING IN THE SIMPLE BEAUTY OF NATURE DURING OUR FIELD TRIPS."
OUT OF MY WAY!
THUMP

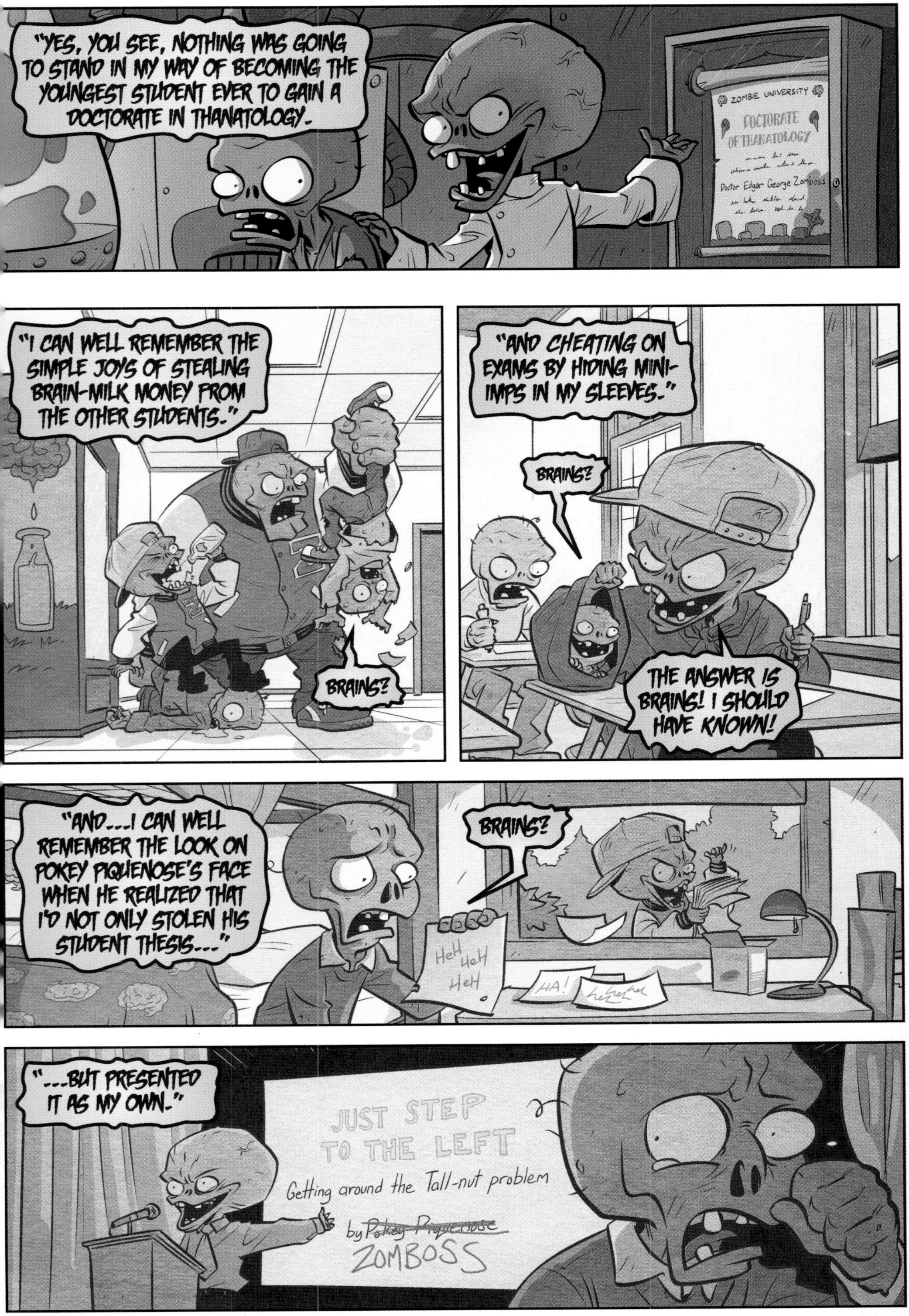
"YES, YOU SEE, NOTHING WAS GOING TO STAND IN MY WAY OF BECOMING THE YOUNGEST STUDENT EVER TO GAIN A DOCTORATE IN THANATOLOGY.
ZOMBIE UNIVERSITY
DOCTORATE OF THANATOLOGY
Doctor Edgar George Zomboss
"I CAN WELL REMEMBER THE SIMPLE JOYS OF STEALING BRAIN-MILK MONEY FROM THE OTHER STUDENTS."
BRAINS?
"AND CHEATING ON EXAMS BY HIDING MINI-IMPS IN MY SLEEVES."
BRAINS?
THE ANSWER IS BRAINS! I SHOULD HAVE KNOWN!
"AND...I CAN WELL REMEMBER THE LOOK ON POKEY PIQUENOSE'S FACE WHEN HE REALIZED THAT I'D NOT ONLY STOLEN HIS STUDENT THESIS..."
BRAINS?
HeH HeH HeH
HA!
"...BUT PRESENTED IT AS MY OWN."
JUST STEP TO THE LEFT
Getting around the Tall-nut problem
by ~~Pokey Piquenose~~ ZOMBOSS

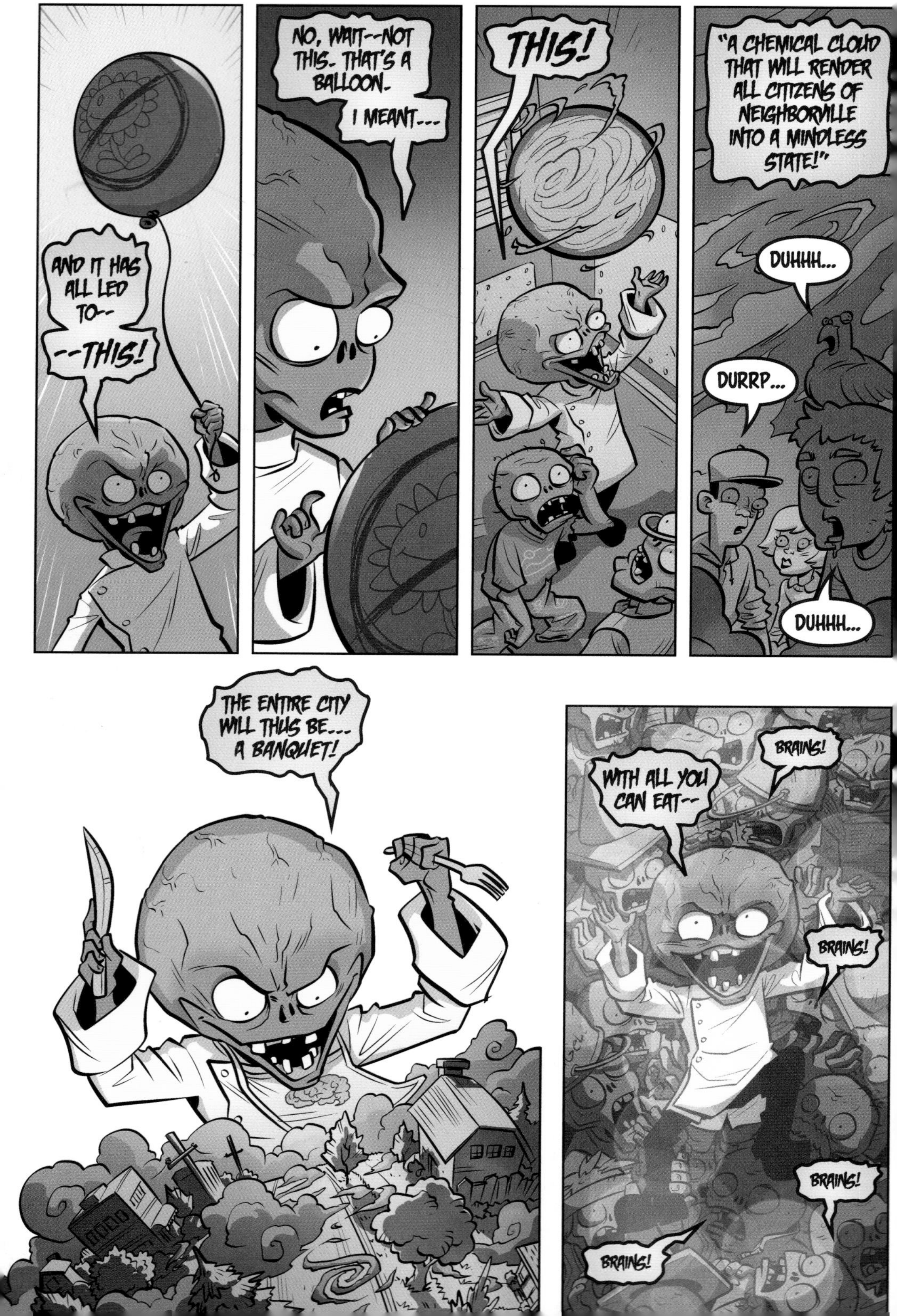
AND IT HAS ALL LED TO--
--THIS!
NO, WAIT--NOT THIS. THAT'S A BALLOON.
I MEANT...
THIS!
"A CHEMICAL CLOUD THAT WILL RENDER ALL CITIZENS OF NEIGHBORVILLE INTO A MINDLESS STATE!"
DUHHH...
DURRP...
DUHHH...
THE ENTIRE CITY WILL THUS BE... A BANQUET!
WITH ALL YOU CAN EAT--
BRAINS!
BRAINS!
BRAINS!
BRAINS!

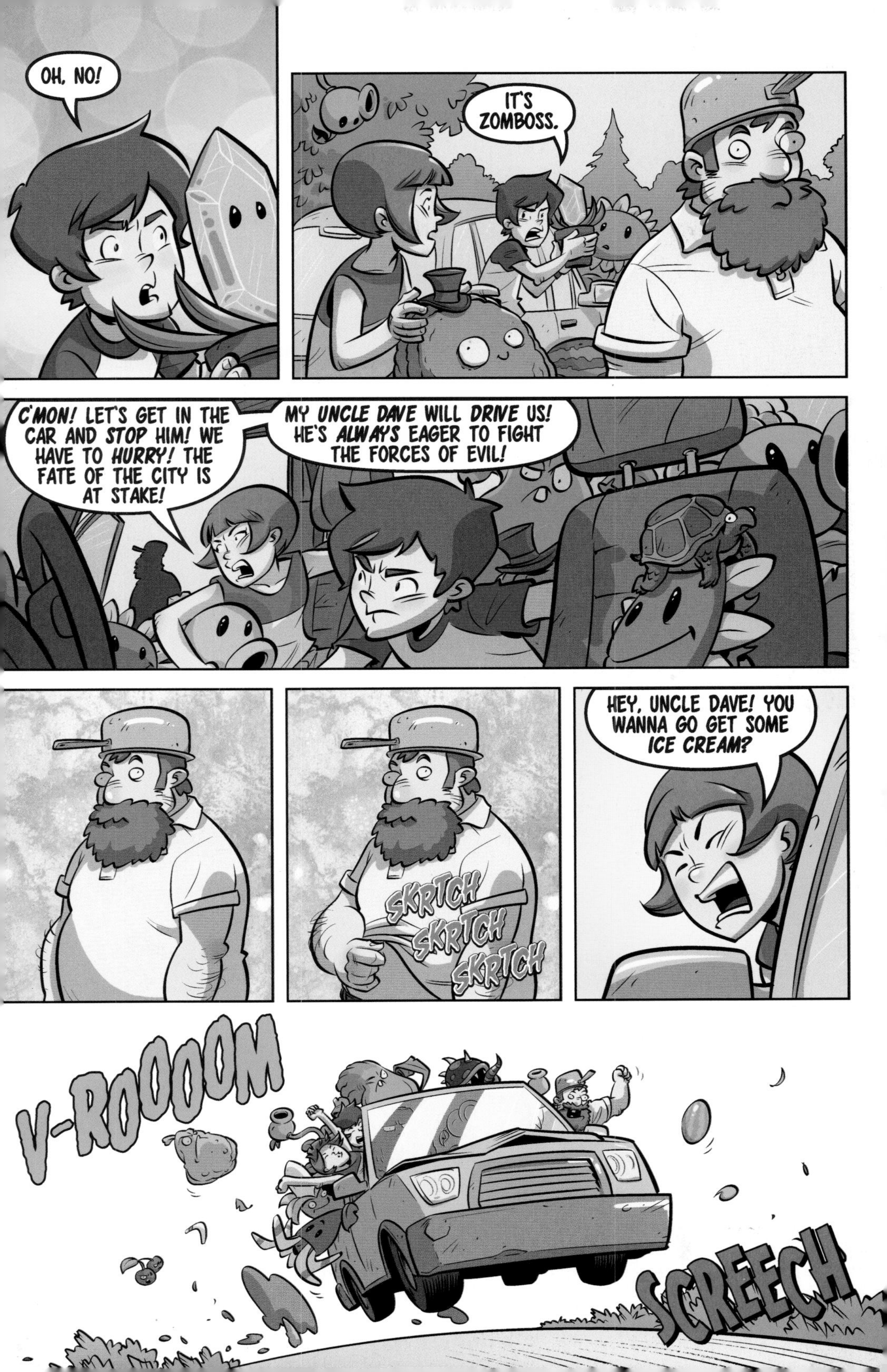
OH, NO!
IT'S ZOMBOSS.
C'MON! LET'S GET IN THE CAR AND STOP HIM! WE HAVE TO HURRY! THE FATE OF THE CITY IS AT STAKE!
MY UNCLE DAVE WILL DRIVE US! HE'S ALWAYS EAGER TO FIGHT THE FORCES OF EVIL!
SKRTCH SKRTCH SKRTCH
HEY, UNCLE DAVE! YOU WANNA GO GET SOME ICE CREAM?
V-ROOOOM
SCREECH

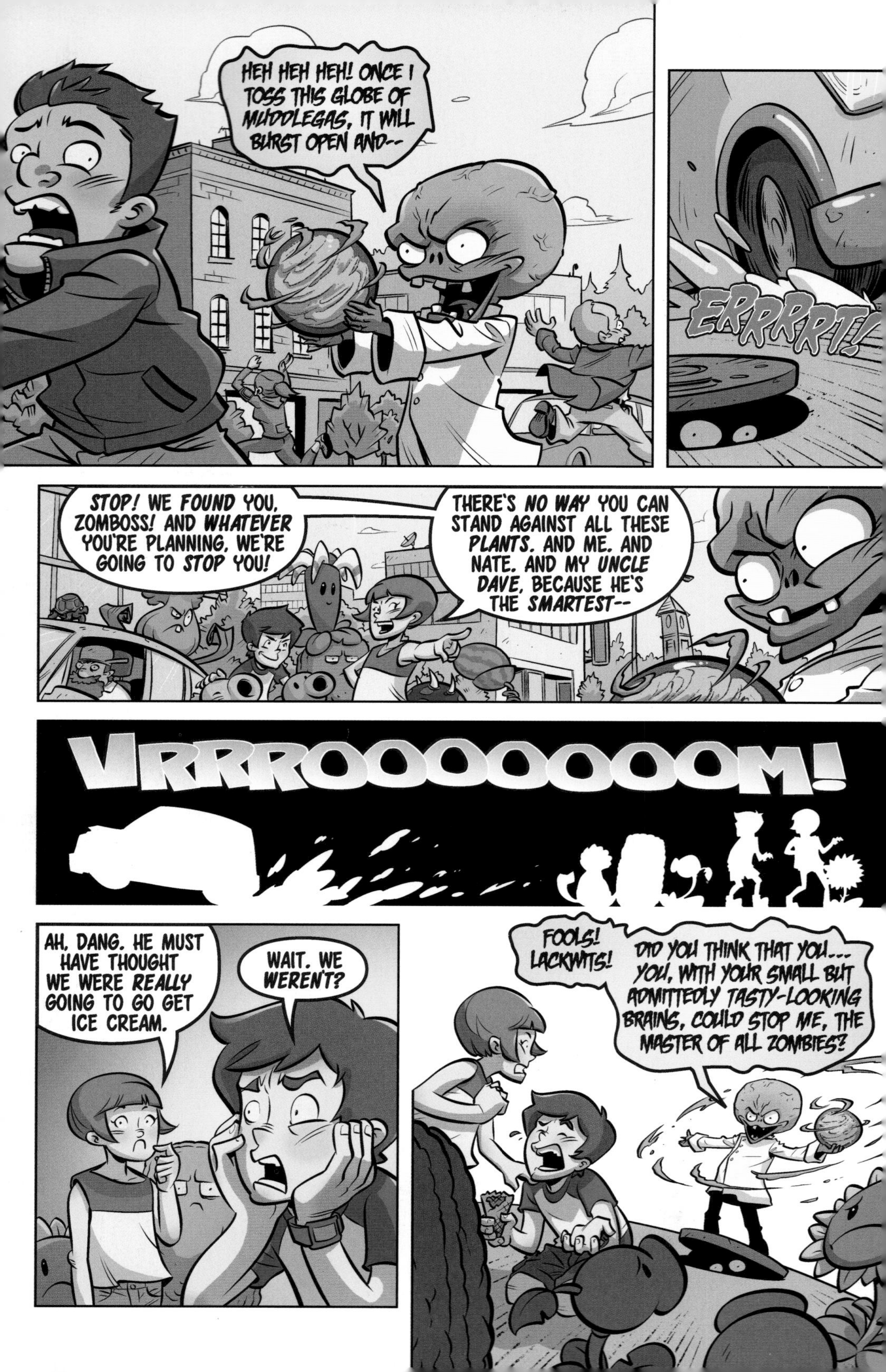
HEH HEH HEH! ONCE I TOSS THIS GLOBE OF MUDDLEGAS, IT WILL BURST OPEN AND--
ERRRRT!
STOP! WE FOUND YOU, ZOMBOSS! AND WHATEVER YOU'RE PLANNING, WE'RE GOING TO STOP YOU!
THERE'S NO WAY YOU CAN STAND AGAINST ALL THESE PLANTS. AND ME. AND NATE. AND MY UNCLE DAVE, BECAUSE HE'S THE SMARTEST--
VRRROOOOOOOM!
AH, DANG. HE MUST HAVE THOUGHT WE WERE REALLY GOING TO GO GET ICE CREAM.
WAIT. WE WEREN'T?
FOOLS! LACKWITS!
DID YOU THINK THAT YOU... YOU, WITH YOUR SMALL BUT ADMITTEDLY TASTY-LOOKING BRAINS, COULD STOP ME, THE MASTER OF ALL ZOMBIES?

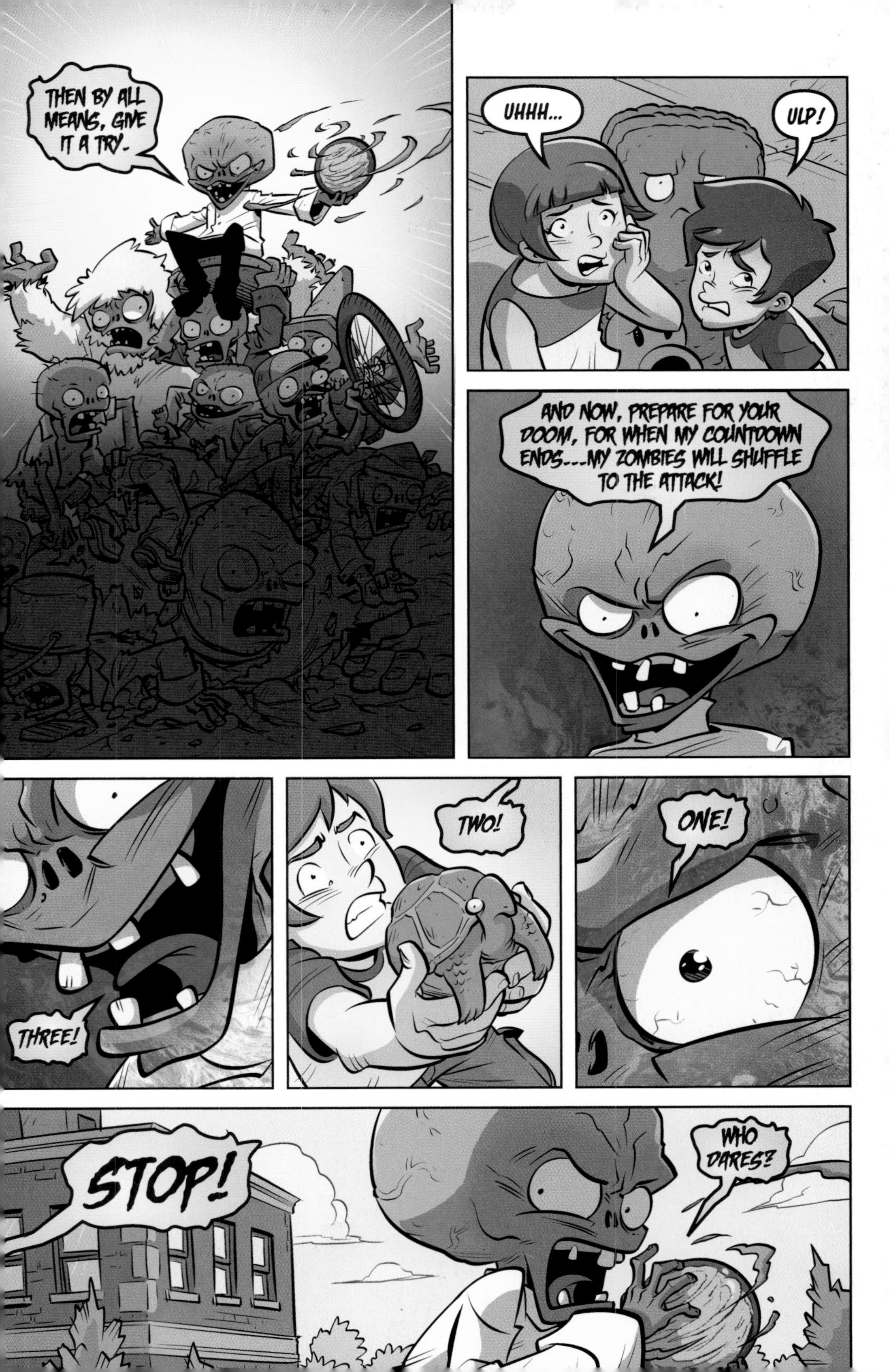
THEN BY ALL MEANS, GIVE IT A TRY.
UHHH...
ULP!
AND NOW, PREPARE FOR YOUR DOOM, FOR WHEN MY COUNTDOWN ENDS...MY ZOMBIES WILL SHUFFLE TO THE ATTACK!
THREE!
TWO!
ONE!
STOP!
WHO DARES?

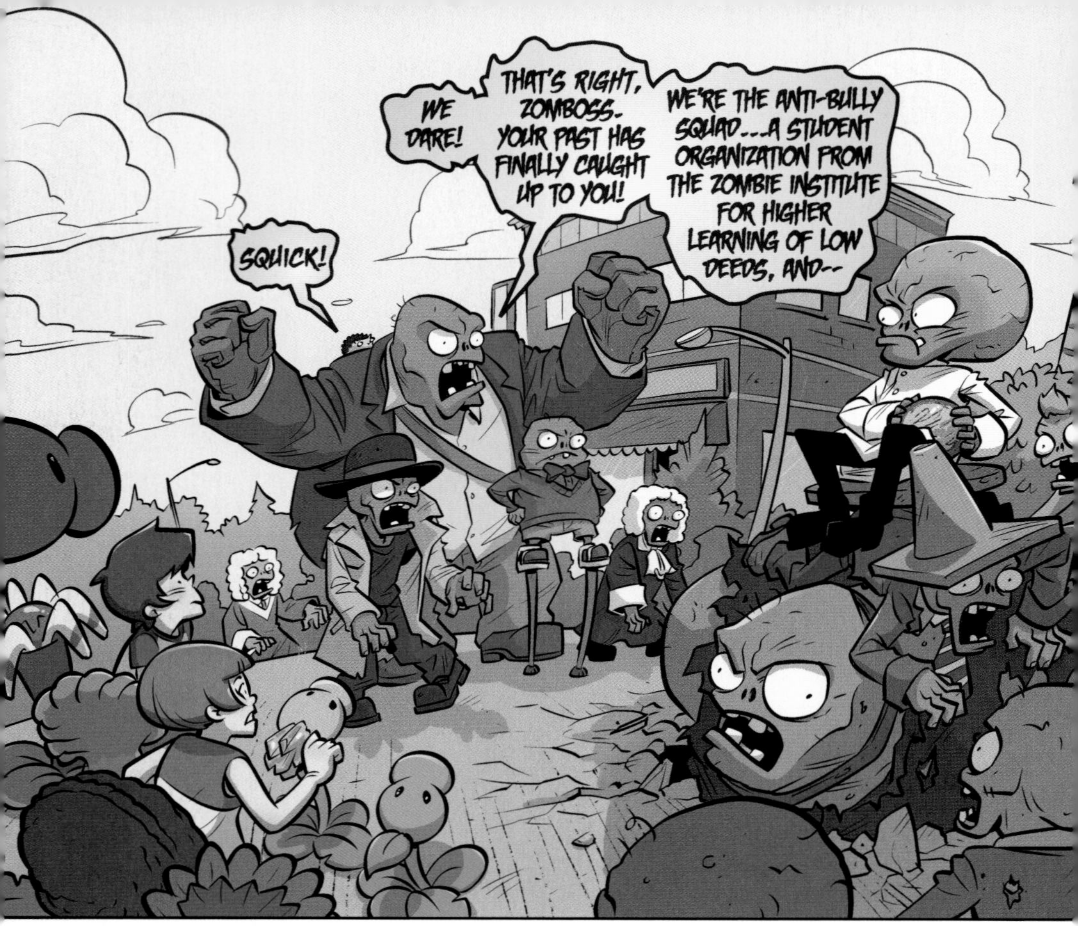
SQUICK!
WE DARE!
THAT'S RIGHT, ZOMBOSS. YOUR PAST HAS FINALLY CAUGHT UP TO YOU!
WE'RE THE ANTI-BULLY SQUAD...A STUDENT ORGANIZATION FROM THE ZOMBIE INSTITUTE FOR HIGHER LEARNING OF LOW DEEDS, AND--

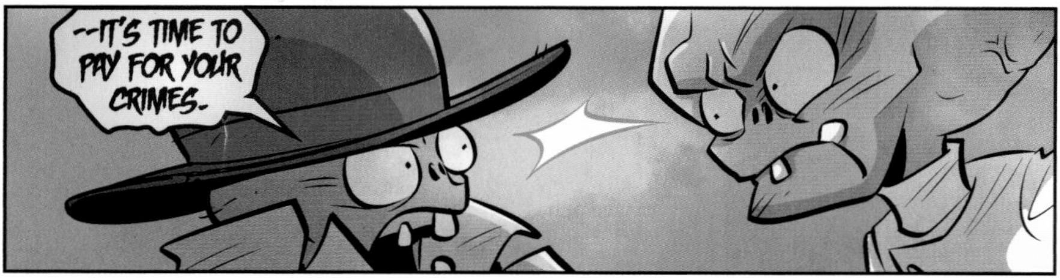
--IT'S TIME TO PAY FOR YOUR CRIMES.

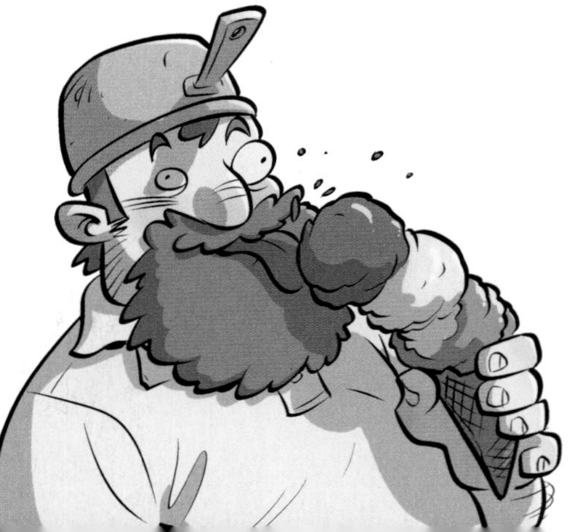

CRAZY DAVE'S ICE-CREAM FACTS

DID YOU KNOW THAT ICE CREAM WAS INVENTED BY PENGUINS? IT'S TRUE! MAYBE. I DON'T KNOW. MAYBE ICE CREAM INVENTED PENGUINS? I LIKE THEM BOTH! HAVE YOU EVER SEEN AN ICE-CREAM-CONE-HEAD ZOMBIE? I HAVEN'T EITHER. STRAWBERRY ICE CREAM IS THE BEST FOR FUELING YOUR TIME MACHINE. *THESE ARE FACTS!*

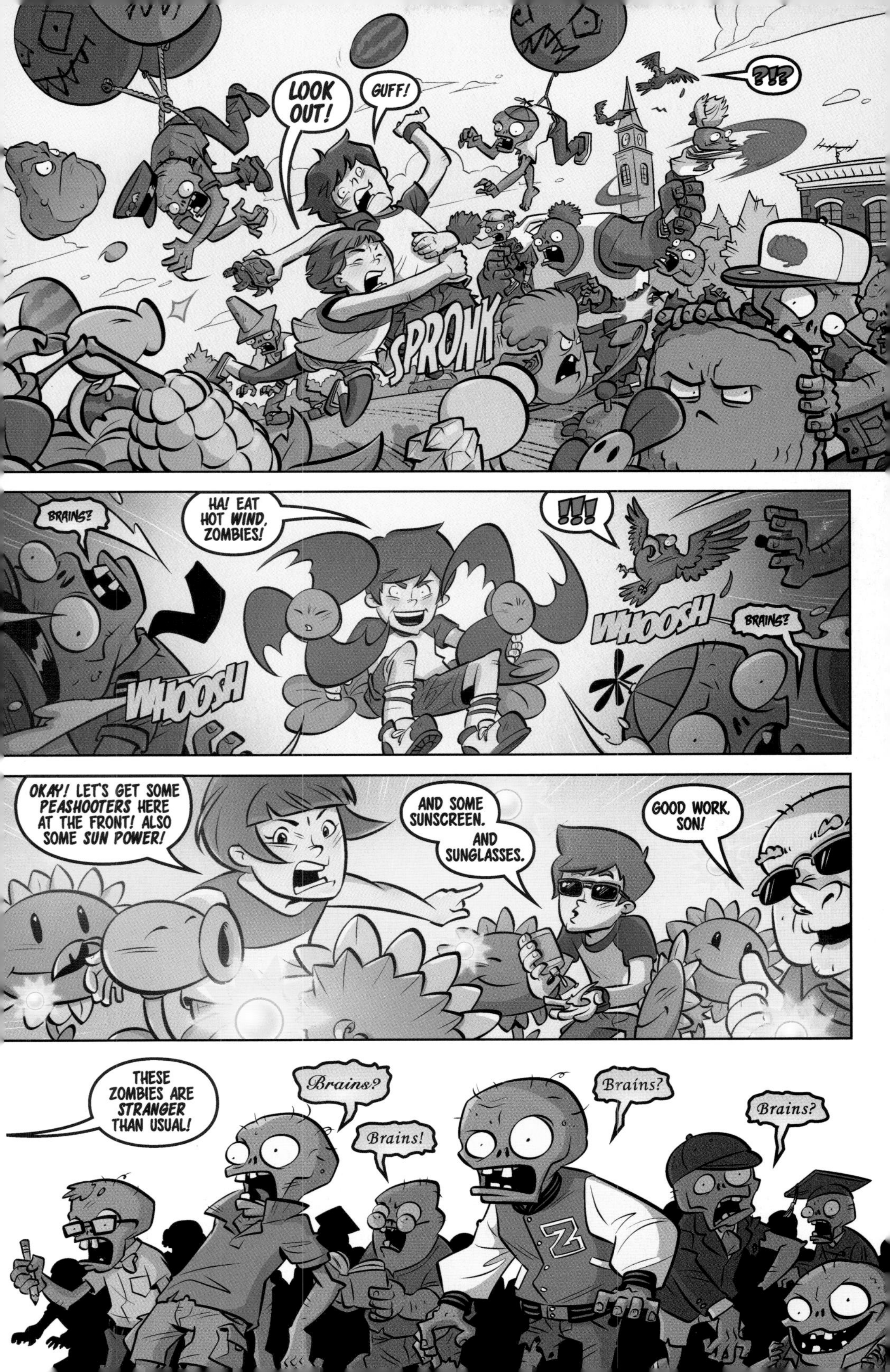
LOOK OUT!
GUFF!
?!?
SPRONK
BRAINS?
HA! EAT HOT WIND, ZOMBIES!
!!!
WHOOSH
WHOOSH
BRAINS?
OKAY! LET'S GET SOME PEASHOOTERS HERE AT THE FRONT! ALSO SOME SUN POWER!
AND SOME SUNSCREEN.
AND SUNGLASSES.
GOOD WORK, SON!
THESE ZOMBIES ARE STRANGER THAN USUAL!
Brains?
Brains!
Brains?
Brains?

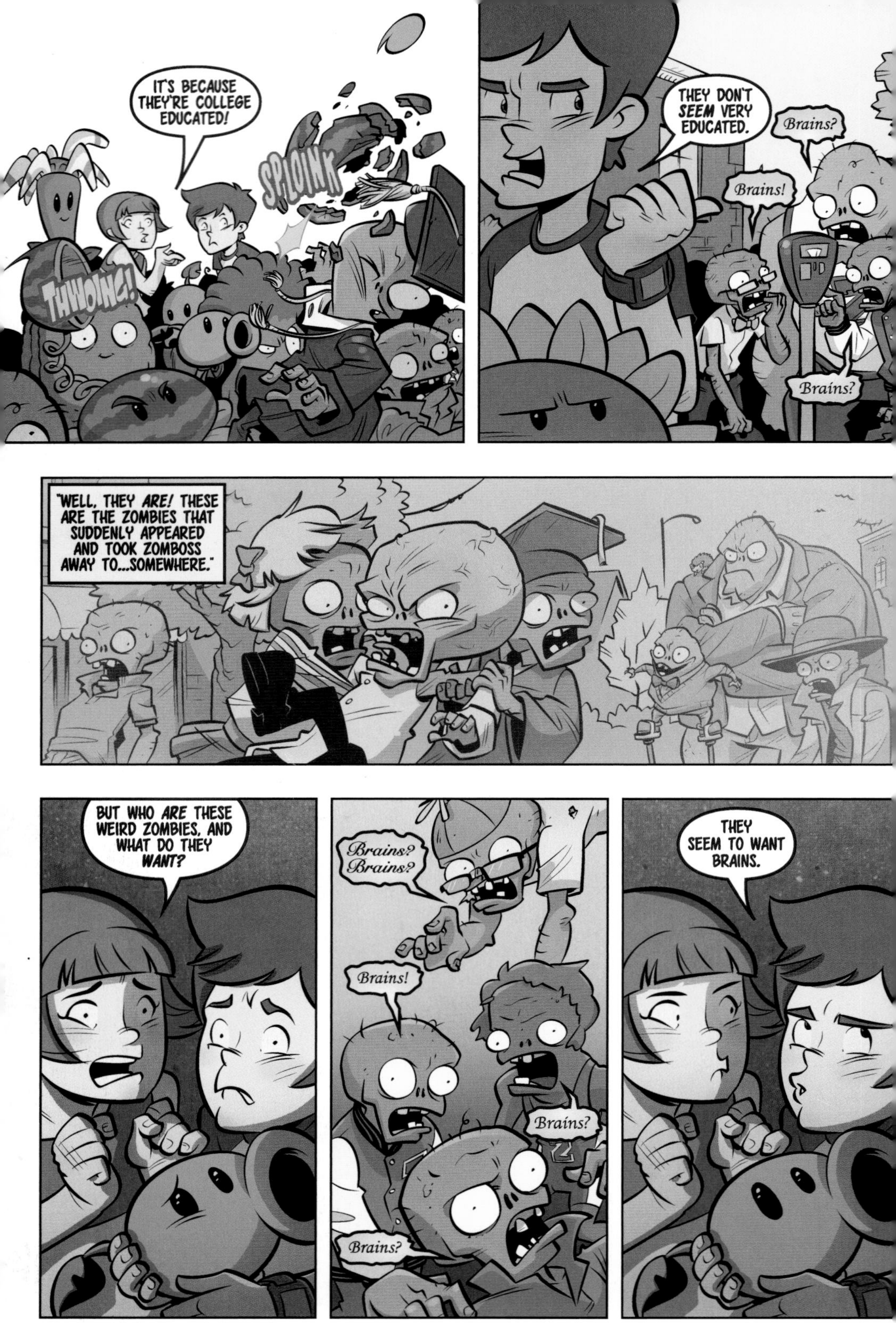

IT'S BECAUSE THEY'RE COLLEGE EDUCATED!
SPLOINK
THWOING!
THEY DON'T SEEM VERY EDUCATED.
Brains?
Brains!
Brains?
"WELL, THEY ARE! THESE ARE THE ZOMBIES THAT SUDDENLY APPEARED AND TOOK ZOMBOSS AWAY TO...SOMEWHERE."
BUT WHO ARE THESE WEIRD ZOMBIES, AND WHAT DO THEY WANT?
Brains? Brains?
Brains!
Brains?
Brains?
THEY SEEM TO WANT BRAINS.

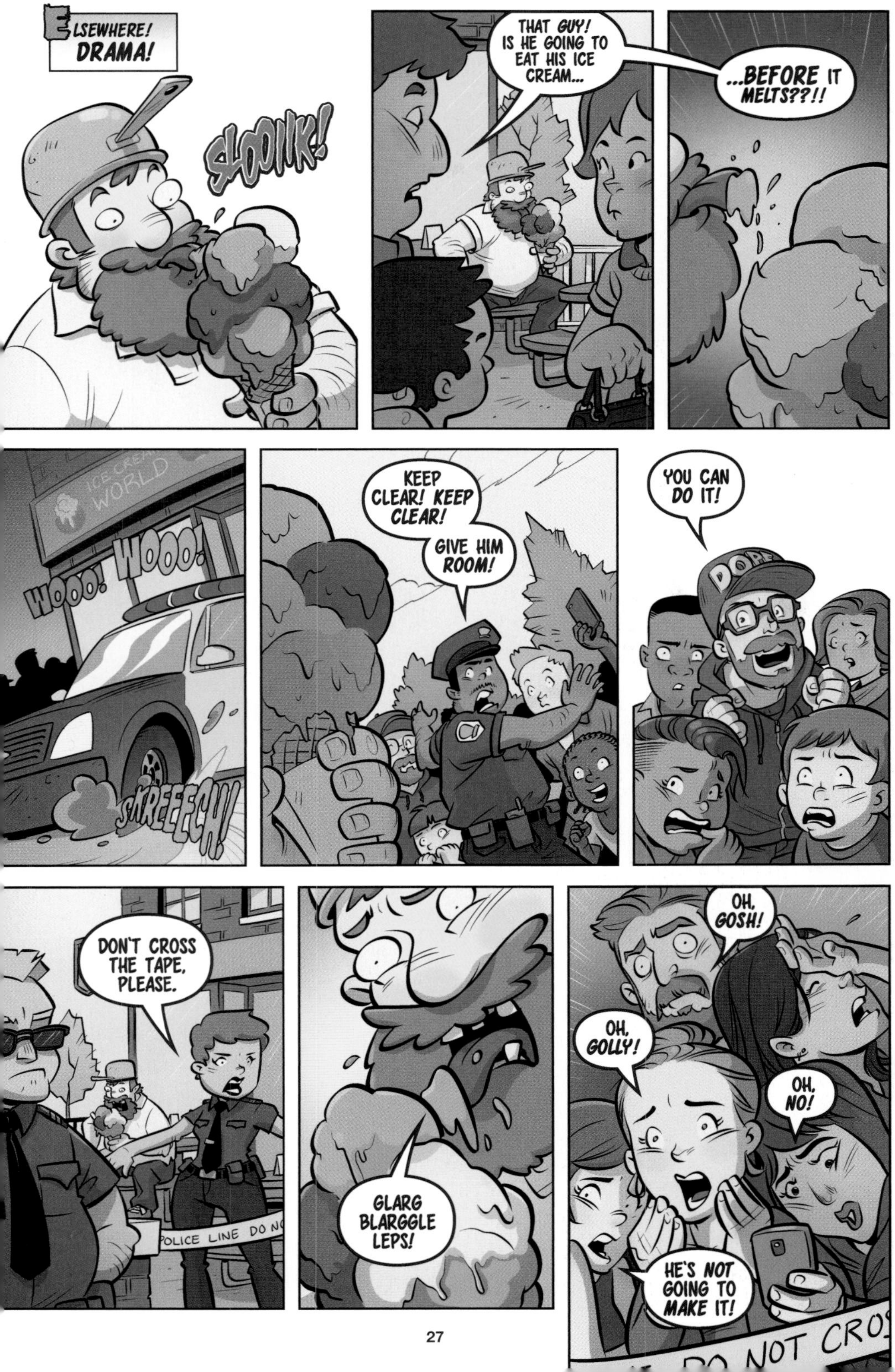
ELSEWHERE! DRAMA!
SLOOIIK!
THAT GUY! IS HE GOING TO EAT HIS ICE CREAM...
...BEFORE IT MELTS??!!
ICE CREAM WORLD
WOOO! WOOO!
SKREEEECH!
KEEP CLEAR! KEEP CLEAR!
GIVE HIM ROOM!
YOU CAN DO IT!
DOPE
DON'T CROSS THE TAPE, PLEASE.
POLICE LINE DO N
GLARG BLARGGLE LEPS!
OH, GOSH!
OH, GOLLY!
OH, NO!
HE'S NOT GOING TO MAKE IT!
DO NOT CROS

MEANWHILE...

YOU CAN'T LEAVE ME ROTTING IN JAIL! **LET ME OUT!**

OR AT LEAST GET ME SOME DIFFERENT READING MATERIAL!

JAIL QUARTERLY
The Magazine All About
Rotting in Jail!
101 NEW WAYS TO ROT
How to end boredom
Find Joy with pebble collect

ALSO MEANWHILE...

HERE THEY COME!

BIRD SEED

"GET READY WITH THE BIRDSEED!"

JAIL QUARTERLY

THROWWW!

HURL!

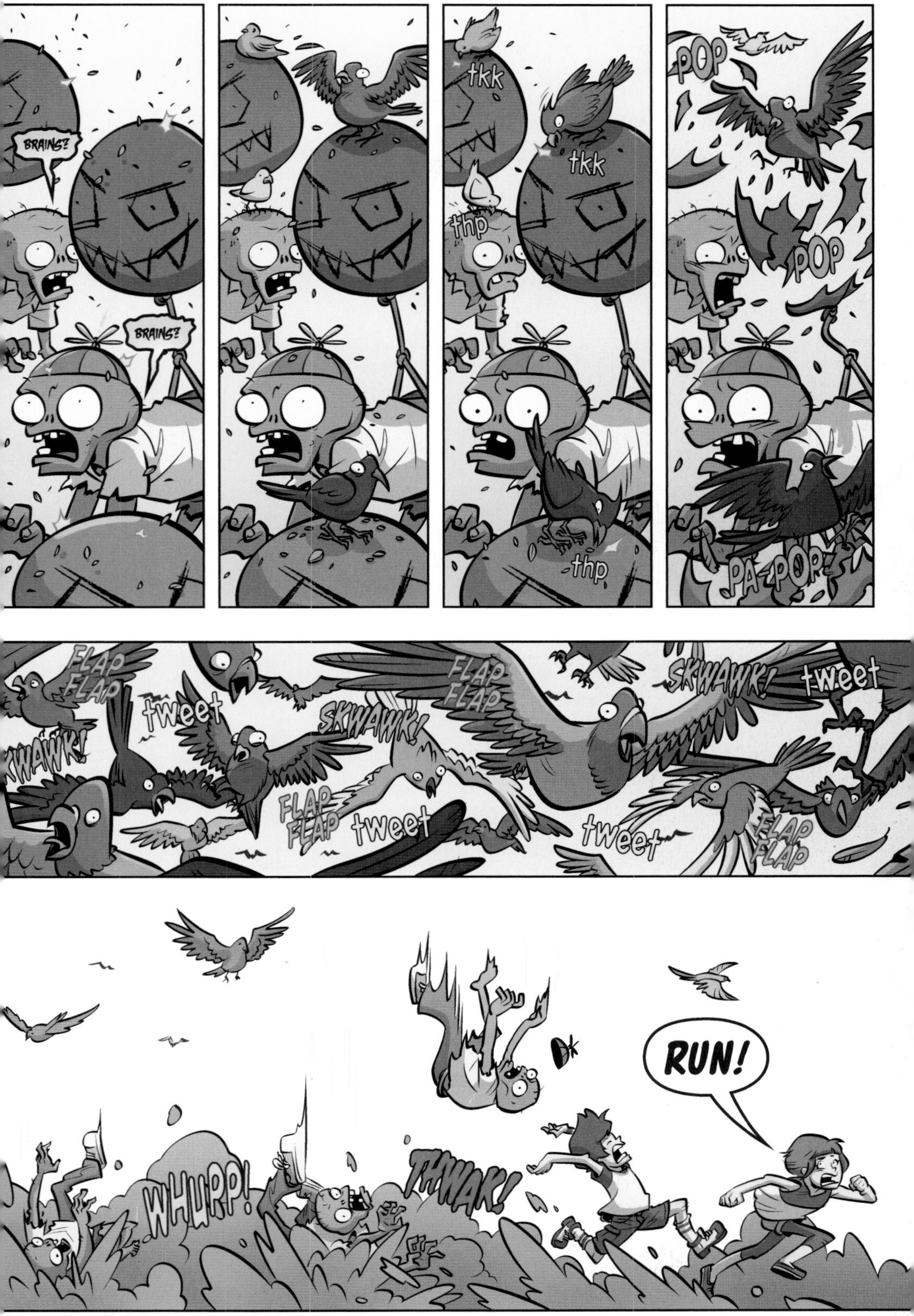
BRAINS?
BRAINS?
tkk
tkk
thp
thp
POP
POP
PA-POP!
FLAP FLAP
SKWAWK!
tweet
SKWAWK!
FLAP FLAP
SKWAWK!
tweet
FLAP FLAP
tweet
tweet
FLAP FLAP
WHUPP!
THWAK!
RUN!

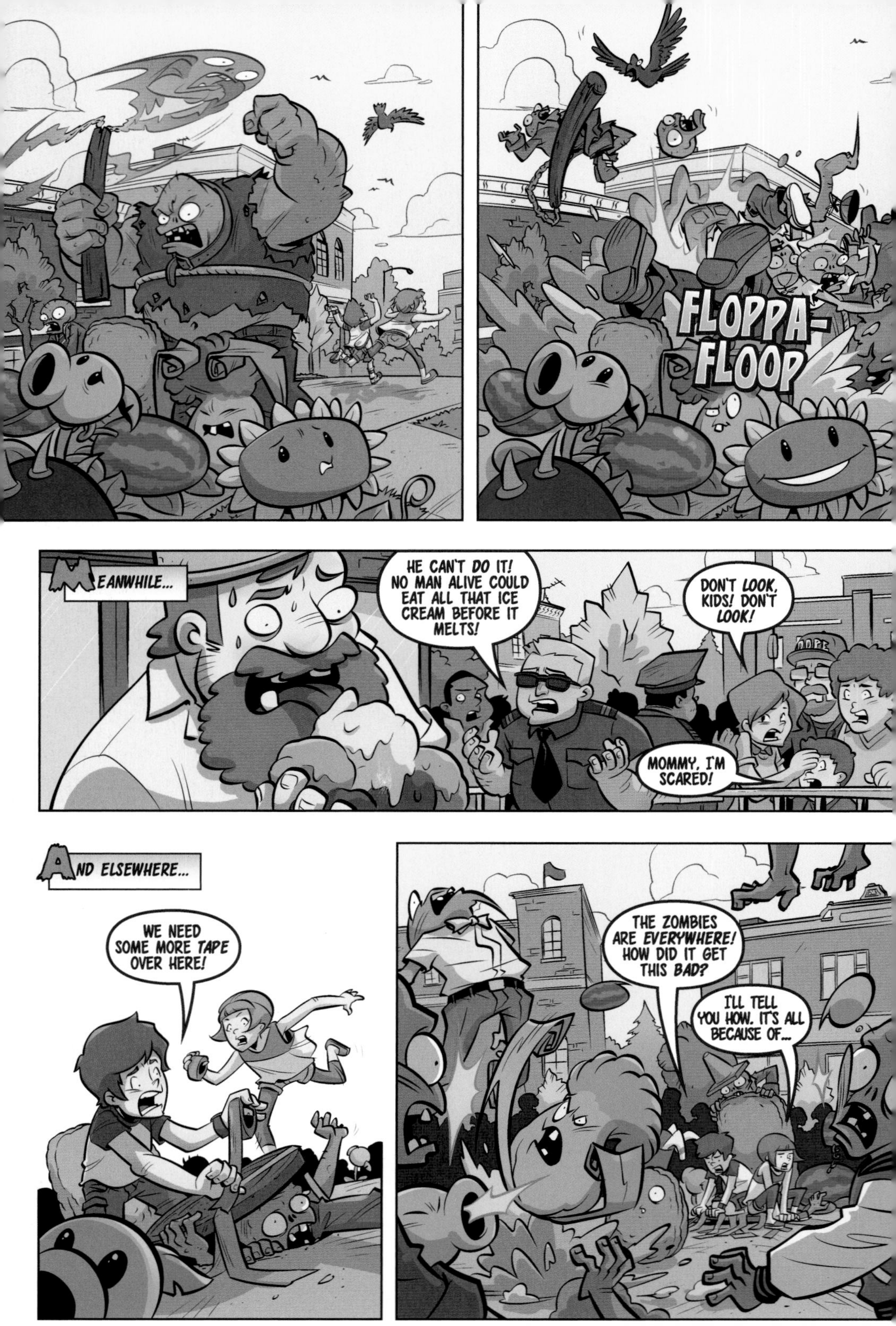
FLOPPA-FLOOP
MEANWHILE...
HE CAN'T DO IT! NO MAN ALIVE COULD EAT ALL THAT ICE CREAM BEFORE IT MELTS!
DON'T LOOK, KIDS! DON'T LOOK!
MOMMY, I'M SCARED!
AND ELSEWHERE...
WE NEED SOME MORE TAPE OVER HERE!
THE ZOMBIES ARE EVERYWHERE! HOW DID IT GET THIS BAD?
I'LL TELL YOU HOW. IT'S ALL BECAUSE OF...

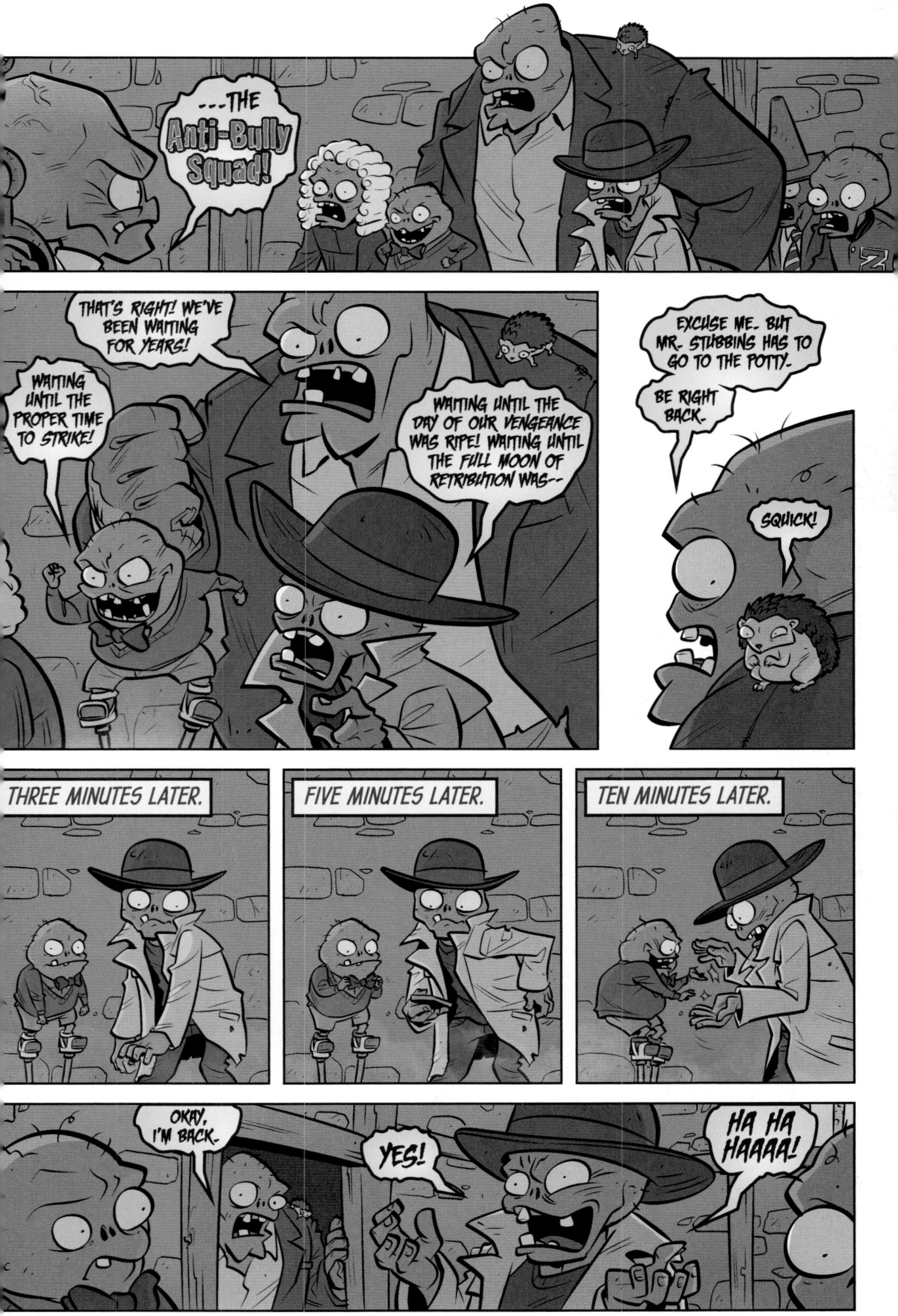

...THE
Anti-Bully Squad!
THAT'S RIGHT! WE'VE BEEN WAITING FOR YEARS!
WAITING UNTIL THE PROPER TIME TO STRIKE!
WAITING UNTIL THE DAY OF OUR VENGEANCE WAS RIPE! WAITING UNTIL THE FULL MOON OF RETRIBUTION WAS--
EXCUSE ME. BUT MR. STUBBINS HAS TO GO TO THE POTTY.
BE RIGHT BACK.
SQUICK!
THREE MINUTES LATER.
FIVE MINUTES LATER.
TEN MINUTES LATER.
OKAY, I'M BACK.
YES!
HA HA HAAAA!

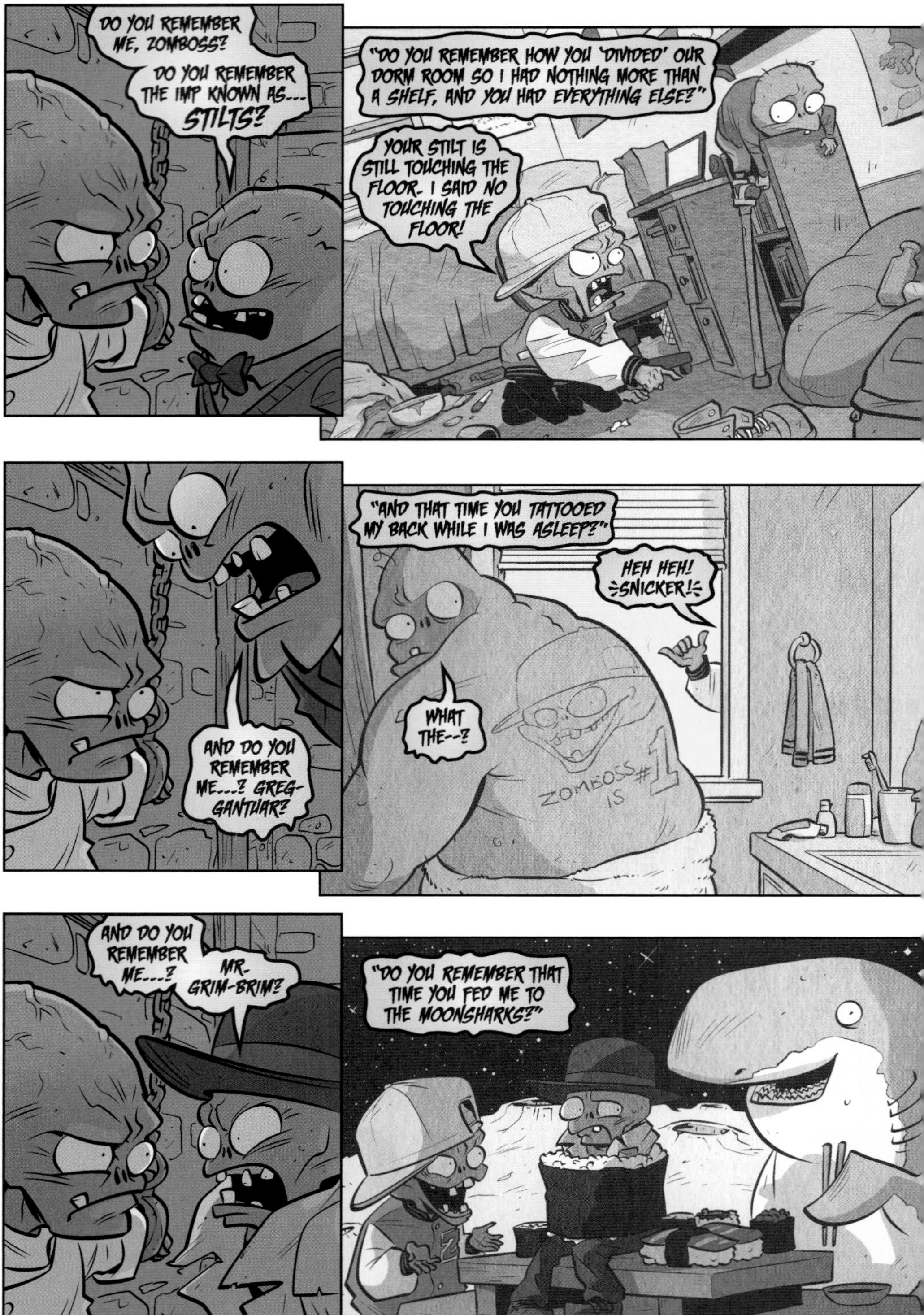

DO YOU REMEMBER ME, ZOMBOSS?
DO YOU REMEMBER THE IMP KNOWN AS... STILTS?
"DO YOU REMEMBER HOW YOU 'DIVIDED' OUR DORM ROOM SO I HAD NOTHING MORE THAN A SHELF, AND YOU HAD EVERYTHING ELSE?"
YOUR STILT IS STILL TOUCHING THE FLOOR. I SAID NO TOUCHING THE FLOOR!
AND DO YOU REMEMBER ME...? GREG-GANTUAR?
"AND THAT TIME YOU TATTOOED MY BACK WHILE I WAS ASLEEP?"
HEH HEH! SNICKER!
WHAT THE--?
ZOMBOSS IS #1
AND DO YOU REMEMBER ME...?
MR. GRIM-BRIM?
"DO YOU REMEMBER THAT TIME YOU FED ME TO THE MOONSHARKS?"

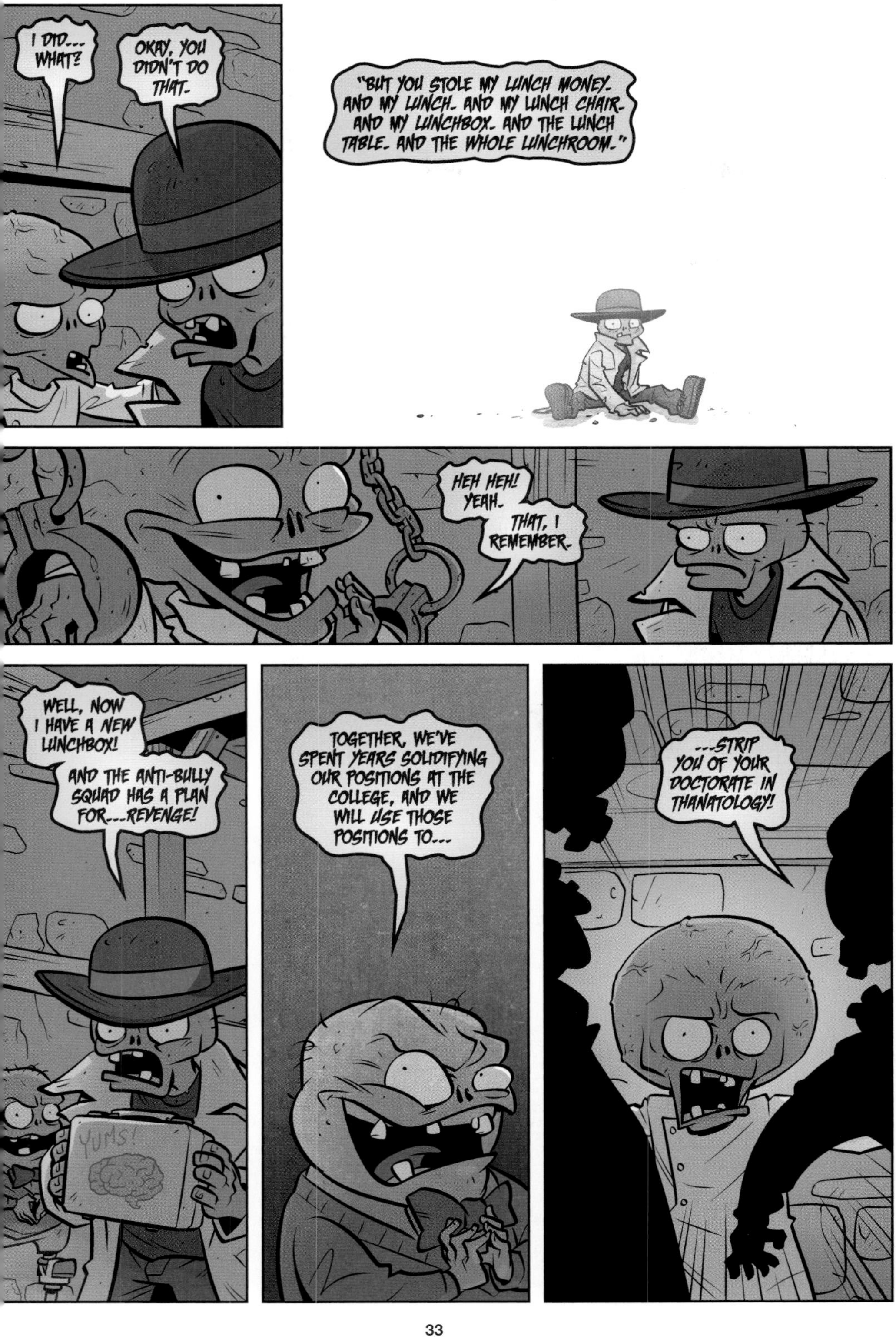
I DID... WHAT?
OKAY, YOU DIDN'T DO THAT.
"BUT YOU STOLE MY LUNCH MONEY. AND MY LUNCH. AND MY LUNCH CHAIR. AND MY LUNCHBOX. AND THE LUNCH TABLE. AND THE WHOLE LUNCHROOM."
HEH HEH! YEAH.
THAT, I REMEMBER.
WELL, NOW I HAVE A NEW LUNCHBOX!
AND THE ANTI-BULLY SQUAD HAS A PLAN FOR...REVENGE!
YUMS!
TOGETHER, WE'VE SPENT YEARS SOLIDIFYING OUR POSITIONS AT THE COLLEGE, AND WE WILL USE THOSE POSITIONS TO...
...STRIP YOU OF YOUR DOCTORATE IN THANATOLOGY!

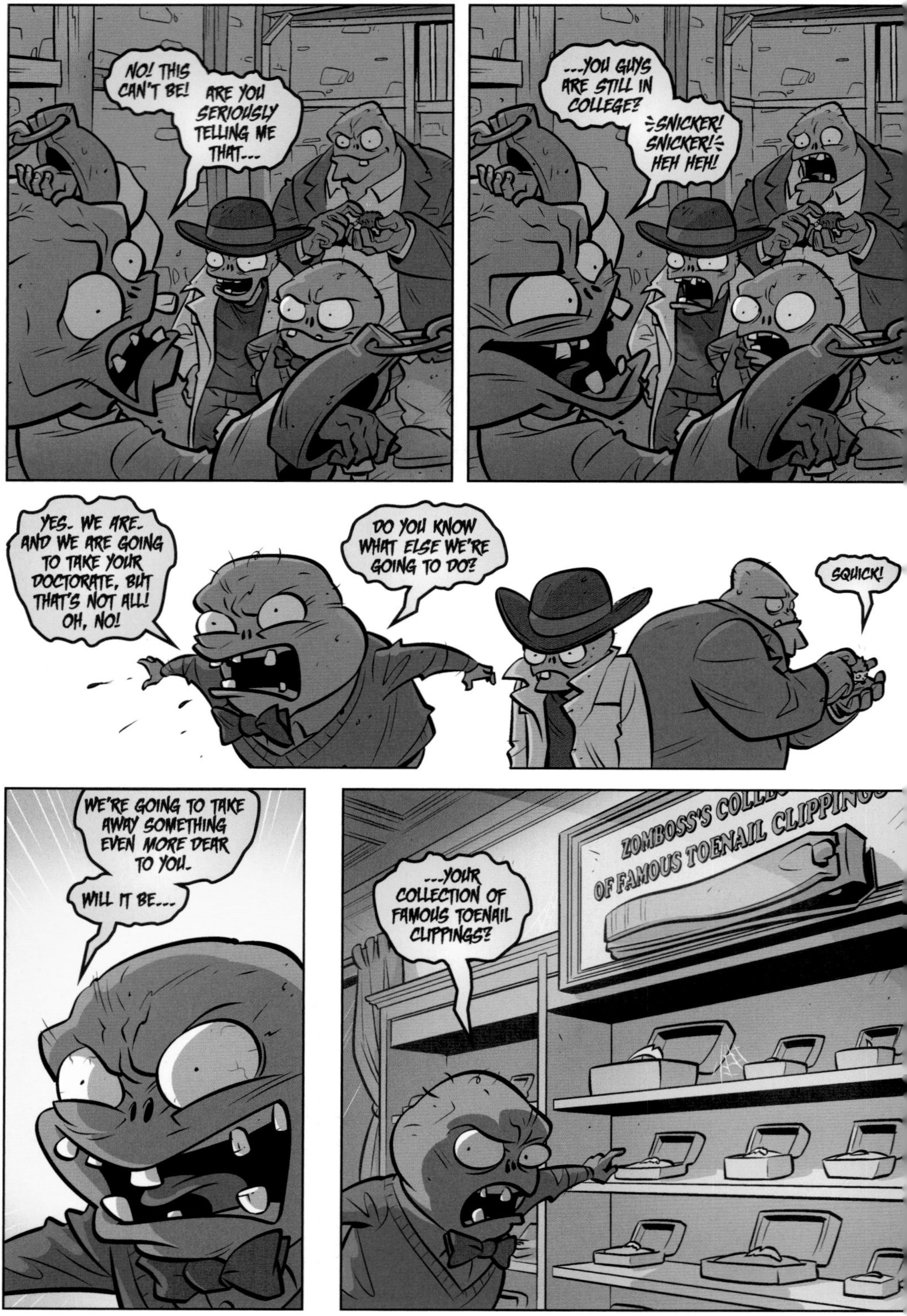
NO! THIS CAN'T BE!
ARE YOU SERIOUSLY TELLING ME THAT...
...YOU GUYS ARE STILL IN COLLEGE?
SNICKER! SNICKER! HEH HEH!
YES. WE ARE. AND WE ARE GOING TO TAKE YOUR DOCTORATE, BUT THAT'S NOT ALL! OH, NO!
DO YOU KNOW WHAT ELSE WE'RE GOING TO DO?
SQUICK!
WE'RE GOING TO TAKE AWAY SOMETHING EVEN MORE DEAR TO YOU.
WILL IT BE...
...YOUR COLLECTION OF FAMOUS TOENAIL CLIPPINGS?
ZOMBOSS'S COLLE
OF FAMOUS TOENAIL CLIPPING

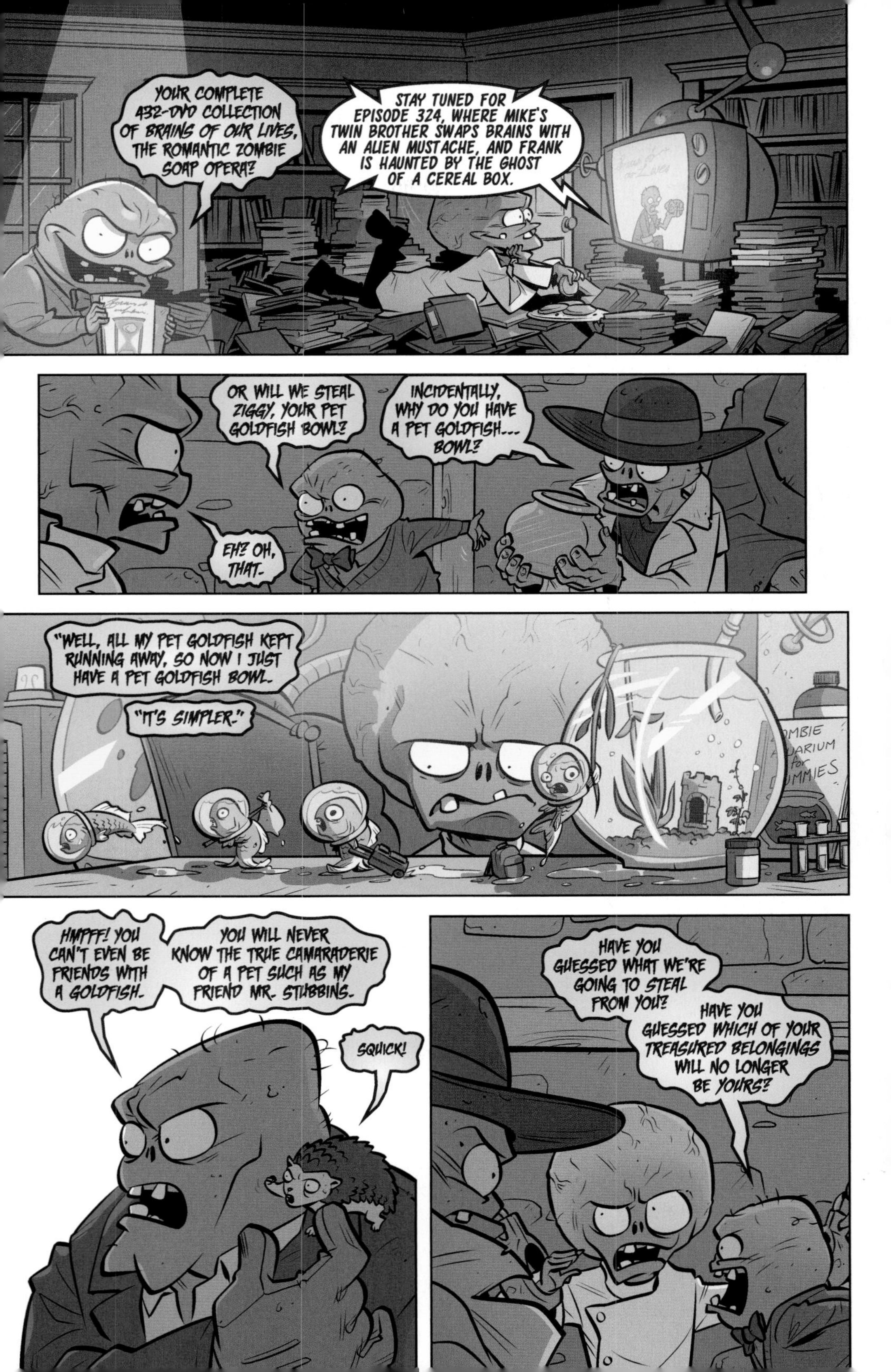
YOUR COMPLETE 432-DVD COLLECTION OF BRAINS OF OUR LIVES, THE ROMANTIC ZOMBIE SOAP OPERA?
STAY TUNED FOR EPISODE 324, WHERE MIKE'S TWIN BROTHER SWAPS BRAINS WITH AN ALIEN MUSTACHE, AND FRANK IS HAUNTED BY THE GHOST OF A CEREAL BOX.
OR WILL WE STEAL ZIGGY, YOUR PET GOLDFISH BOWL?
INCIDENTALLY, WHY DO YOU HAVE A PET GOLDFISH... BOWL?
EH? OH, THAT.
"WELL, ALL MY PET GOLDFISH KEPT RUNNING AWAY, SO NOW I JUST HAVE A PET GOLDFISH BOWL.
"IT'S SIMPLER."
HMPFF! YOU CAN'T EVEN BE FRIENDS WITH A GOLDFISH.
YOU WILL NEVER KNOW THE TRUE CAMARADERIE OF A PET SUCH AS MY FRIEND MR. STUBBINS.
SQUICK!
HAVE YOU GUESSED WHAT WE'RE GOING TO STEAL FROM YOU?
HAVE YOU GUESSED WHICH OF YOUR TREASURED BELONGINGS WILL NO LONGER BE YOURS?

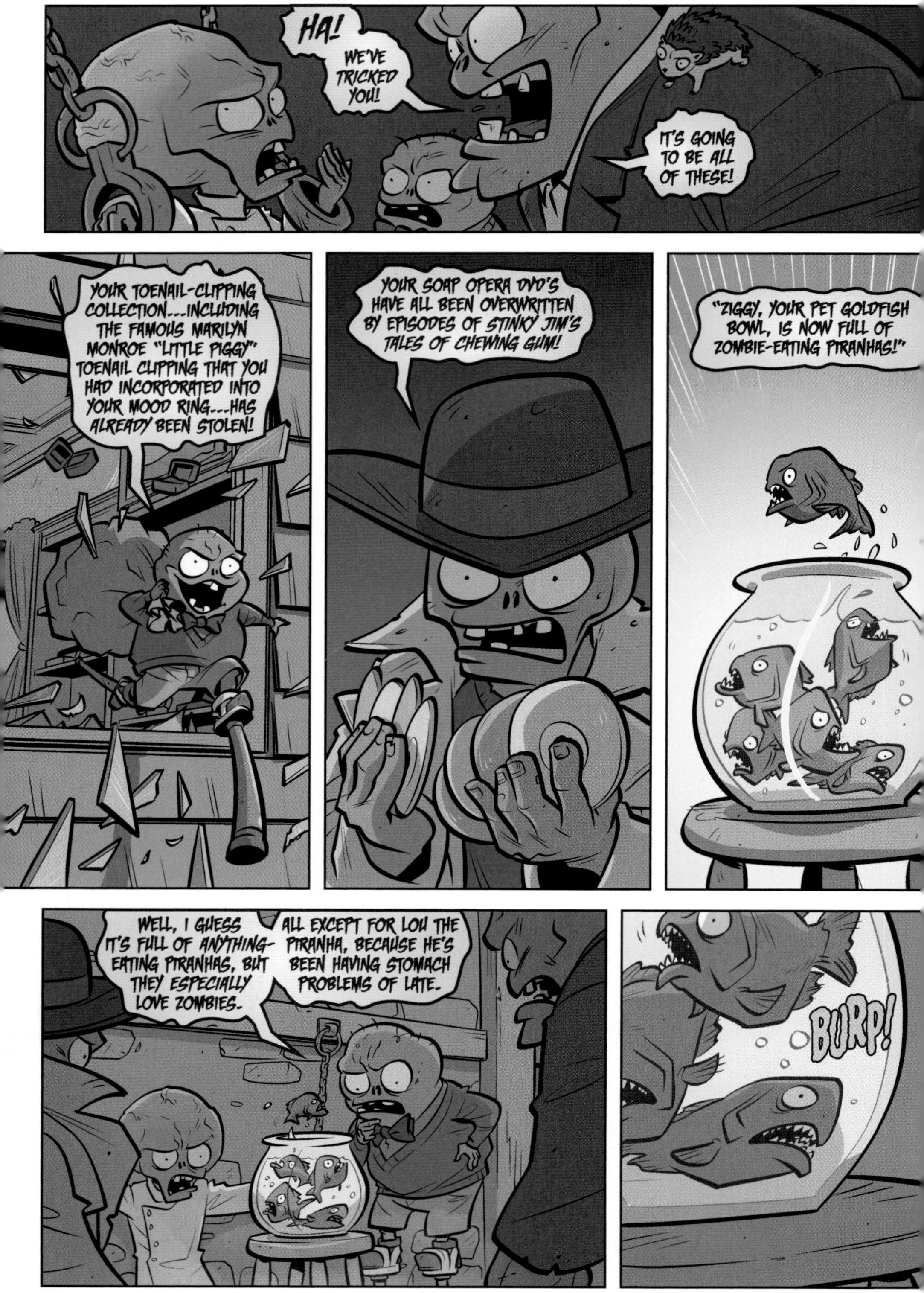
HA!
WE'VE TRICKED YOU!
IT'S GOING TO BE ALL OF THESE!
YOUR TOENAIL-CLIPPING COLLECTION...INCLUDING THE FAMOUS MARILYN MONROE "LITTLE PIGGY" TOENAIL CLIPPING THAT YOU HAD INCORPORATED INTO YOUR MOOD RING...HAS ALREADY BEEN STOLEN!
YOUR SOAP OPERA DVD'S HAVE ALL BEEN OVERWRITTEN BY EPISODES OF STINKY JIM'S TALES OF CHEWING GUM!
"ZIGGY, YOUR PET GOLDFISH BOWL, IS NOW FULL OF ZOMBIE-EATING PIRANHAS!"
WELL, I GUESS IT'S FULL OF ANYTHING-EATING PIRANHAS, BUT THEY ESPECIALLY LOVE ZOMBIES.
ALL EXCEPT FOR LOU THE PIRANHA, BECAUSE HE'S BEEN HAVING STOMACH PROBLEMS OF LATE.
BURP!

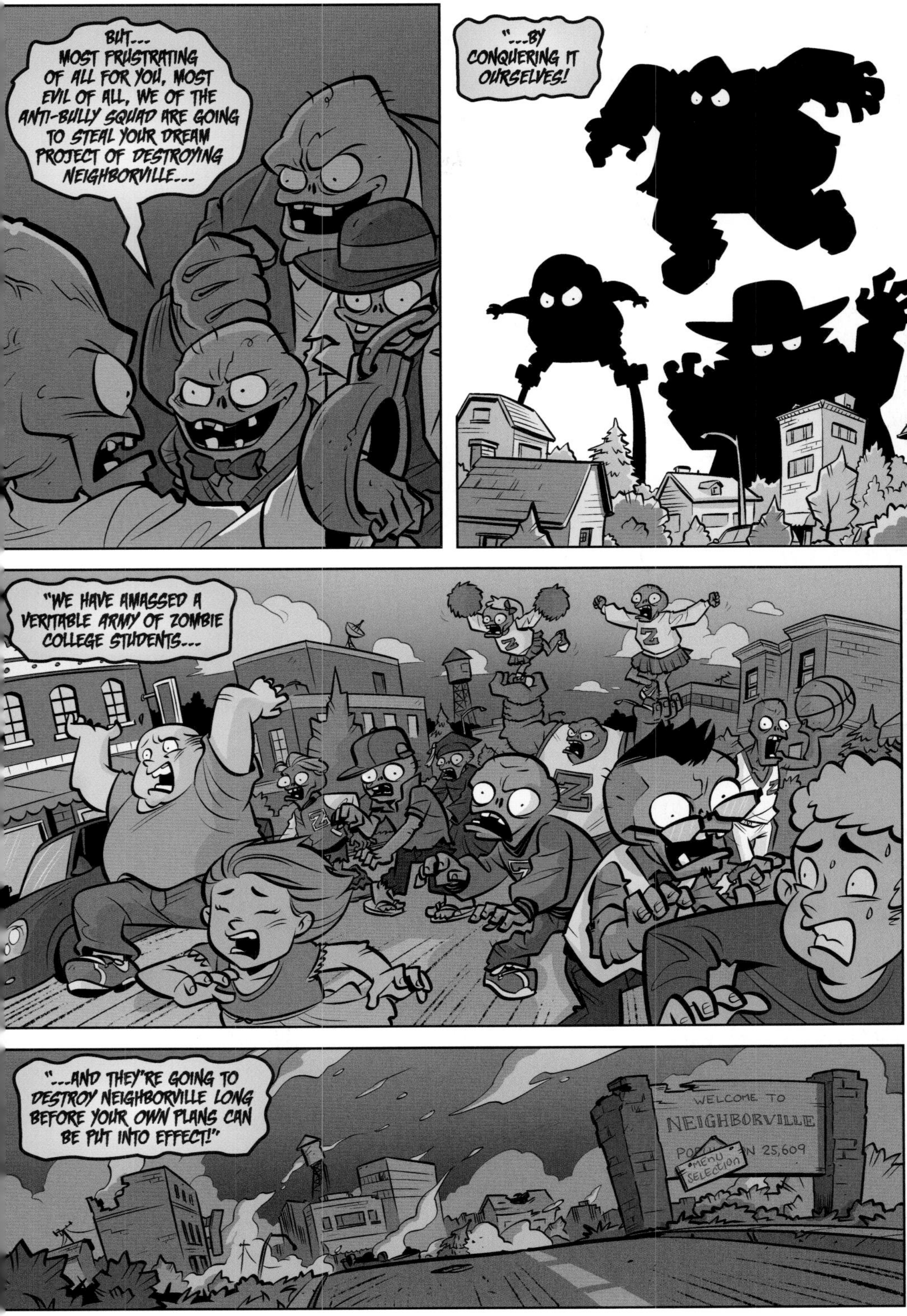
BUT... MOST FRUSTRATING OF ALL FOR YOU, MOST EVIL OF ALL, WE OF THE ANTI-BULLY SQUAD ARE GOING TO STEAL YOUR DREAM PROJECT OF DESTROYING NEIGHBORVILLE...
"...BY CONQUERING IT OURSELVES!
"WE HAVE AMASSED A VERITABLE ARMY OF ZOMBIE COLLEGE STUDENTS...
"...AND THEY'RE GOING TO DESTROY NEIGHBORVILLE LONG BEFORE YOUR OWN PLANS CAN BE PUT INTO EFFECT!"
WELCOME TO
NEIGHBORVILLE
25,609
MENU SELECTION

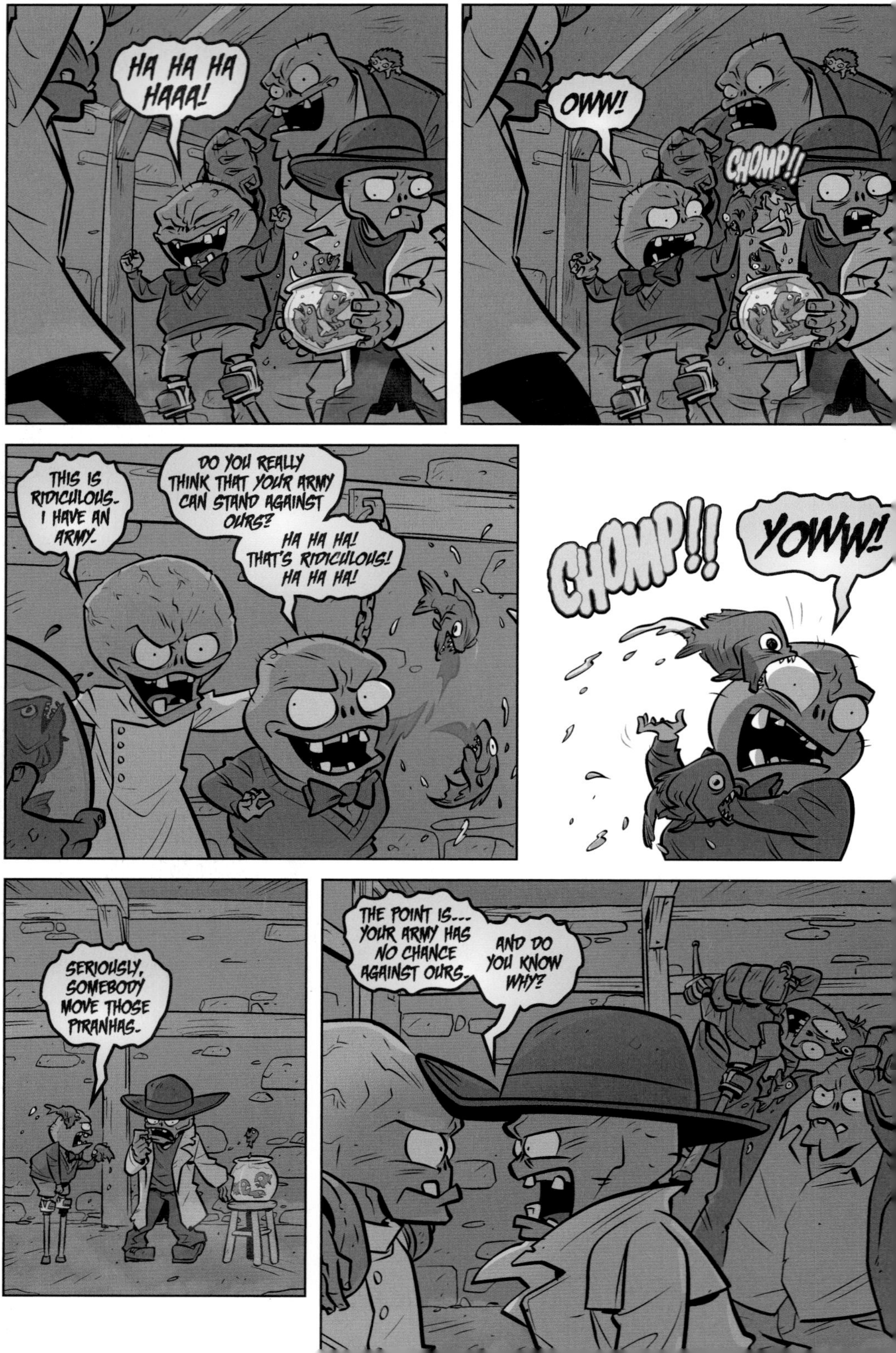
HA HA HA HAAA!
OWW!
CHOMP!!
THIS IS RIDICULOUS. I HAVE AN ARMY.
DO YOU REALLY THINK THAT YOUR ARMY CAN STAND AGAINST OURS?
HA HA HA! THAT'S RIDICULOUS! HA HA HA!
CHOMP!!
YOWW!
SERIOUSLY, SOMEBODY MOVE THOSE PIRANHAS.
THE POINT IS... YOUR ARMY HAS NO CHANCE AGAINST OURS.
AND DO YOU KNOW WHY?

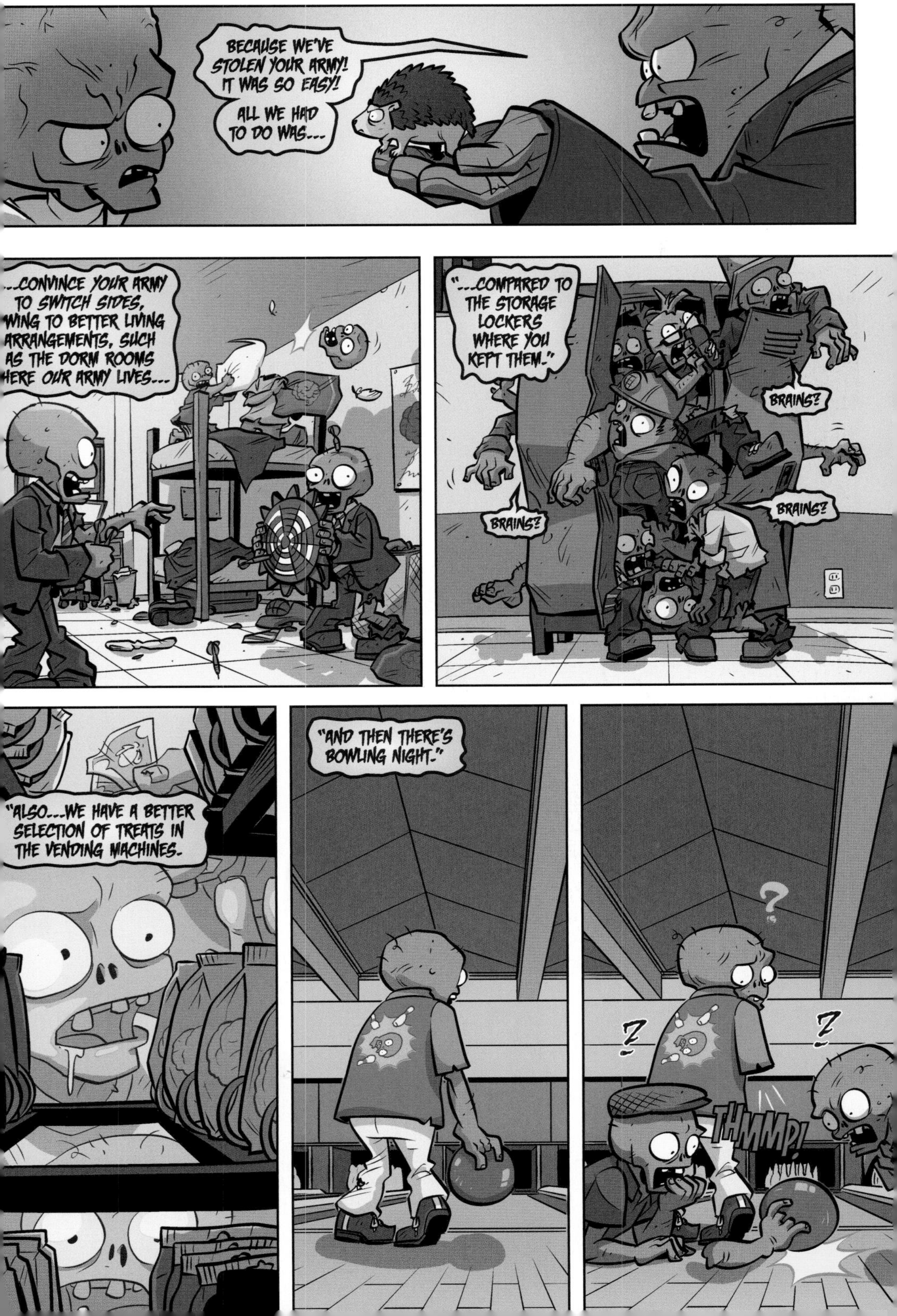

BECAUSE WE'VE STOLEN YOUR ARMY! IT WAS SO EASY!
ALL WE HAD TO DO WAS...
...CONVINCE YOUR ARMY TO SWITCH SIDES, OWING TO BETTER LIVING ARRANGEMENTS, SUCH AS THE DORM ROOMS WHERE OUR ARMY LIVES...
"...COMPARED TO THE STORAGE LOCKERS WHERE YOU KEPT THEM."
BRAINS?
BRAINS?
BRAINS?
"ALSO...WE HAVE A BETTER SELECTION OF TREATS IN THE VENDING MACHINES.
"AND THEN THERE'S BOWLING NIGHT."
?
Z
Z
THMMP!

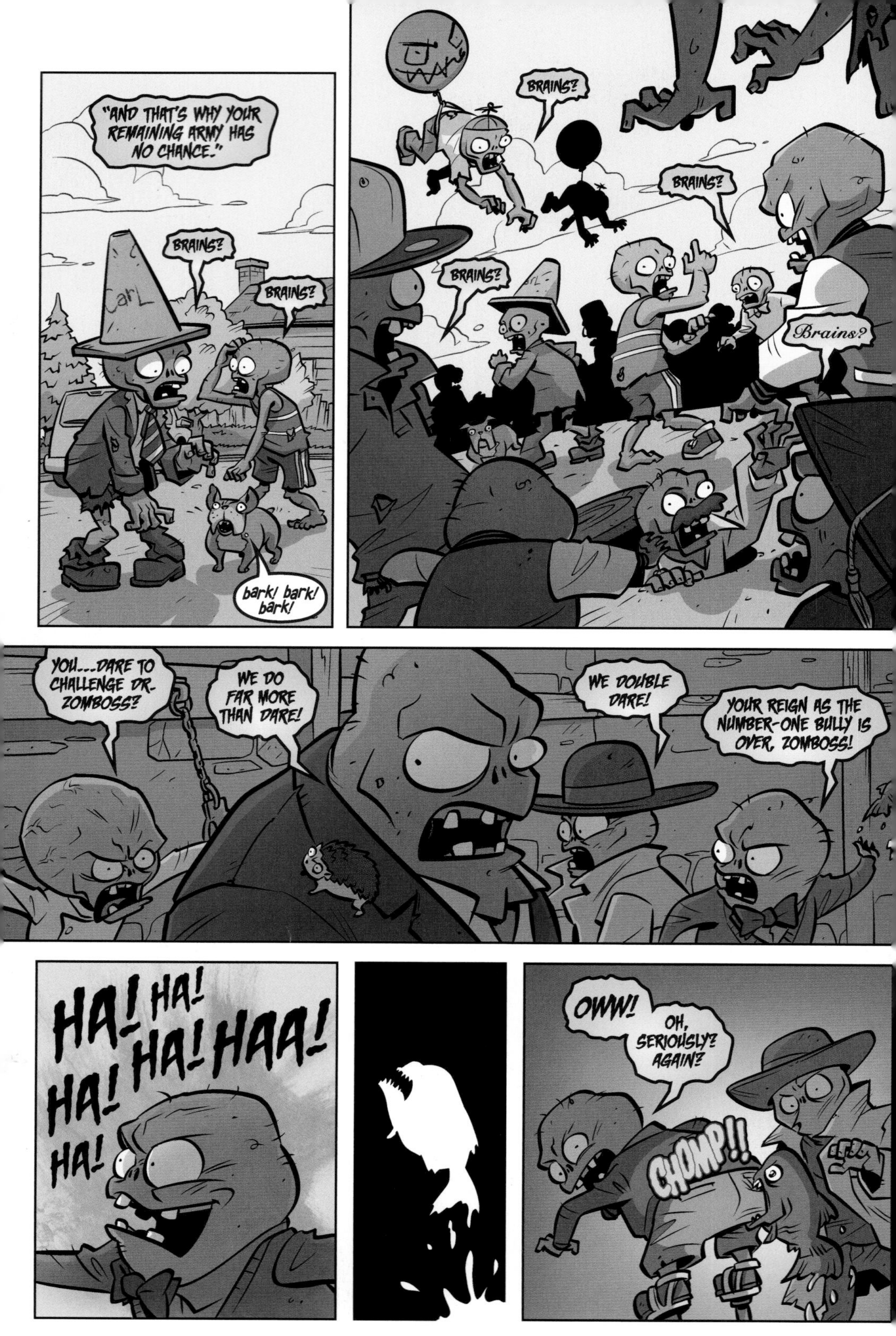
"AND THAT'S WHY YOUR REMAINING ARMY HAS NO CHANCE."
BRAINS?
BRAINS?
bark! bark! bark!
BRAINS?
BRAINS?
BRAINS?
Brains?
YOU...DARE TO CHALLENGE DR. ZOMBOSS?
WE DO FAR MORE THAN DARE!
WE DOUBLE DARE!
YOUR REIGN AS THE NUMBER-ONE BULLY IS OVER, ZOMBOSS!
HA! HA! HA! HA! HAA! HA!
OWW!
OH, SERIOUSLY? AGAIN?
CHOMP!!

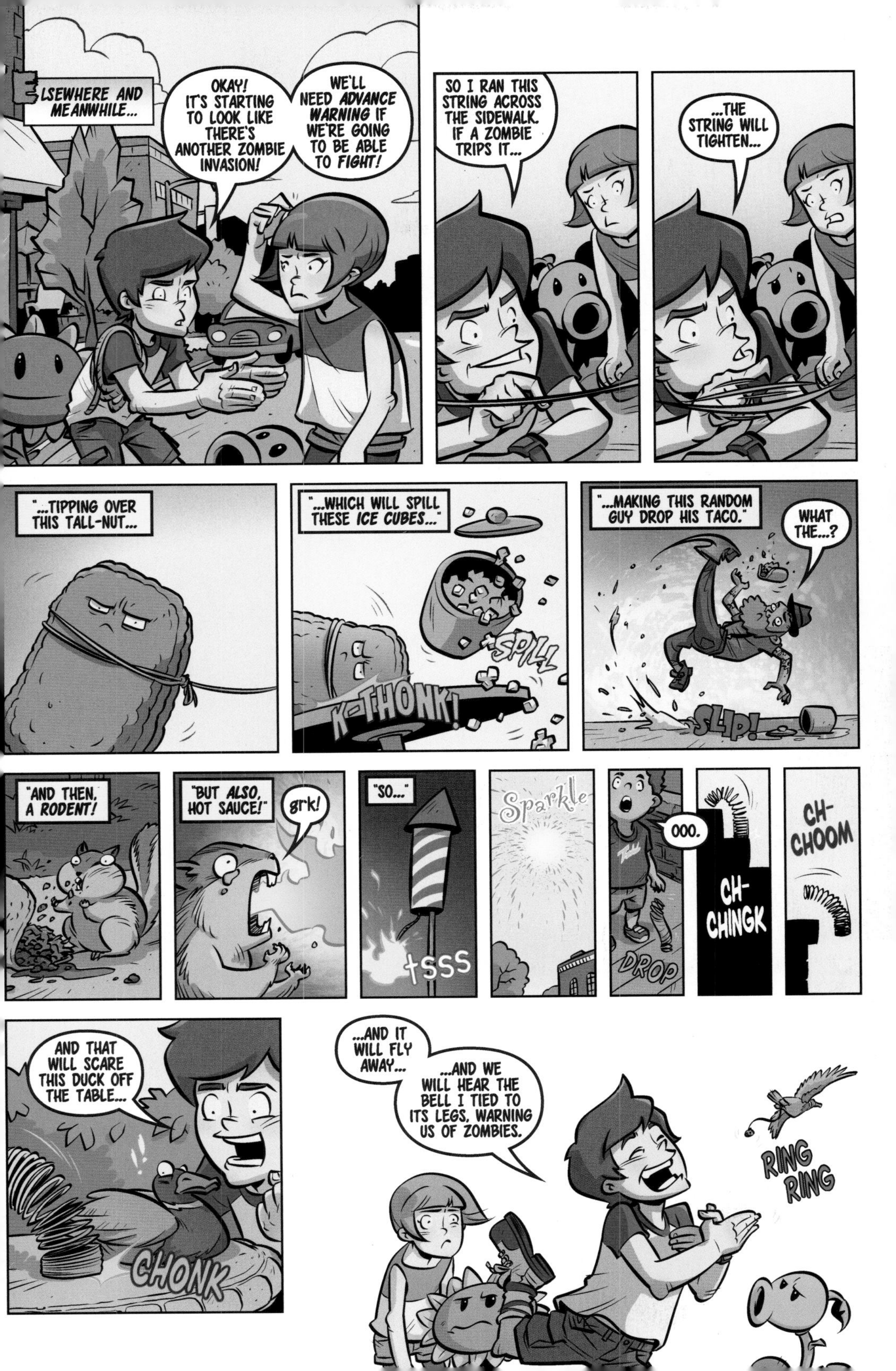
ELSEWHERE AND MEANWHILE...
OKAY! IT'S STARTING TO LOOK LIKE THERE'S ANOTHER ZOMBIE INVASION!
WE'LL NEED ADVANCE WARNING IF WE'RE GOING TO BE ABLE TO FIGHT!
SO I RAN THIS STRING ACROSS THE SIDEWALK. IF A ZOMBIE TRIPS IT...
...THE STRING WILL TIGHTEN...
"...TIPPING OVER THIS TALL-NUT...
"...WHICH WILL SPILL THESE ICE CUBES..."
SPILL
K-THONK!
"...MAKING THIS RANDOM GUY DROP HIS TACO."
WHAT THE...?
SLIP!
"AND THEN, A RODENT!
"BUT ALSO, HOT SAUCE!"
grk!
"SO..."
tSSS
Sparkle
OOO.
DROP
CH-CHINGK
CH-CHOOM
AND THAT WILL SCARE THIS DUCK OFF THE TABLE...
!
CHONK
...AND IT WILL FLY AWAY...
...AND WE WILL HEAR THE BELL I TIED TO ITS LEGS, WARNING US OF ZOMBIES.
RING RING

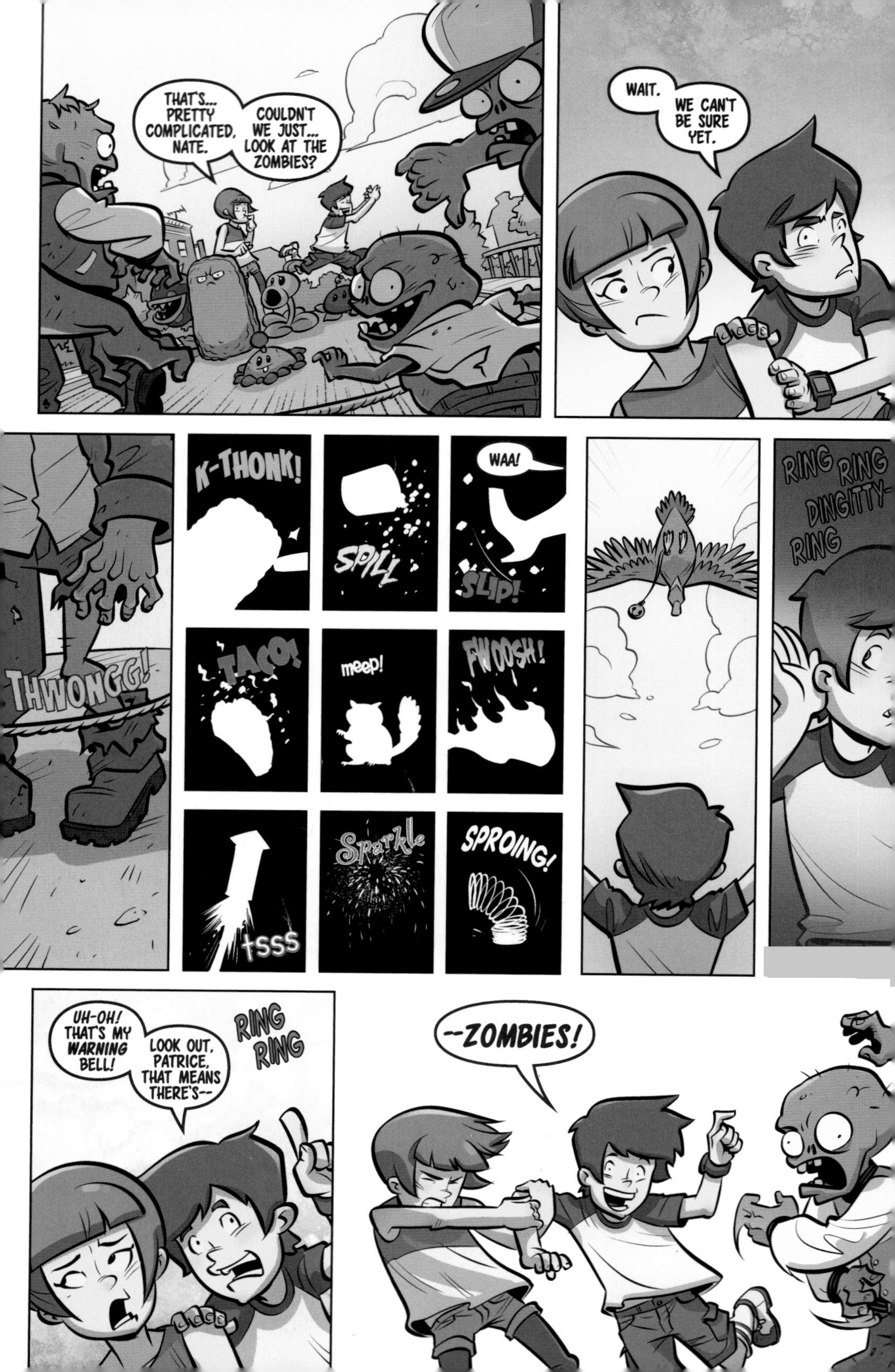
THAT'S... PRETTY COMPLICATED, NATE.
COULDN'T WE JUST... LOOK AT THE ZOMBIES?
WAIT.
WE CAN'T BE SURE YET.
THWONGG!
K-THONK!
SPILL
WAA!
SLIP!
TACO!
meep!
FWOOSH!
tsss
Sparkle
SPROING!
RING RING DINGITTY-RING
UH-OH! THAT'S MY WARNING BELL!
LOOK OUT, PATRICE, THAT MEANS THERE'S--
RING RING
--ZOMBIES!

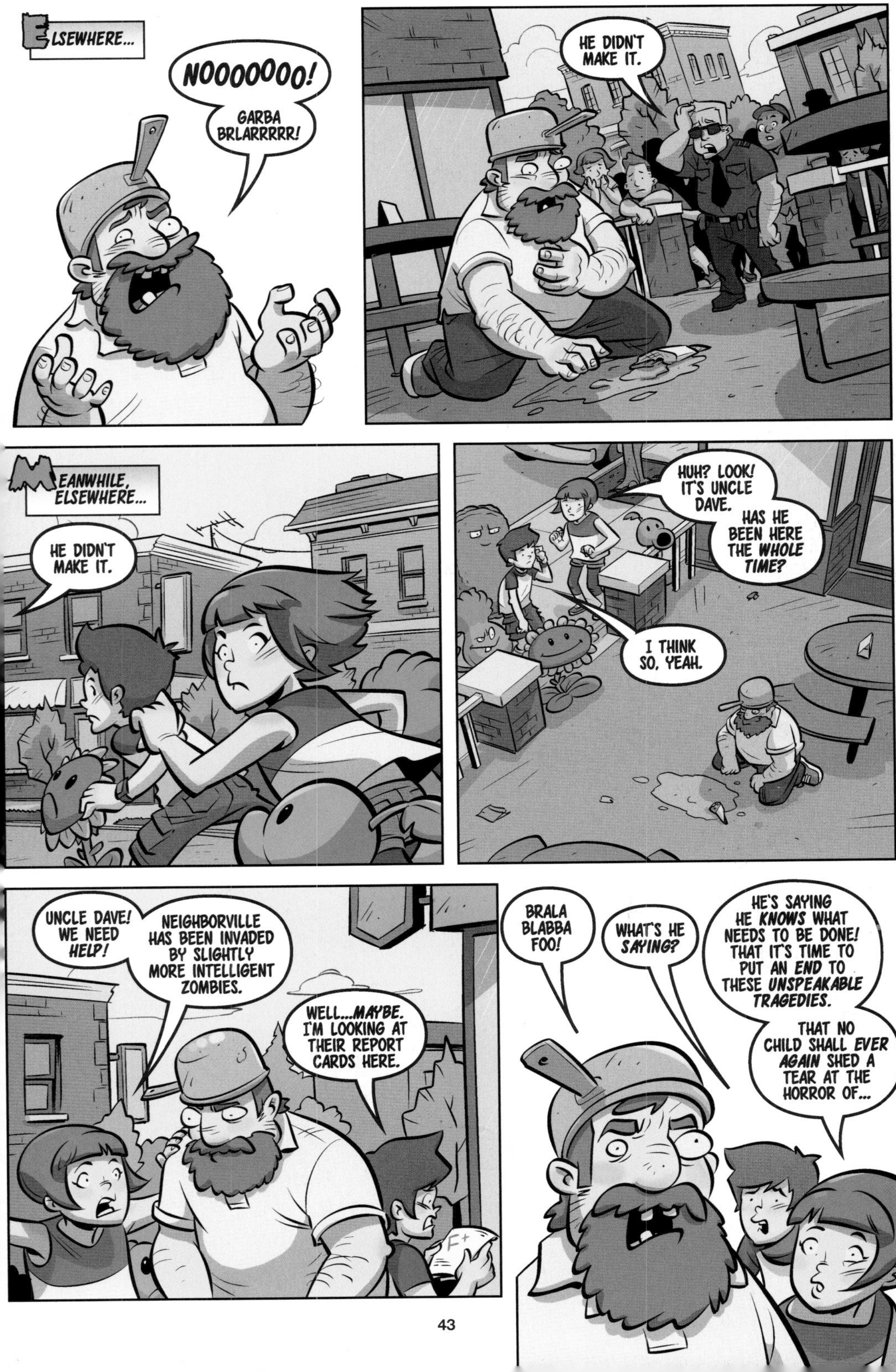
ELSEWHERE...
NOOOOOOO!
GARBA BRLARRRRR!
HE DIDN'T MAKE IT.
MEANWHILE, ELSEWHERE...
HE DIDN'T MAKE IT.
HUH? LOOK! IT'S UNCLE DAVE.
HAS HE BEEN HERE THE WHOLE TIME?
I THINK SO, YEAH.
UNCLE DAVE! WE NEED HELP!
NEIGHBORVILLE HAS BEEN INVADED BY SLIGHTLY MORE INTELLIGENT ZOMBIES.
WELL...MAYBE. I'M LOOKING AT THEIR REPORT CARDS HERE.
F+
BRALA BLABBA FOO!
WHAT'S HE SAYING?
HE'S SAYING HE KNOWS WHAT NEEDS TO BE DONE! THAT IT'S TIME TO PUT AN END TO THESE UNSPEAKABLE TRAGEDIES.
THAT NO CHILD SHALL EVER AGAIN SHED A TEAR AT THE HORROR OF...

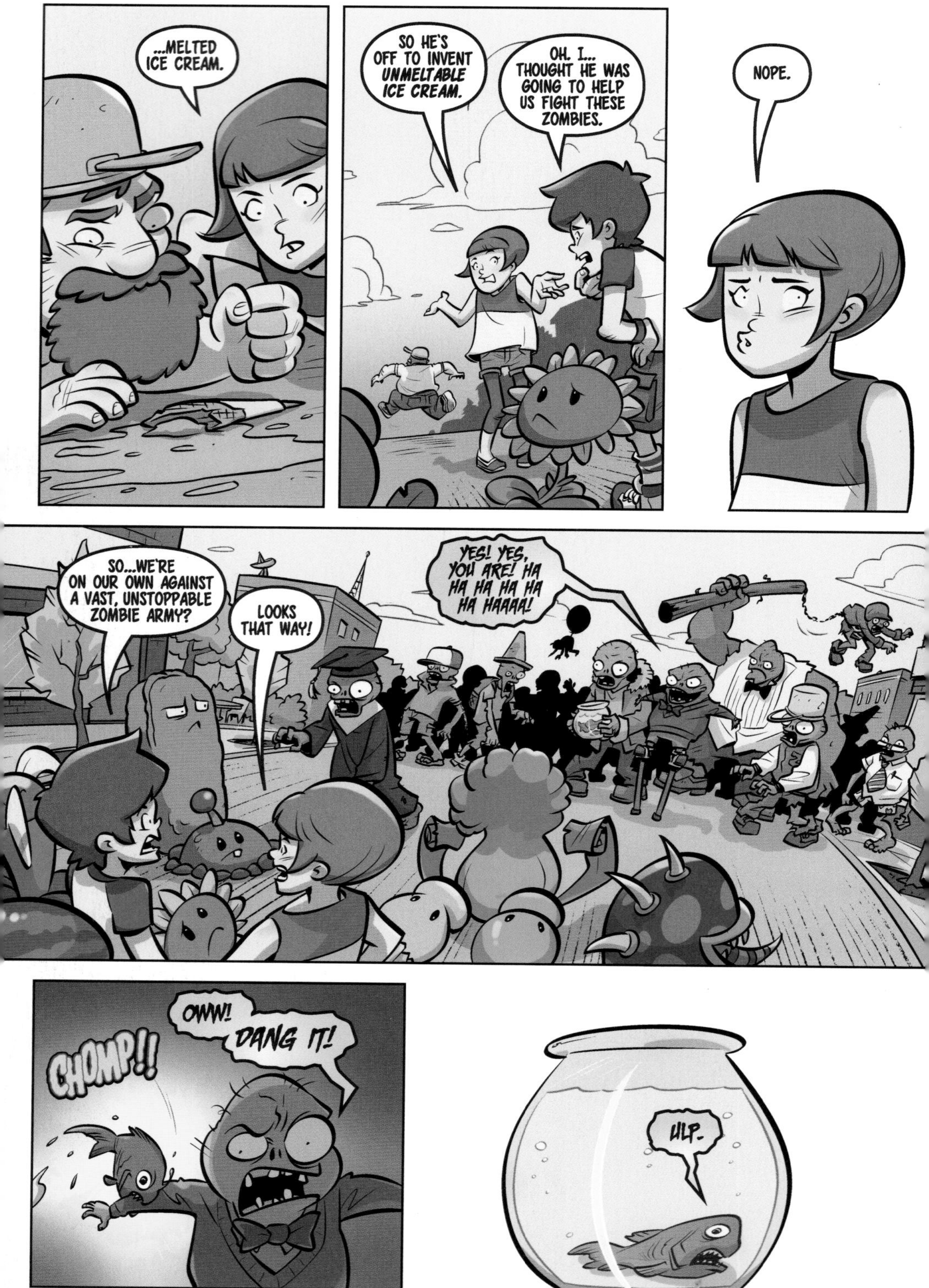
...MELTED ICE CREAM.
SO HE'S OFF TO INVENT UNMELTABLE ICE CREAM.
OH. I... THOUGHT HE WAS GOING TO HELP US FIGHT THESE ZOMBIES.
NOPE.
SO...WE'RE ON OUR OWN AGAINST A VAST, UNSTOPPABLE ZOMBIE ARMY?
LOOKS THAT WAY!
YES! YES, YOU ARE! HA HA HA HA HA HA HAAAA!
CHOMP!!
OWW!
DANG IT!
ULP.

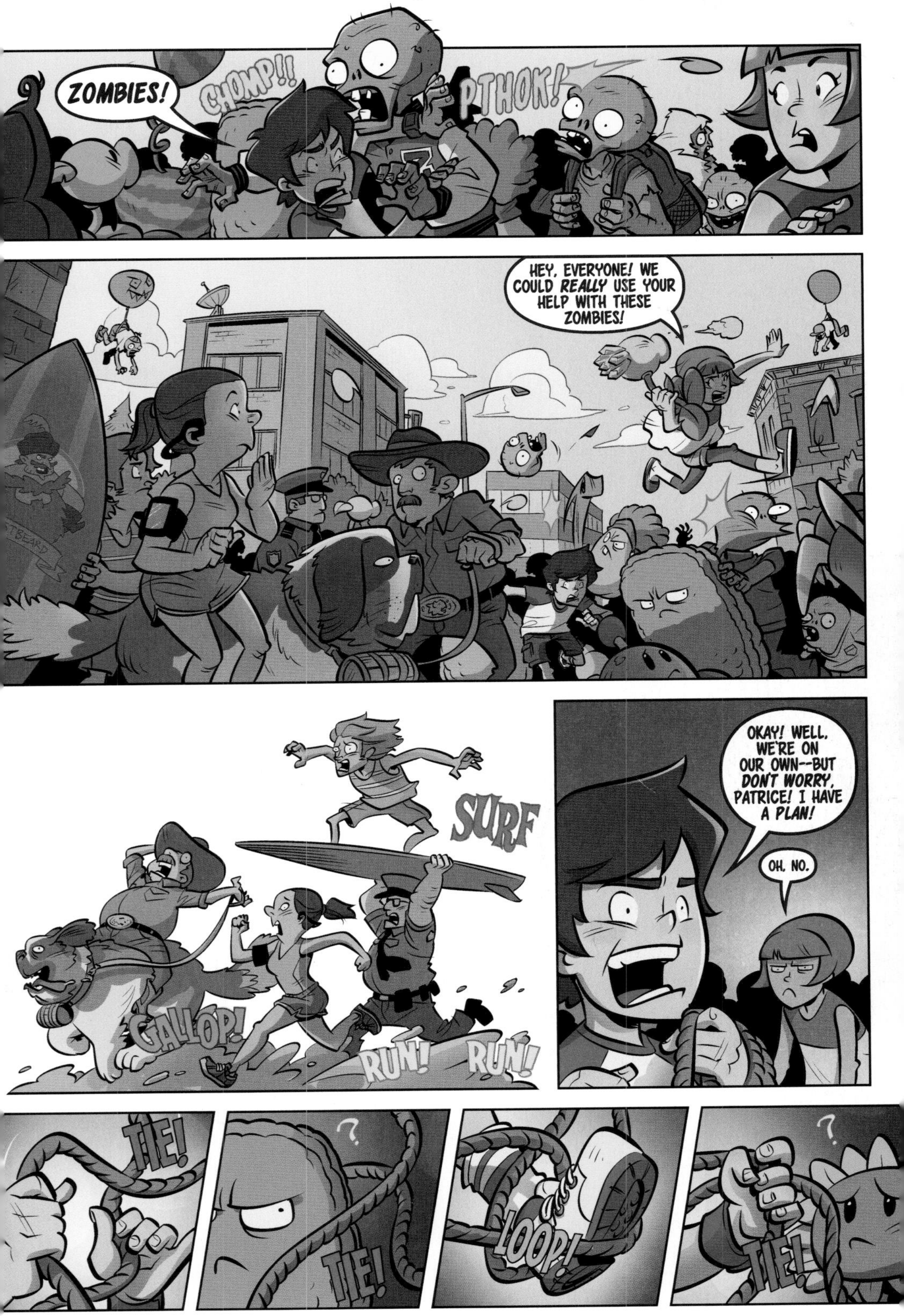

ZOMBIES!
CHOMP!!
PTHOK!
HEY, EVERYONE! WE COULD REALLY USE YOUR HELP WITH THESE ZOMBIES!
SURF
GALLOP!
RUN!
RUN!
OKAY! WELL, WE'RE ON OUR OWN--BUT DON'T WORRY, PATRICE! I HAVE A PLAN!
OH, NO.
TIE!
?
TIE!
LOOP!
?
TIE!

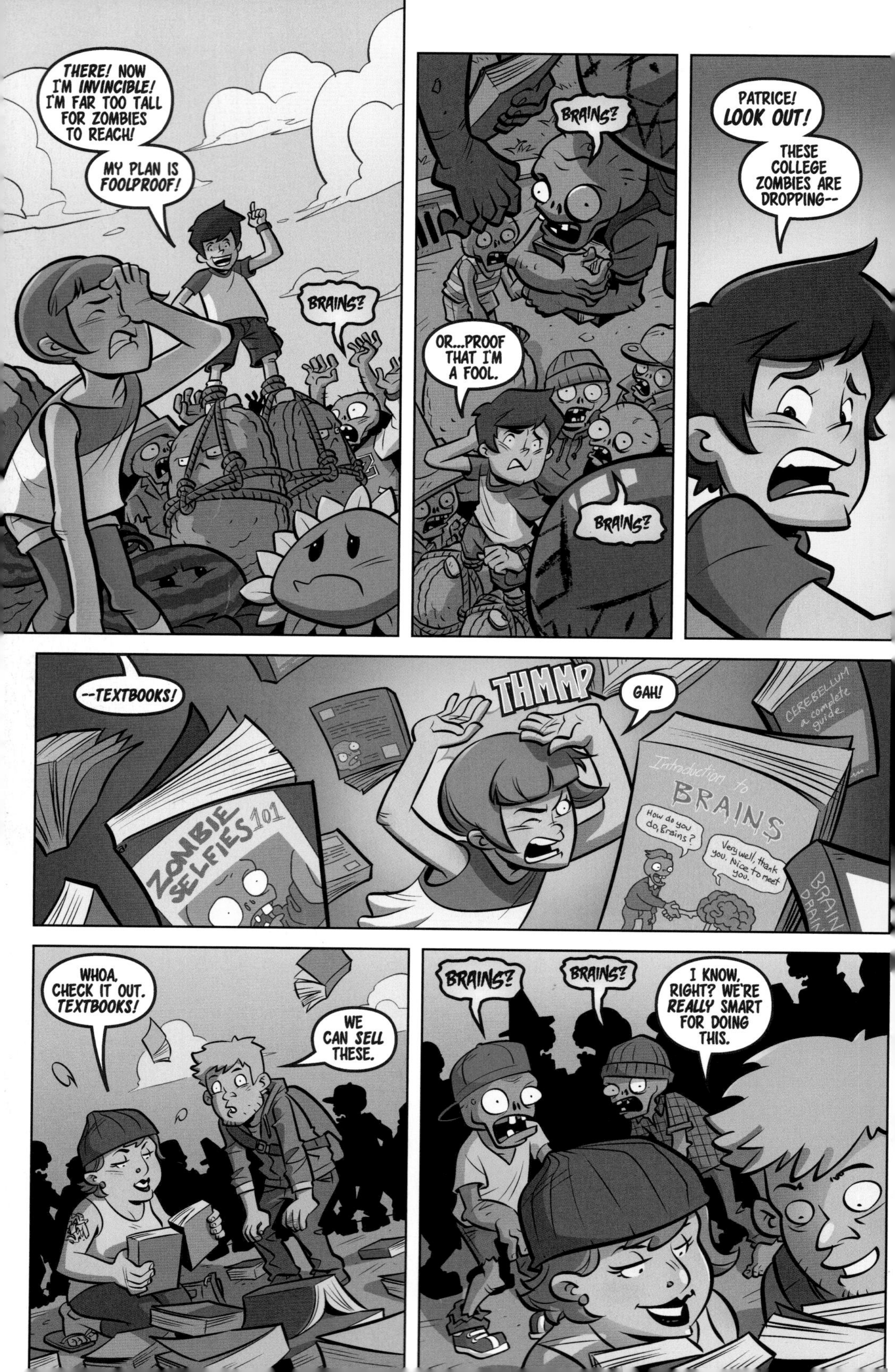
THERE! NOW I'M INVINCIBLE! I'M FAR TOO TALL FOR ZOMBIES TO REACH!
MY PLAN IS FOOLPROOF!
BRAINS?
BRAINS?
OR...PROOF THAT I'M A FOOL.
BRAINS?
PATRICE! LOOK OUT!
THESE COLLEGE ZOMBIES ARE DROPPING--
--TEXTBOOKS!
THMMP
GAH!
ZOMBIE SELFIES 101
CEREBELLUM a complete guide
Introduction to BRAINS
How do you do, Brains?
Very well, thank you. Nice to meet you.
WHOA, CHECK IT OUT. TEXTBOOKS!
WE CAN SELL THESE.
BRAINS?
BRAINS?
I KNOW, RIGHT? WE'RE REALLY SMART FOR DOING THIS.

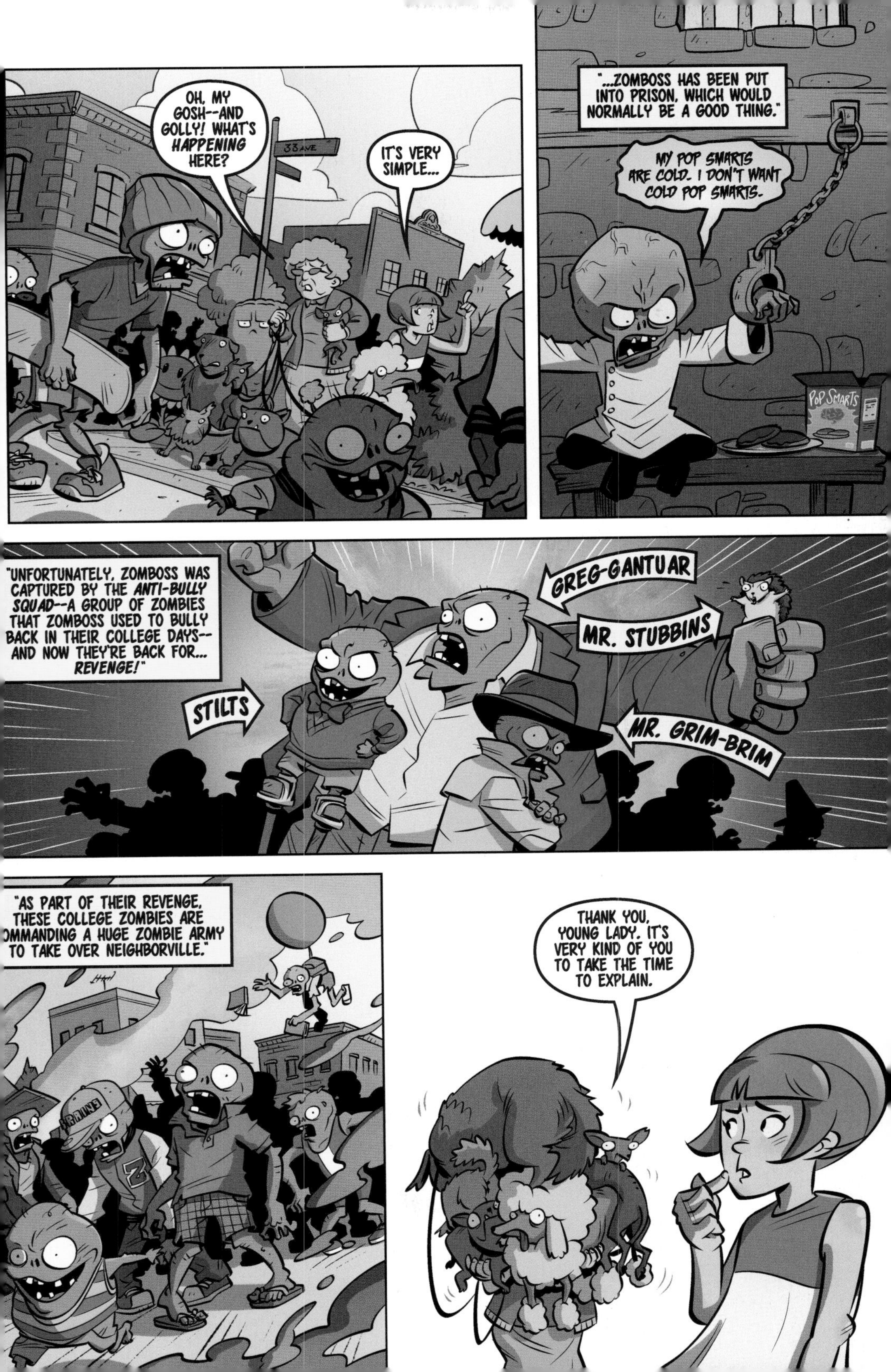
OH, MY GOSH--AND GOLLY! WHAT'S HAPPENING HERE?
33 AVE
IT'S VERY SIMPLE...
"...ZOMBOSS HAS BEEN PUT INTO PRISON, WHICH WOULD NORMALLY BE A GOOD THING."
MY POP SMARTS ARE COLD. I DON'T WANT COLD POP SMARTS.
POP SMARTS
"UNFORTUNATELY, ZOMBOSS WAS CAPTURED BY THE ANTI-BULLY SQUAD--A GROUP OF ZOMBIES THAT ZOMBOSS USED TO BULLY BACK IN THEIR COLLEGE DAYS--AND NOW THEY'RE BACK FOR... REVENGE!"
GREG-GANTUAR
MR. STUBBINS
STILTS
MR. GRIM-BRIM
"AS PART OF THEIR REVENGE, THESE COLLEGE ZOMBIES ARE OMMANDING A HUGE ZOMBIE ARMY TO TAKE OVER NEIGHBORVILLE."
BRAINS
THANK YOU, YOUNG LADY. IT'S VERY KIND OF YOU TO TAKE THE TIME TO EXPLAIN.

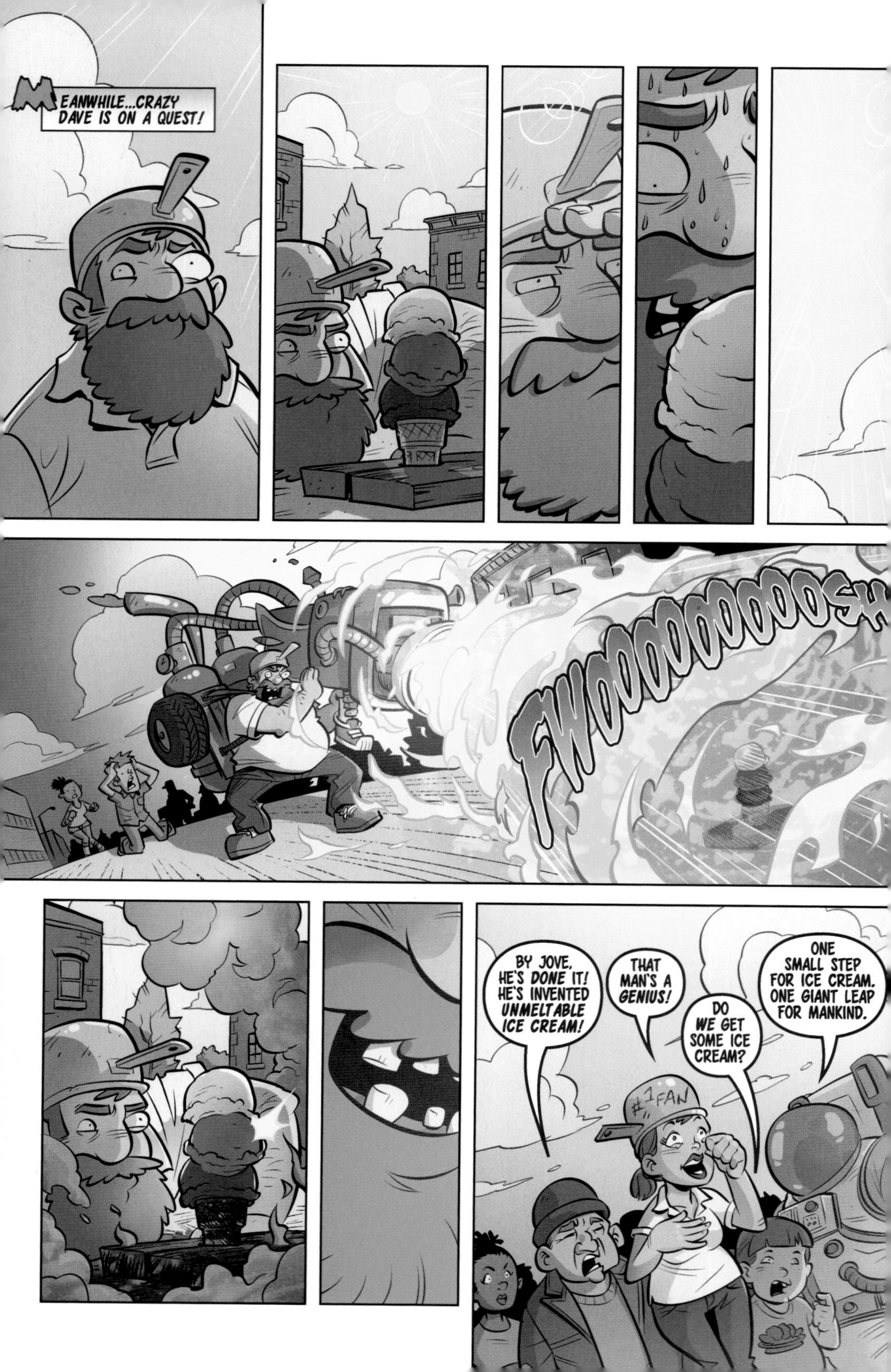
MEANWHILE...CRAZY DAVE IS ON A QUEST!
FWOOOOOOOOOOSH
BY JOVE, HE'S DONE IT! HE'S INVENTED UNMELTABLE ICE CREAM!
THAT MAN'S A GENIUS!
DO WE GET SOME ICE CREAM?
ONE SMALL STEP FOR ICE CREAM. ONE GIANT LEAP FOR MANKIND.
#1 FAN

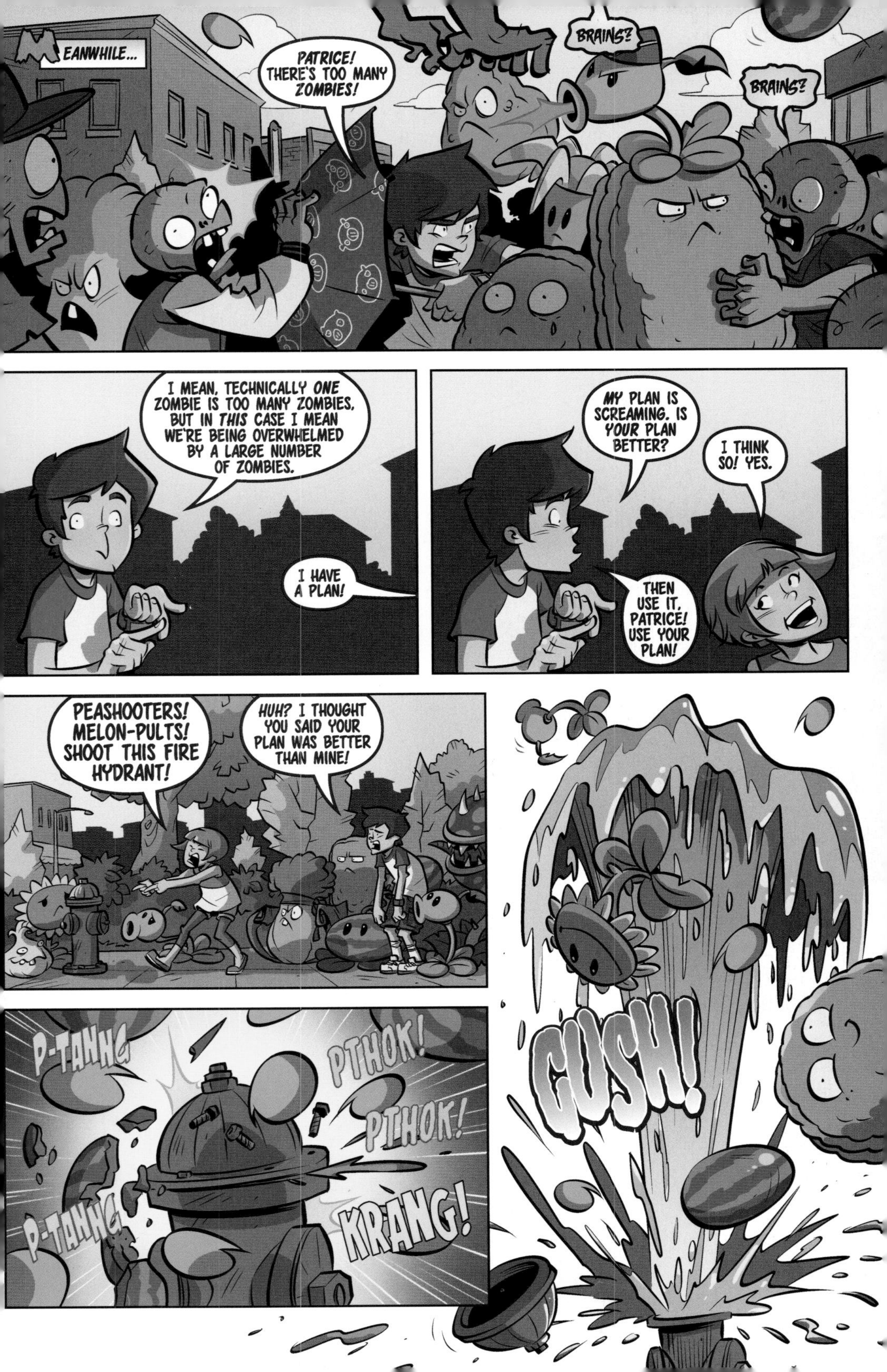
MEANWHILE...
PATRICE! THERE'S TOO MANY ZOMBIES!
BRAINS?
BRAINS?
I MEAN, TECHNICALLY ONE ZOMBIE IS TOO MANY ZOMBIES, BUT IN THIS CASE I MEAN WE'RE BEING OVERWHELMED BY A LARGE NUMBER OF ZOMBIES.
I HAVE A PLAN!
MY PLAN IS SCREAMING. IS YOUR PLAN BETTER?
I THINK SO! YES.
THEN USE IT, PATRICE! USE YOUR PLAN!
PEASHOOTERS! MELON-PULTS! SHOOT THIS FIRE HYDRANT!
HUH? I THOUGHT YOU SAID YOUR PLAN WAS BETTER THAN MINE!
P-TANNG
PTHOK!
PTHOK!
P-TANNG
KRANG!
GUSH!

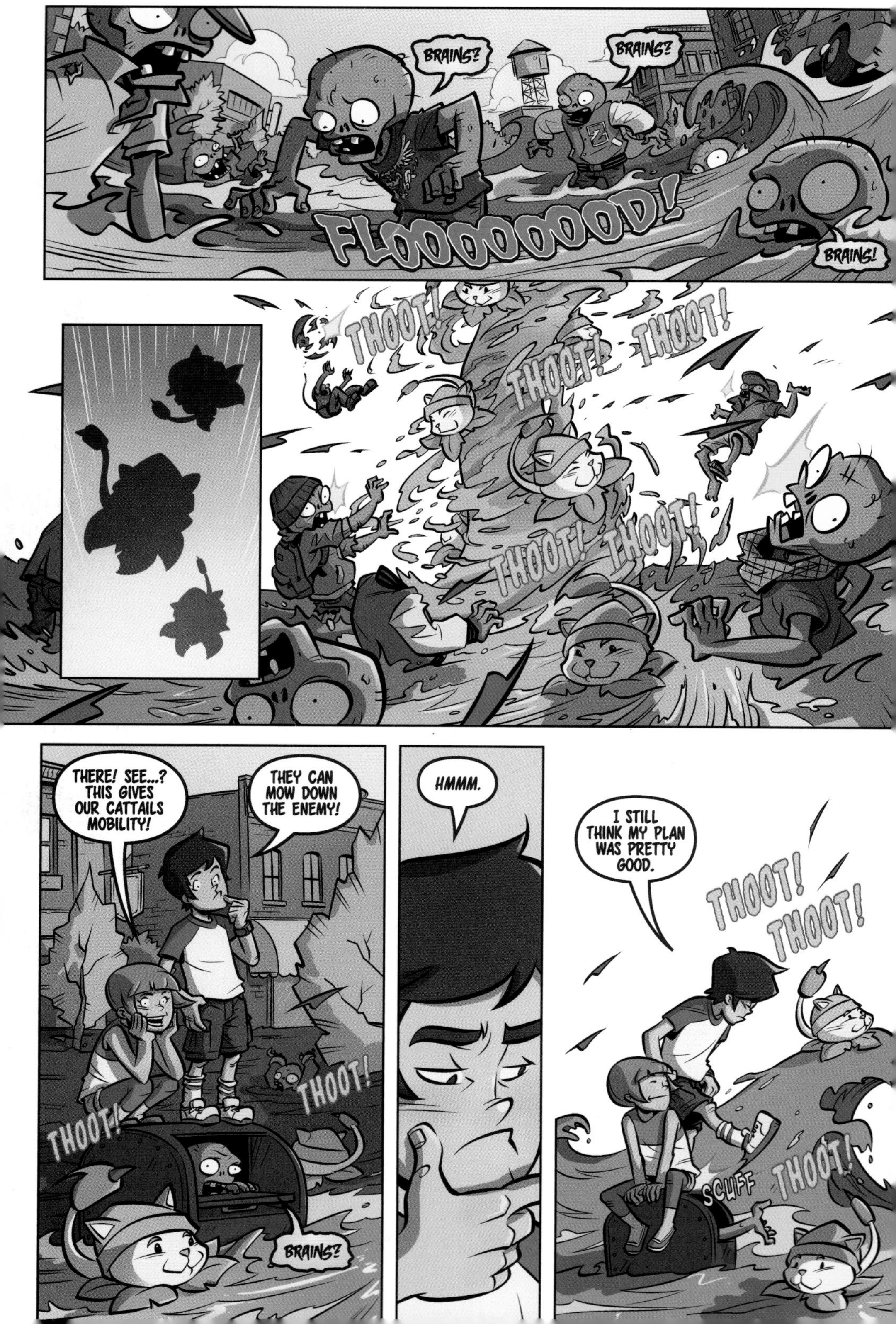
BRAINS?
BRAINS?
FLOOOOOOOD!
BRAINS!
THOOT!
THOOT!
THOOT!
THOOT!
THOOT!
THERE! SEE...? THIS GIVES OUR CATTAILS MOBILITY!
THEY CAN MOW DOWN THE ENEMY!
THOOT!
THOOT!
BRAINS?
HMMM.
I STILL THINK MY PLAN WAS PRETTY GOOD.
THOOT!
THOOT!
SCUFF
THOOT!

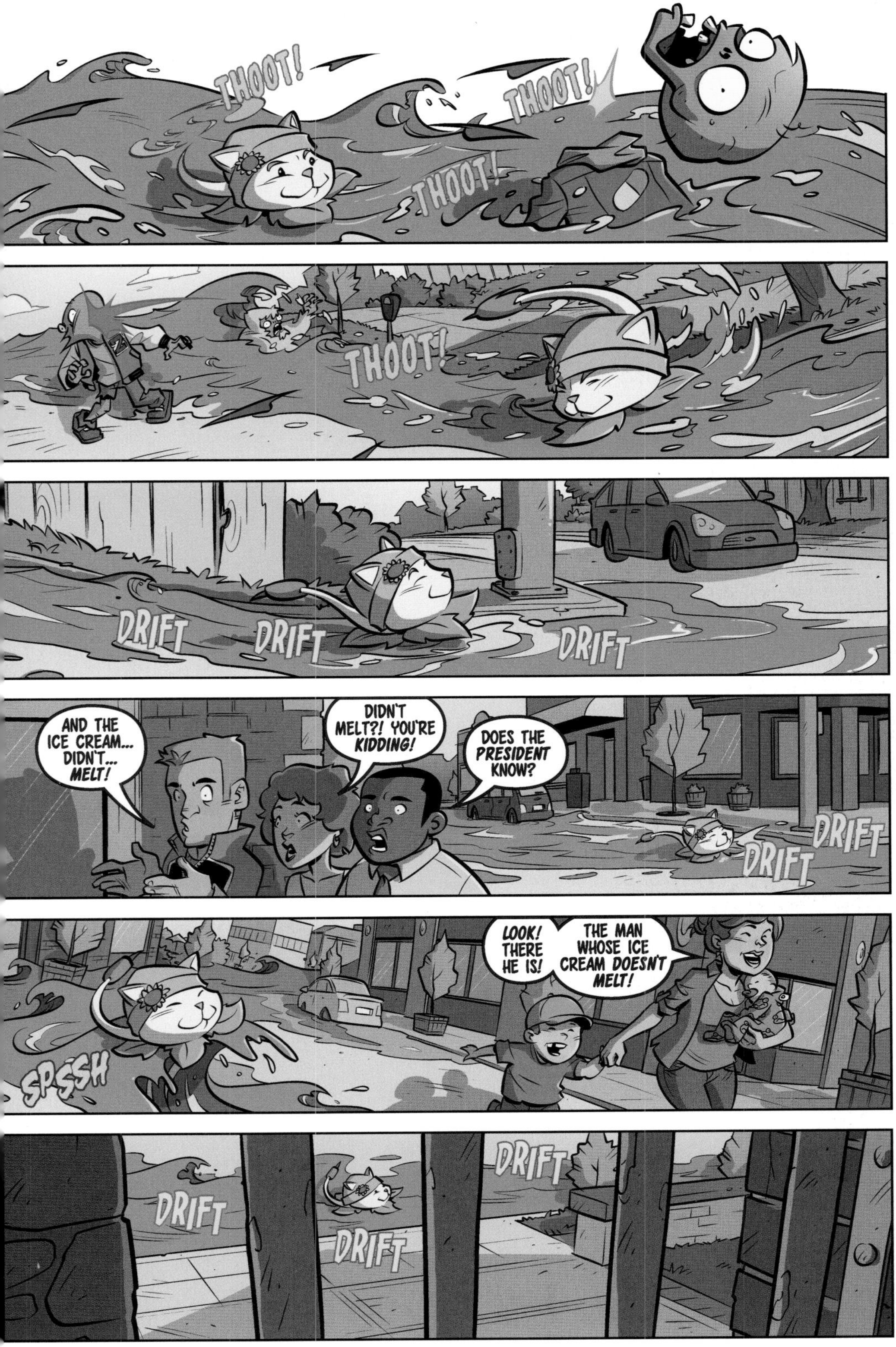
THOOT!
THOOT!
THOOT!
THOOT!
DRIFT
DRIFT
DRIFT
AND THE ICE CREAM... DIDN'T... MELT!
DIDN'T MELT?! YOU'RE KIDDING!
DOES THE PRESIDENT KNOW?
DRIFT
DRIFT
SPSSH
LOOK! THERE HE IS!
THE MAN WHOSE ICE CREAM DOESN'T MELT!
DRIFT
DRIFT
DRIFT

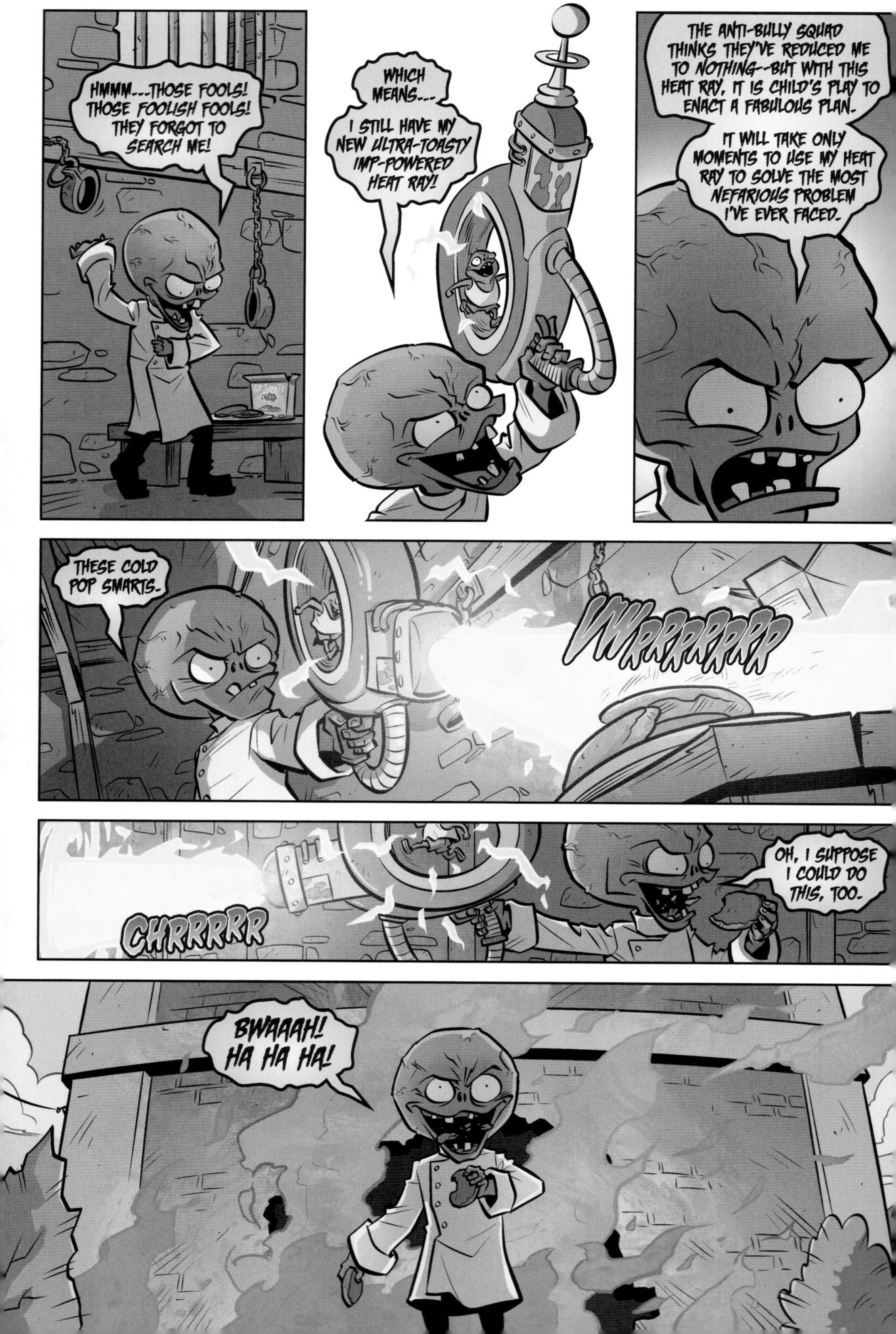
HMMM...THOSE FOOLS! THOSE FOOLISH FOOLS! THEY FORGOT TO SEARCH ME!
WHICH MEANS...
I STILL HAVE MY NEW ULTRA-TOASTY IMP-POWERED HEAT RAY!
THE ANTI-BULLY SQUAD THINKS THEY'VE REDUCED ME TO NOTHING--BUT WITH THIS HEAT RAY, IT IS CHILD'S PLAY TO ENACT A FABULOUS PLAN.
IT WILL TAKE ONLY MOMENTS TO USE MY HEAT RAY TO SOLVE THE MOST NEFARIOUS PROBLEM I'VE EVER FACED.
THESE COLD POP SMARTS.
VWRRRRRRR
CHRRRRR
OH, I SUPPOSE I COULD DO THIS, TOO.
BWAAAH! HA HA HA!

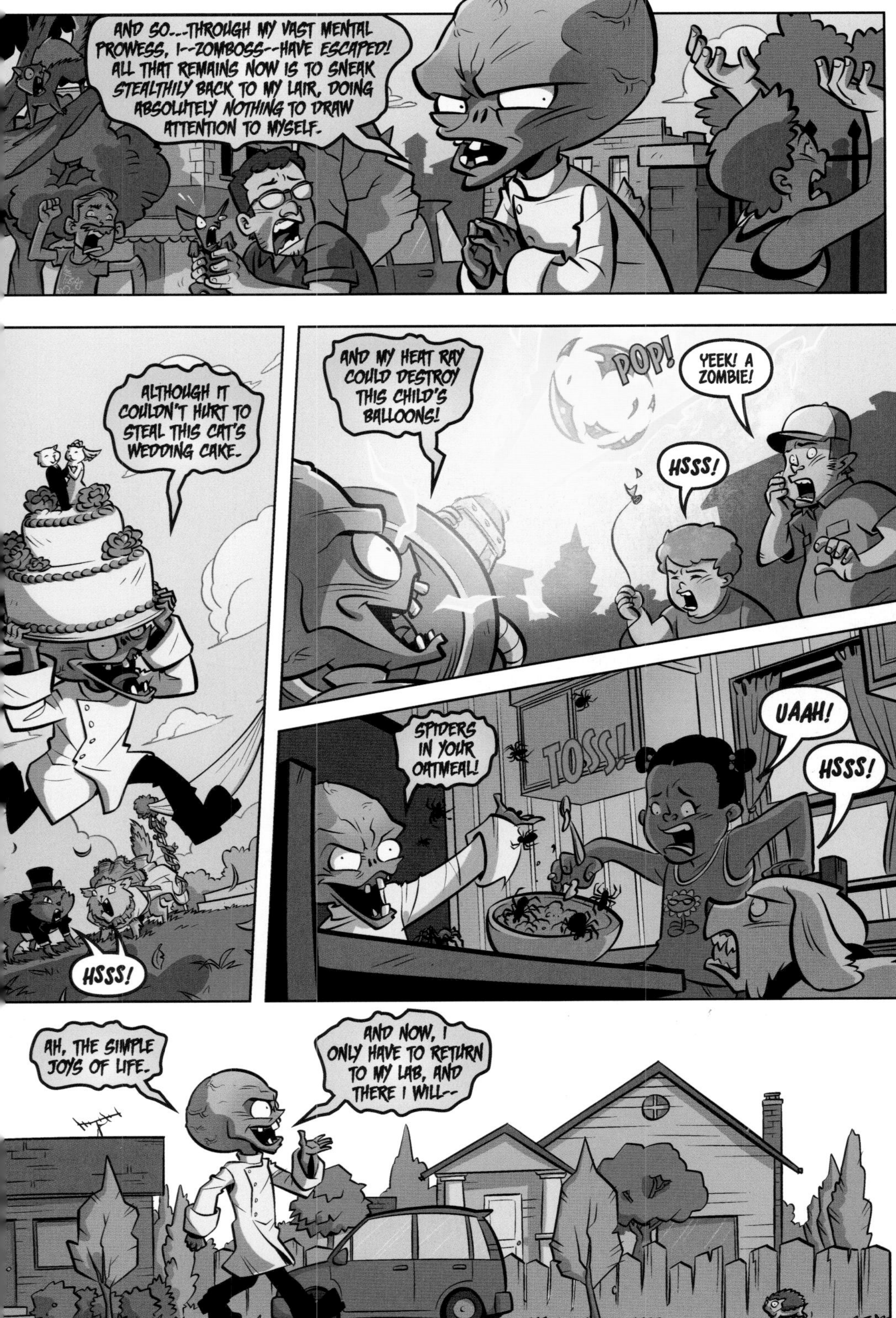

AND SO...THROUGH MY VAST MENTAL PROWESS, I--ZOMBOSS--HAVE ESCAPED! ALL THAT REMAINS NOW IS TO SNEAK STEALTHILY BACK TO MY LAIR, DOING ABSOLUTELY NOTHING TO DRAW ATTENTION TO MYSELF.
ALTHOUGH IT COULDN'T HURT TO STEAL THIS CAT'S WEDDING CAKE.
HSSS!
AND MY HEAT RAY COULD DESTROY THIS CHILD'S BALLOONS!
POP!
YEEK! A ZOMBIE!
HSSS!
SPIDERS IN YOUR OATMEAL!
TOSS!
UAAH!
HSSS!
AH, THE SIMPLE JOYS OF LIFE.
AND NOW, I ONLY HAVE TO RETURN TO MY LAB, AND THERE I WILL--

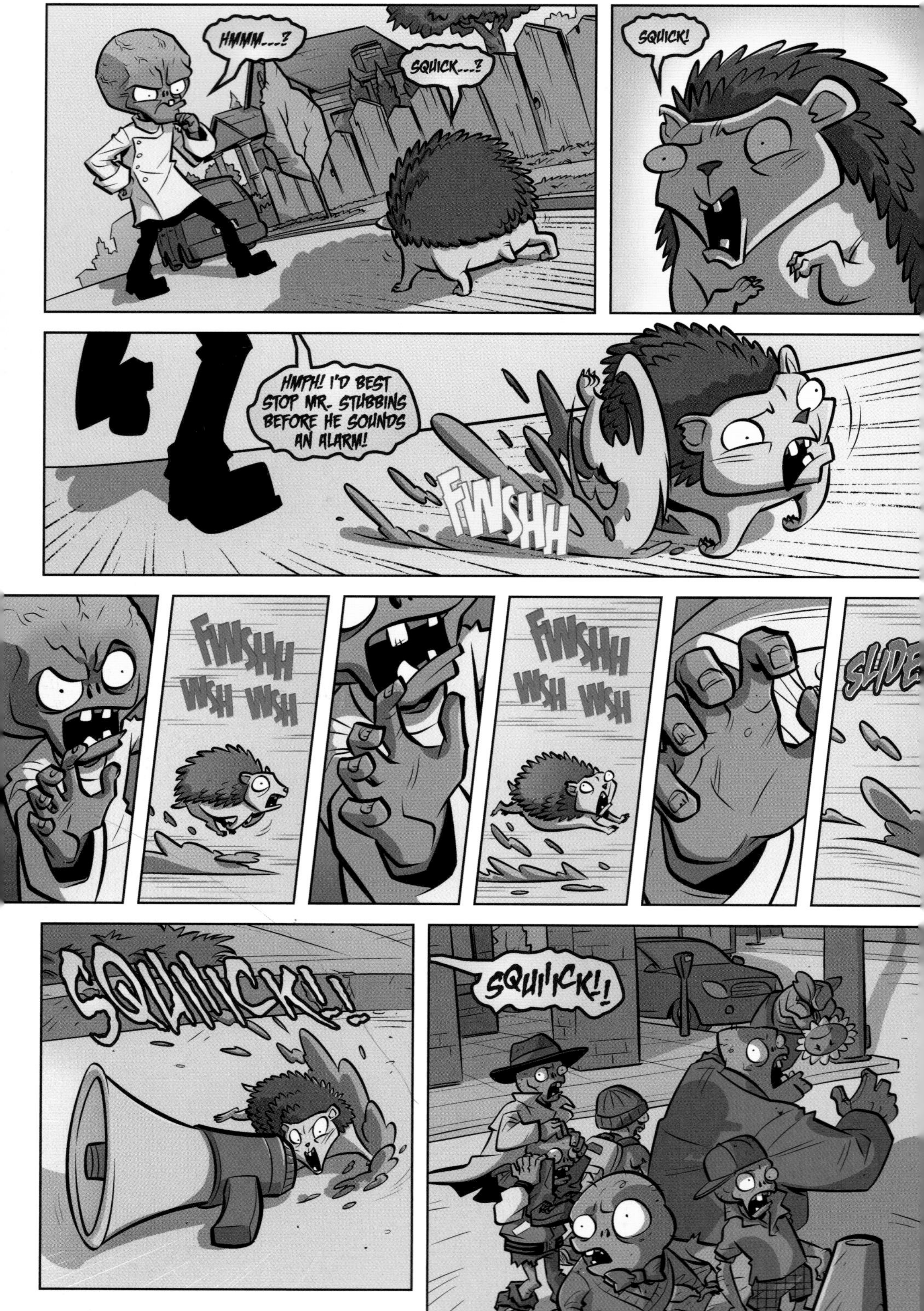
HMMM...?
SQUICK...?
SQUICK!
HMPH! I'D BEST STOP MR. STUBBINS BEFORE HE SOUNDS AN ALARM!
FWSHH
FWSHH
WSH WSH
FWSHH
WSH WSH
SLIDE
SQUIICK!!
SQUI'ICK!!

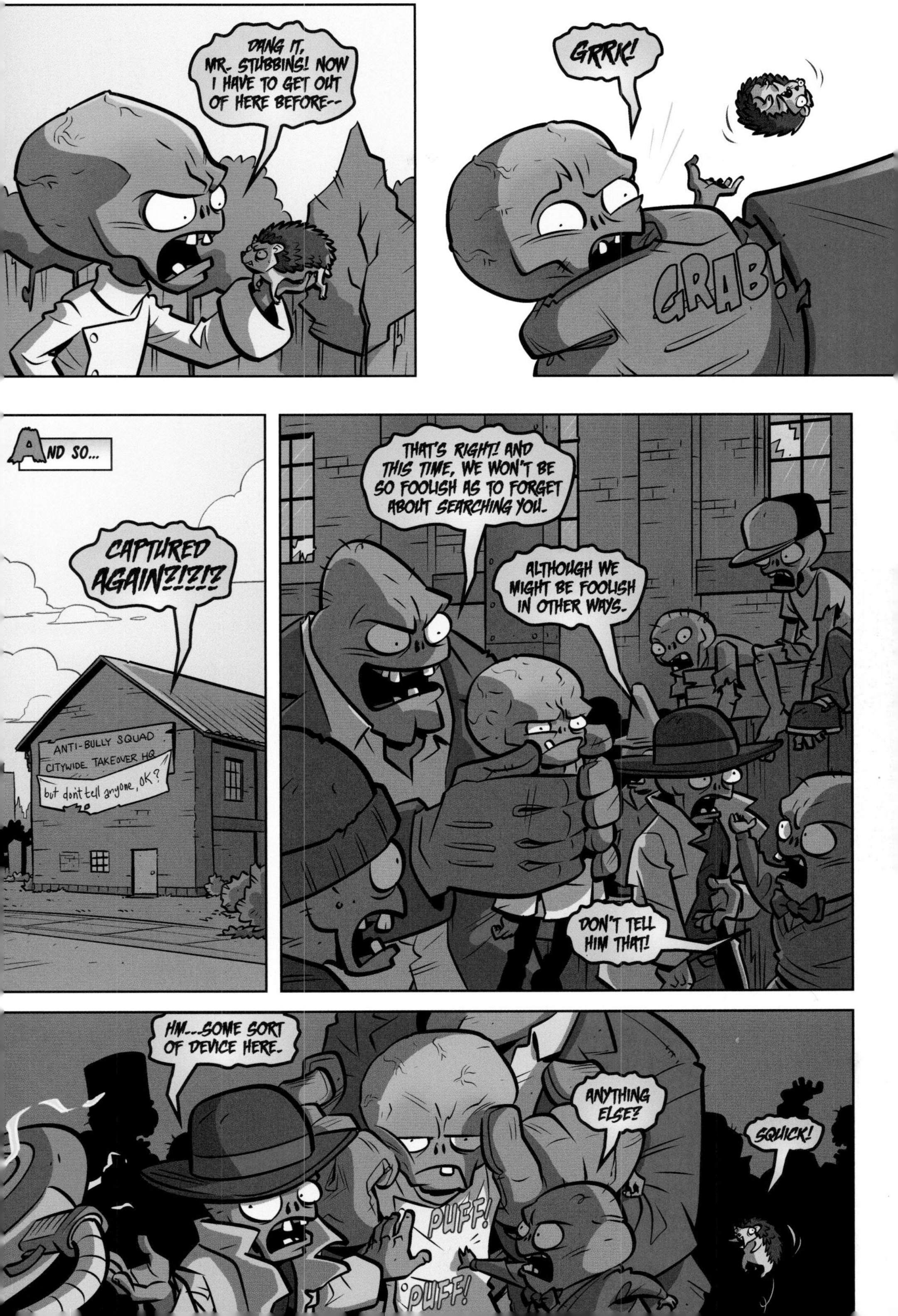
DANG IT, MR. STUBBINS! NOW I HAVE TO GET OUT OF HERE BEFORE--
GRRK!
GRAB!
AND SO...
CAPTURED AGAIN?!?!?!?
ANTI-BULLY SQUAD
CITYWIDE TAKEOVER HQ
but don't tell anyone, OK?
THAT'S RIGHT! AND THIS TIME, WE WON'T BE SO FOOLISH AS TO FORGET ABOUT SEARCHING YOU.
ALTHOUGH WE MIGHT BE FOOLISH IN OTHER WAYS.
DON'T TELL HIM THAT!
HM...SOME SORT OF DEVICE HERE.
ANYTHING ELSE?
SQUICK!
PUFF!
PUFF!

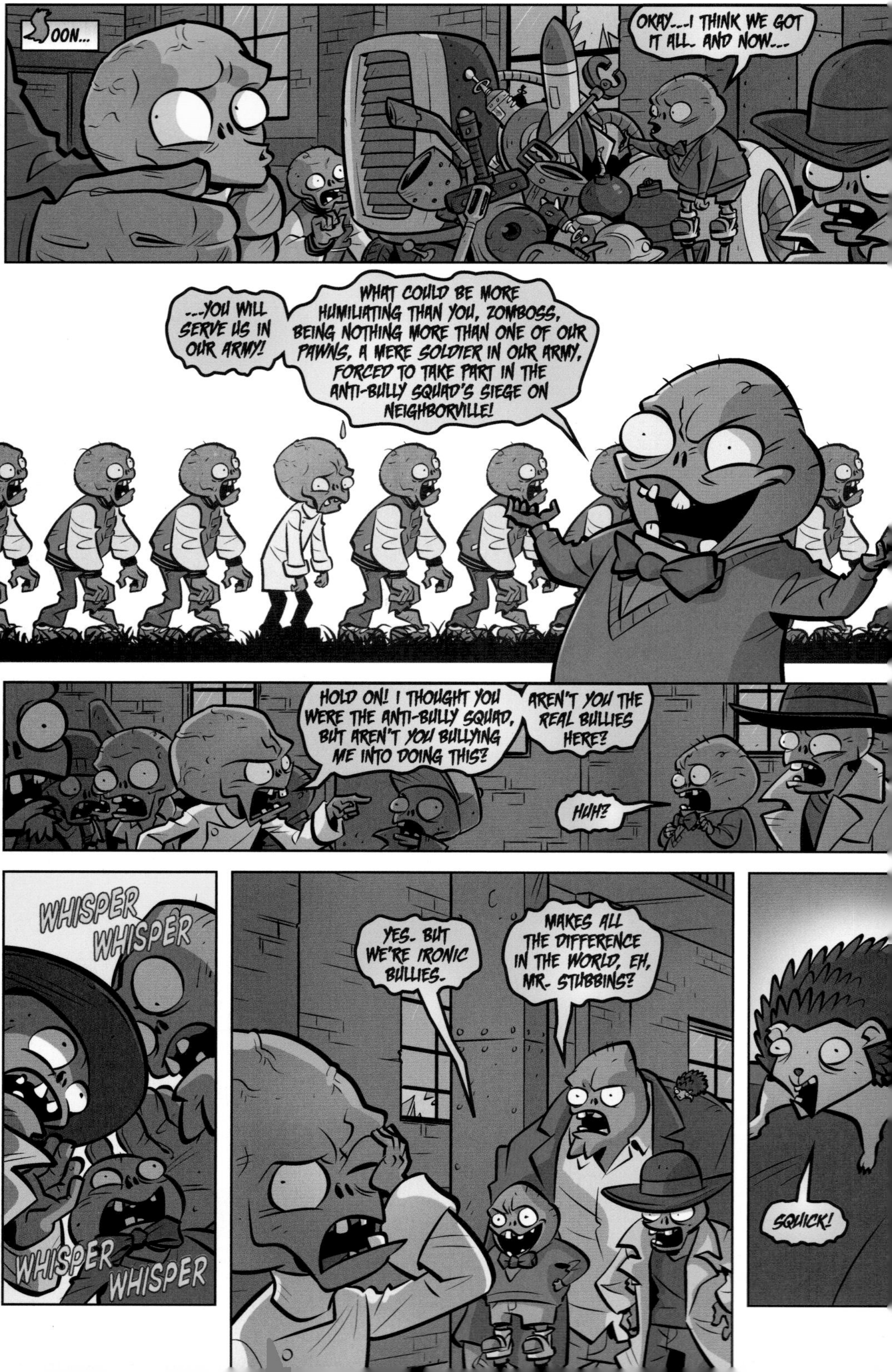
SOON...
OKAY... I THINK WE GOT IT ALL. AND NOW...
...YOU WILL SERVE US IN OUR ARMY!
WHAT COULD BE MORE HUMILIATING THAN YOU, ZOMBOSS, BEING NOTHING MORE THAN ONE OF OUR PAWNS, A MERE SOLDIER IN OUR ARMY, FORCED TO TAKE PART IN THE ANTI-BULLY SQUAD'S SIEGE ON NEIGHBORVILLE!
HOLD ON! I THOUGHT YOU WERE THE ANTI-BULLY SQUAD, BUT AREN'T YOU BULLYING ME INTO DOING THIS?
AREN'T YOU THE REAL BULLIES HERE?
HUH?
WHISPER
WHISPER
WHISPER
WHISPER
YES. BUT WE'RE IRONIC BULLIES.
MAKES ALL THE DIFFERENCE IN THE WORLD, EH, MR. STUBBINS?
SQUICK!

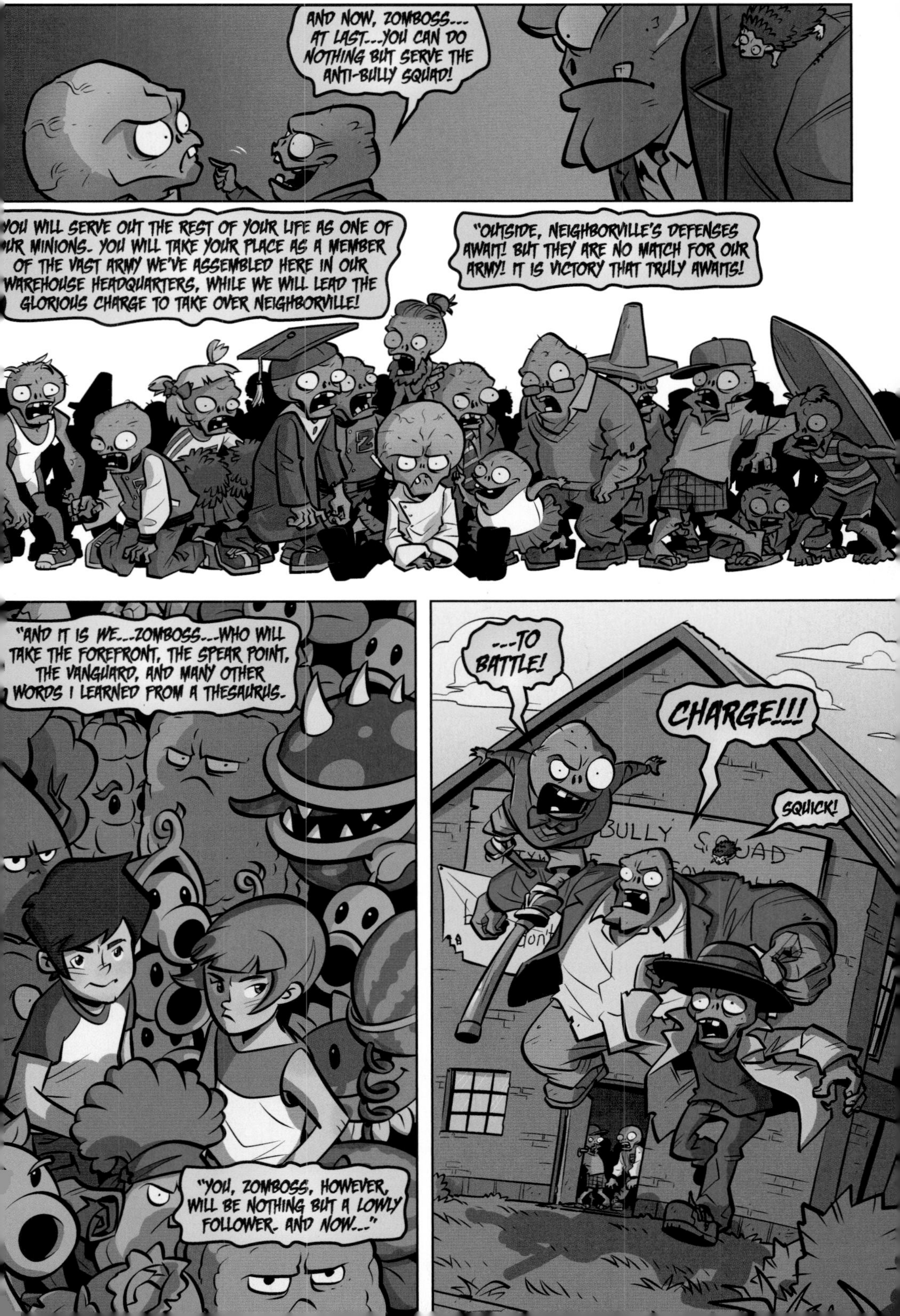
AND NOW, ZOMBOSS... AT LAST...YOU CAN DO NOTHING BUT SERVE THE ANTI-BULLY SQUAD!
YOU WILL SERVE OUT THE REST OF YOUR LIFE AS ONE OF OUR MINIONS. YOU WILL TAKE YOUR PLACE AS A MEMBER OF THE VAST ARMY WE'VE ASSEMBLED HERE IN OUR WAREHOUSE HEADQUARTERS, WHILE WE WILL LEAD THE GLORIOUS CHARGE TO TAKE OVER NEIGHBORVILLE!
"OUTSIDE, NEIGHBORVILLE'S DEFENSES AWAIT! BUT THEY ARE NO MATCH FOR OUR ARMY! IT IS VICTORY THAT TRULY AWAITS!
"AND IT IS WE...ZOMBOSS...WHO WILL TAKE THE FOREFRONT, THE SPEAR POINT, THE VANGUARD, AND MANY OTHER WORDS I LEARNED FROM A THESAURUS.
"YOU, ZOMBOSS, HOWEVER, WILL BE NOTHING BUT A LOWLY FOLLOWER. AND NOW..."
...TO BATTLE!
CHARGE!!!
SQUICK!

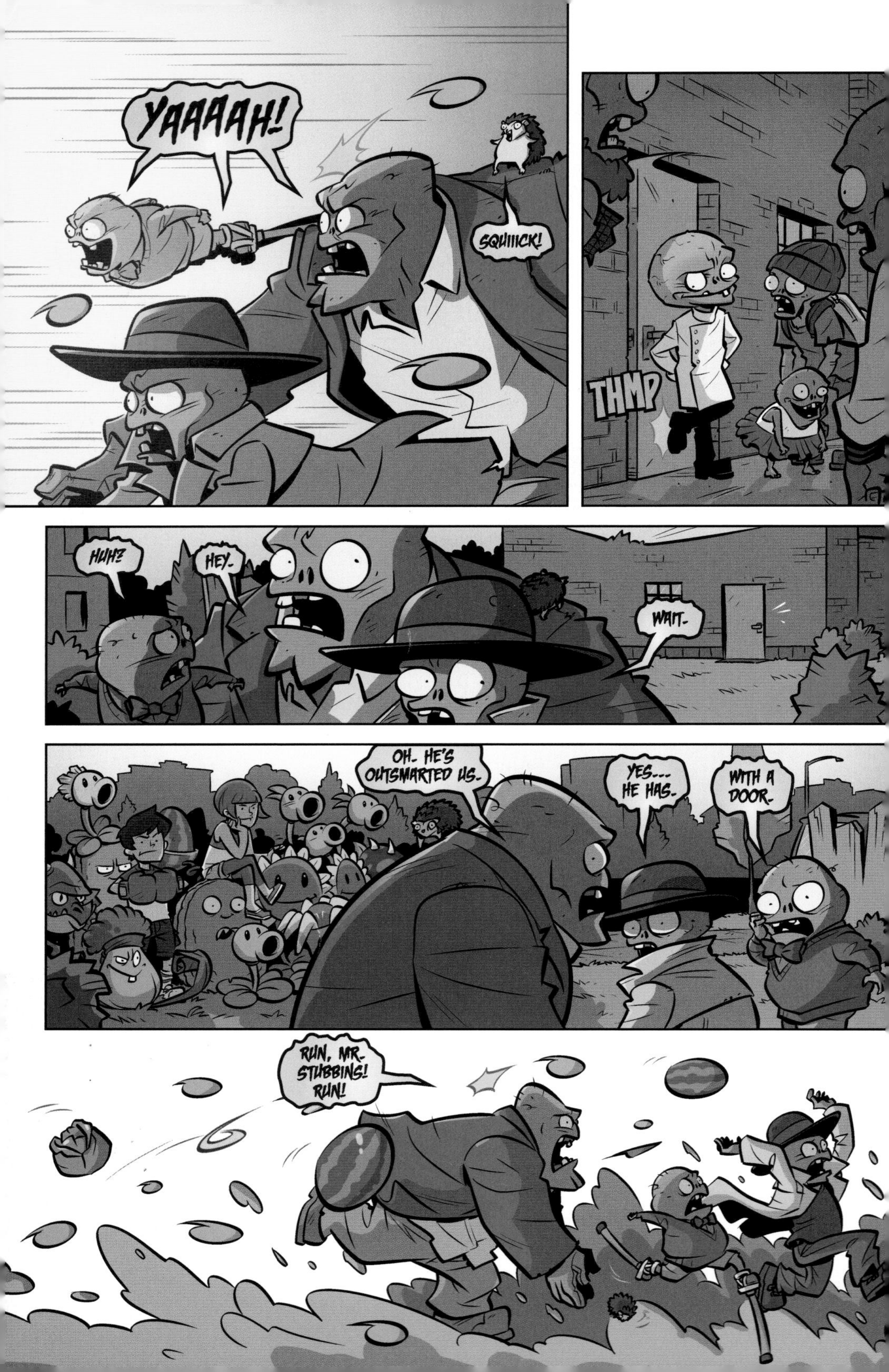
YAAAAH!
SQUIIICK!
THMP
HUH?
HEY.
WAIT.
OH. HE'S OUTSMARTED US.
YES... HE HAS.
WITH A DOOR.
RUN, MR. STUBBINS! RUN!

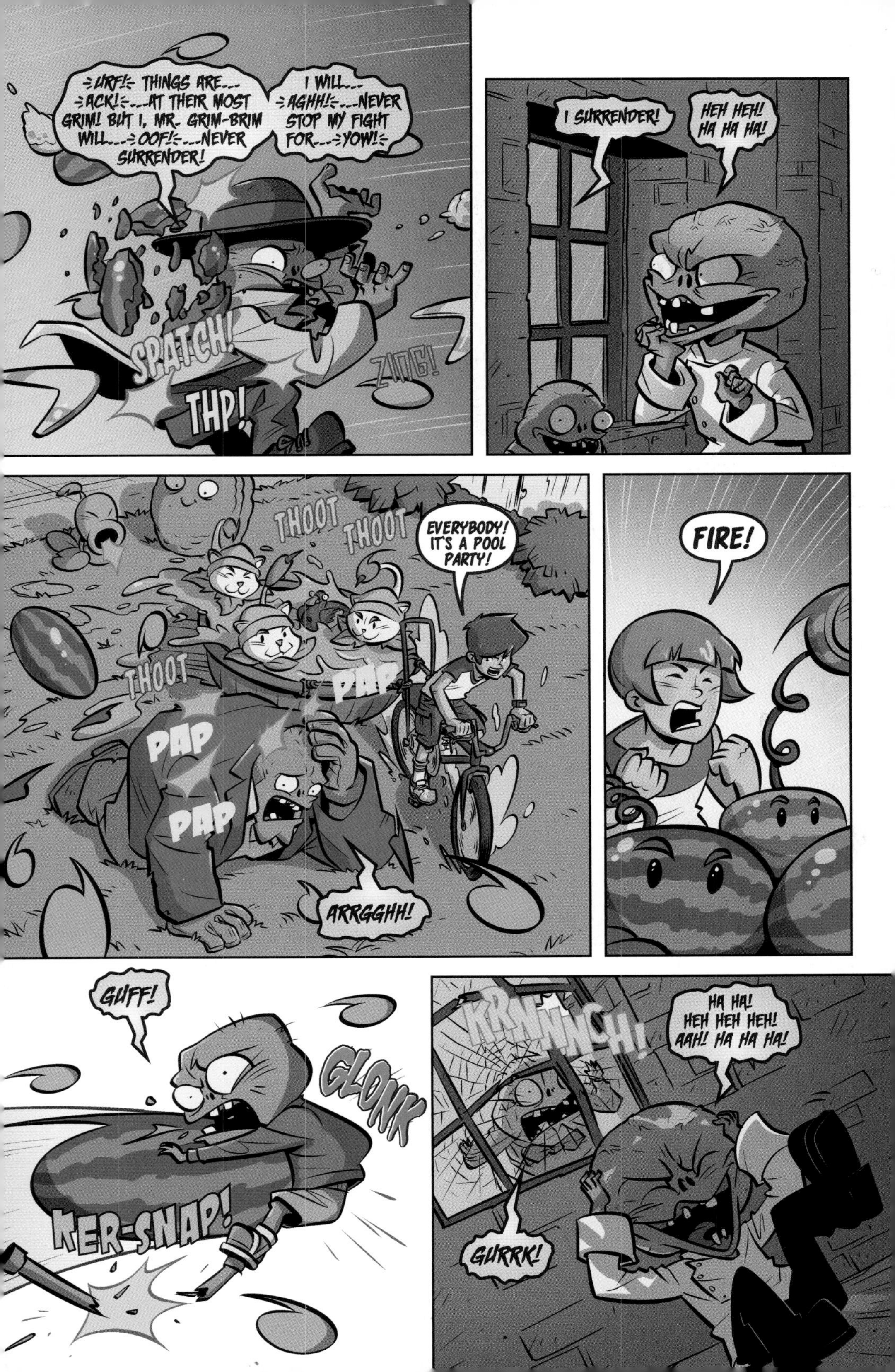

URF! THINGS ARE... ACK! ...AT THEIR MOST GRIM! BUT I, MR. GRIM-BRIM WILL... OOF! ...NEVER SURRENDER!
I WILL... AGHH! ...NEVER STOP MY FIGHT FOR... YOW!
SPATCH!
ZING!
THP!
I SURRENDER!
HEH HEH! HA HA HA!
THOOT
THOOT
EVERYBODY! IT'S A POOL PARTY!
THOOT
PAP
PAP
PAP
ARRGGHH!
FIRE!
GUFF!
GLONK
KER-SNAP!
KRNNNNCH!
HA HA! HEH HEH HEH! AAH! HA HA HA!
GURRK!

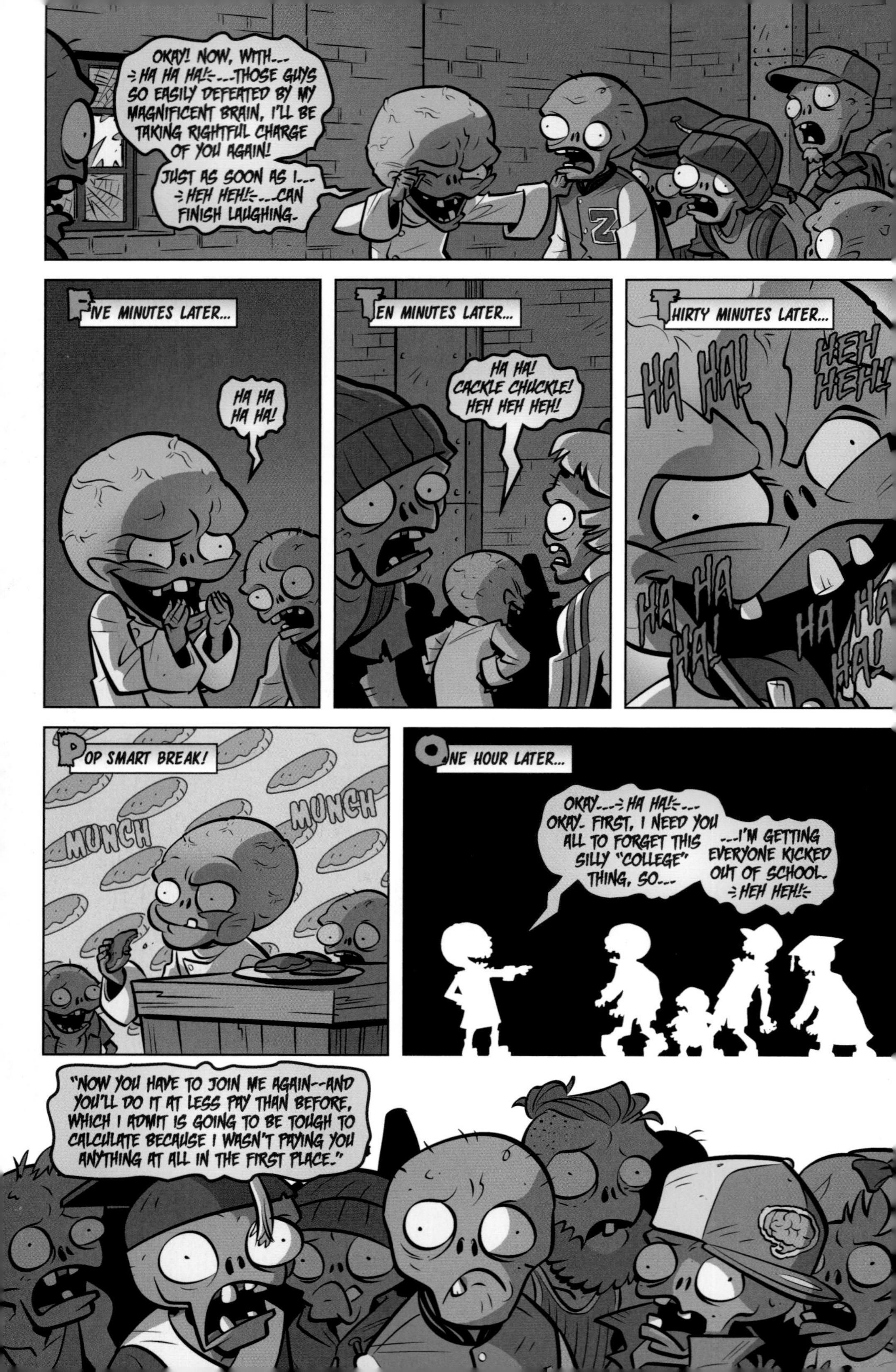

OKAY! NOW, WITH... -HA HA HA!- ...THOSE GUYS SO EASILY DEFEATED BY MY MAGNIFICENT BRAIN, I'LL BE TAKING RIGHTFUL CHARGE OF YOU AGAIN!
JUST AS SOON AS I... -HEH HEH!- ...CAN FINISH LAUGHING.
FIVE MINUTES LATER...
HA HA HA HA!
TEN MINUTES LATER...
HA HA! CACKLE CHUCKLE! HEH HEH HEH!
THIRTY MINUTES LATER...
HA HA!
HEH HEH!
HA HA HA!
HA HA HA!
POP SMART BREAK!
MUNCH
MUNCH
ONE HOUR LATER...
OKAY... -HA HA!- ... OKAY. FIRST, I NEED YOU ALL TO FORGET THIS SILLY "COLLEGE" THING, SO...
...I'M GETTING EVERYONE KICKED OUT OF SCHOOL. -HEH HEH!-
"NOW YOU HAVE TO JOIN ME AGAIN--AND YOU'LL DO IT AT LESS PAY THAN BEFORE, WHICH I ADMIT IS GOING TO BE TOUGH TO CALCULATE BECAUSE I WASN'T PAYING YOU ANYTHING AT ALL IN THE FIRST PLACE."

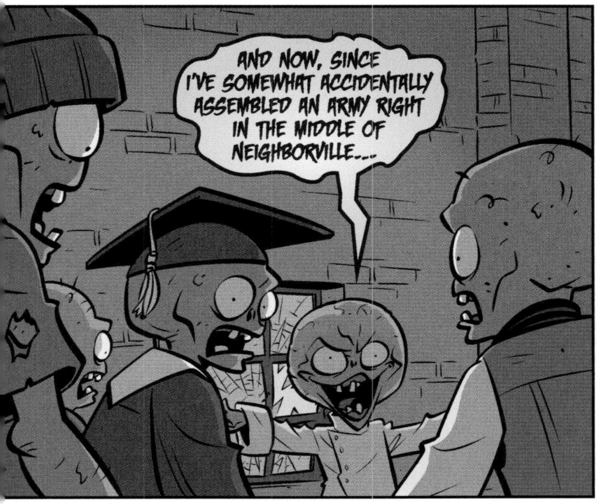
AND NOW, SINCE I'VE SOMEWHAT ACCIDENTALLY ASSEMBLED AN ARMY RIGHT IN THE MIDDLE OF NEIGHBORVILLE...

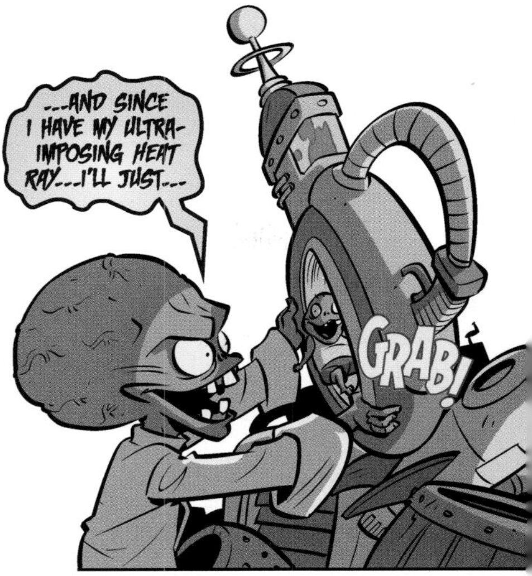
...AND SINCE I HAVE MY ULTRA-IMPOSING HEAT RAY...I'LL JUST...
GRAB!

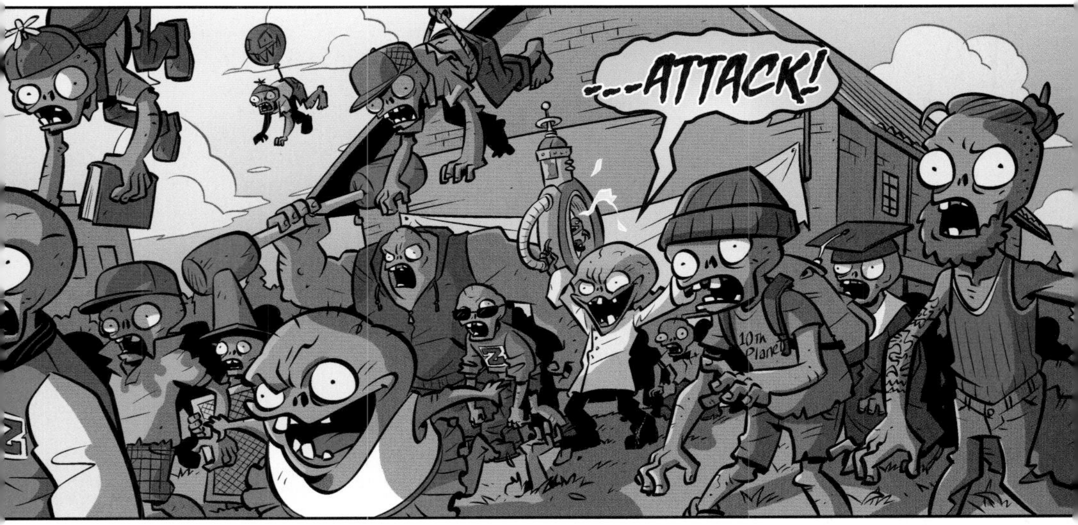
...ATTACK!

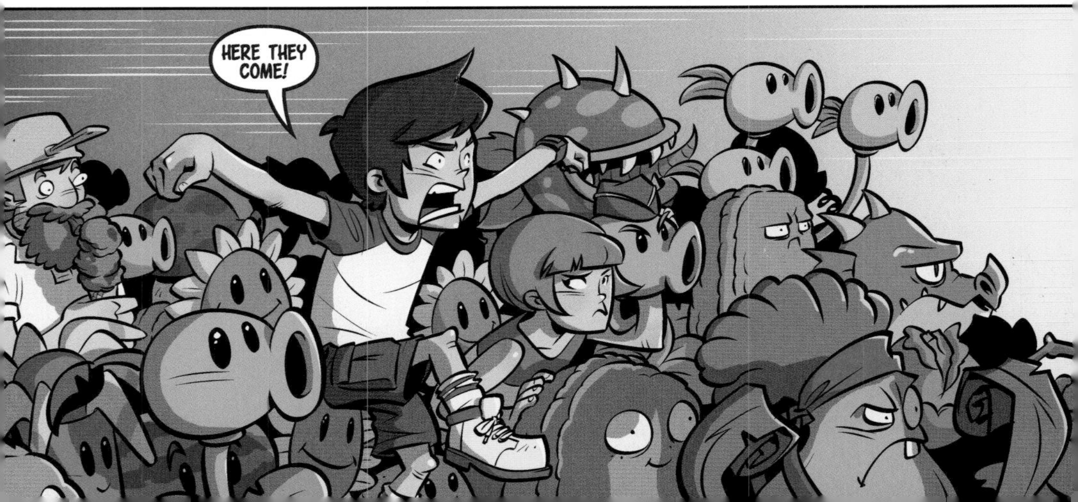
HERE THEY COME!

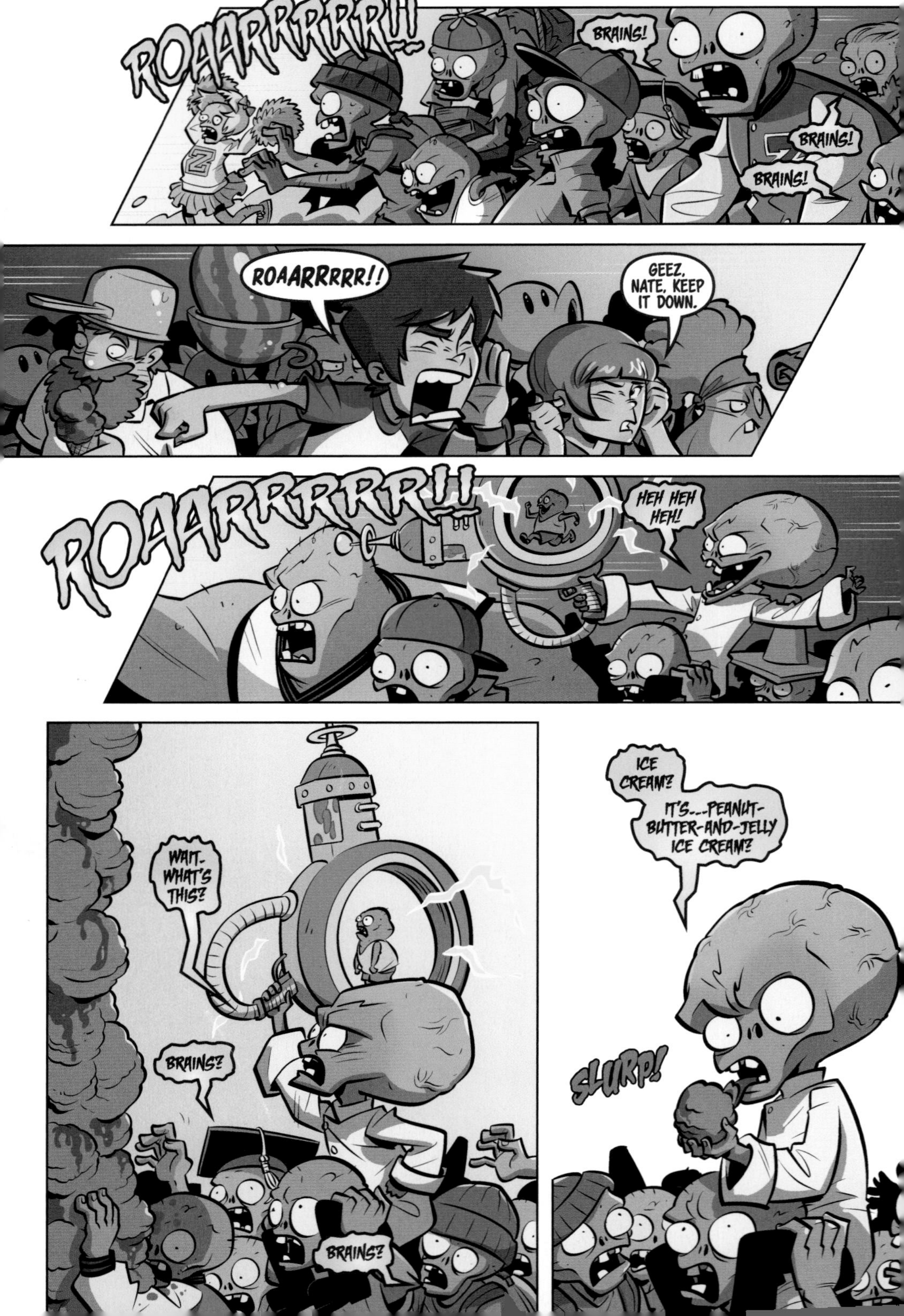
ROAARRRRR!!
BRAINS!
BRAINS!
BRAINS!
ROAARRrrr!!
GEEZ, NATE, KEEP IT DOWN.
ROAARRRRR!!
HEH HEH HEH!
WAIT-WHAT'S THIS?
BRAINS?
BRAINS?
ICE CREAM?
IT'S...PEANUT-BUTTER-AND-JELLY ICE CREAM?
SLURP!

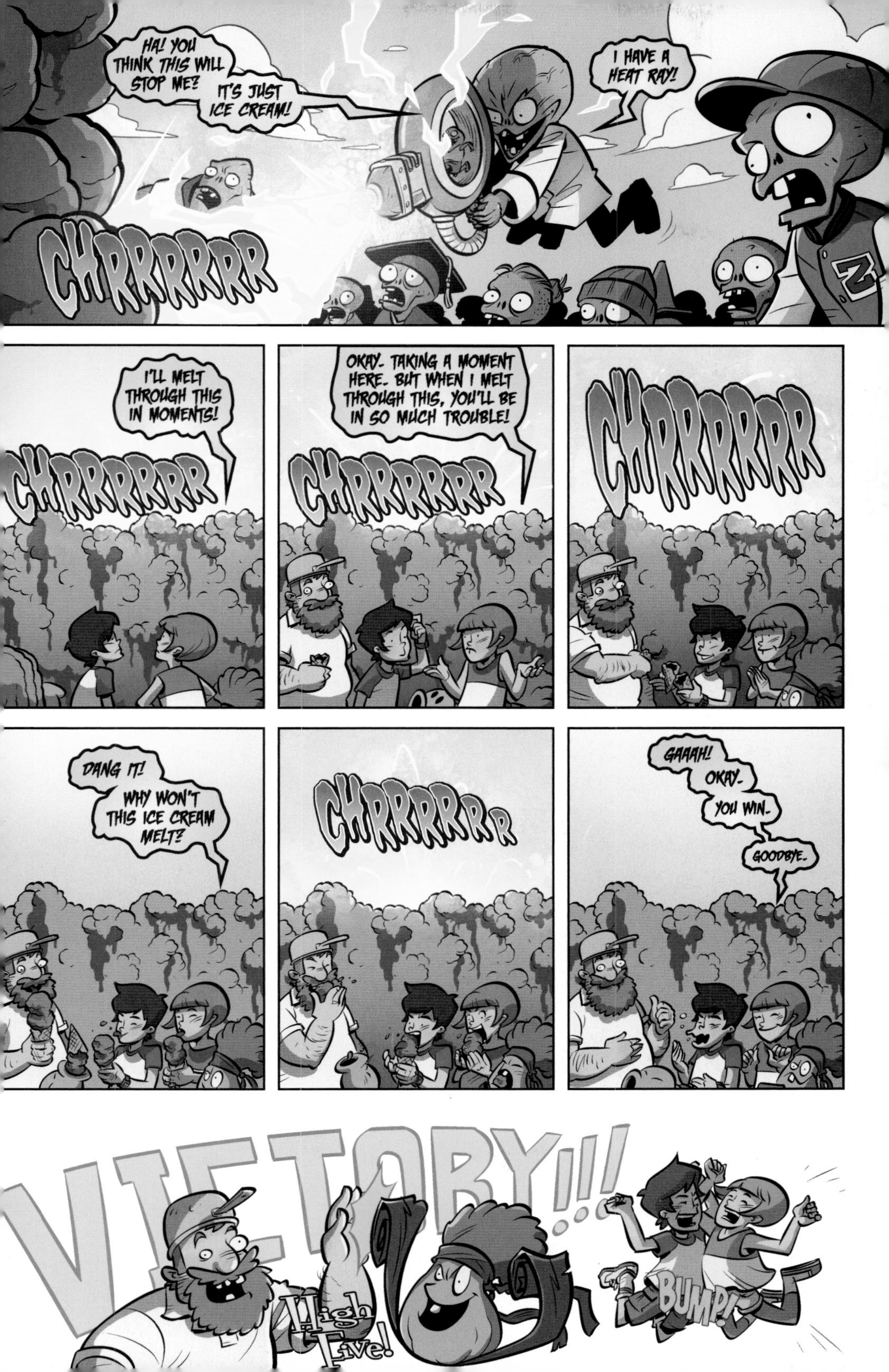
HA! YOU THINK THIS WILL STOP ME?
IT'S JUST ICE CREAM!
I HAVE A HEAT RAY!
CHRRRRRR
I'LL MELT THROUGH THIS IN MOMENTS!
CHRRRRRR
OKAY. TAKING A MOMENT HERE. BUT WHEN I MELT THROUGH THIS, YOU'LL BE IN SO MUCH TROUBLE!
CHRRRRRR
CHRRRRRR
DANG IT!
WHY WON'T THIS ICE CREAM MELT?
CHRRRRRR
GAAAH!
OKAY.
YOU WIN.
GOODBYE.
VICTORY!!!
High Five!
BUMP!

ONE WEEK LATER...

SO.... WE WERE EXPELLED?

AND NOW WE HAVE TO TAKE COLLEGE ALL OVER AGAIN?

THAT'S WHAT THE LETTERS SAID. WE HAVE TO RETAKE ALL OF OUR CLASSES, INCLUDING...

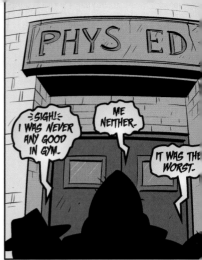

PHYS ED

≈SIGH!≈ I WAS NEVER ANY GOOD IN GYM.

ME NEITHER.

IT WAS THE WORST.

I HEAR THERE'S A NEW SUBSTITUTE COACH. MAYBE HE'LL BE NICE?

I HOPE SO. MAYBE WE CAN JUST--

HA HA HA!

THAT... LAUGHTER? NO! IT CAN'T BE!

HA HA HA HA!

HA!

HA HA! HA!

ZOMBOSS!

HELLO, ANTI-BULLY SQUAD. WELCOME TO GYM CLASS, WHERE WE'RE GOING TO PLAY...

SQUICK!

...DODGEBALL.

THE END!

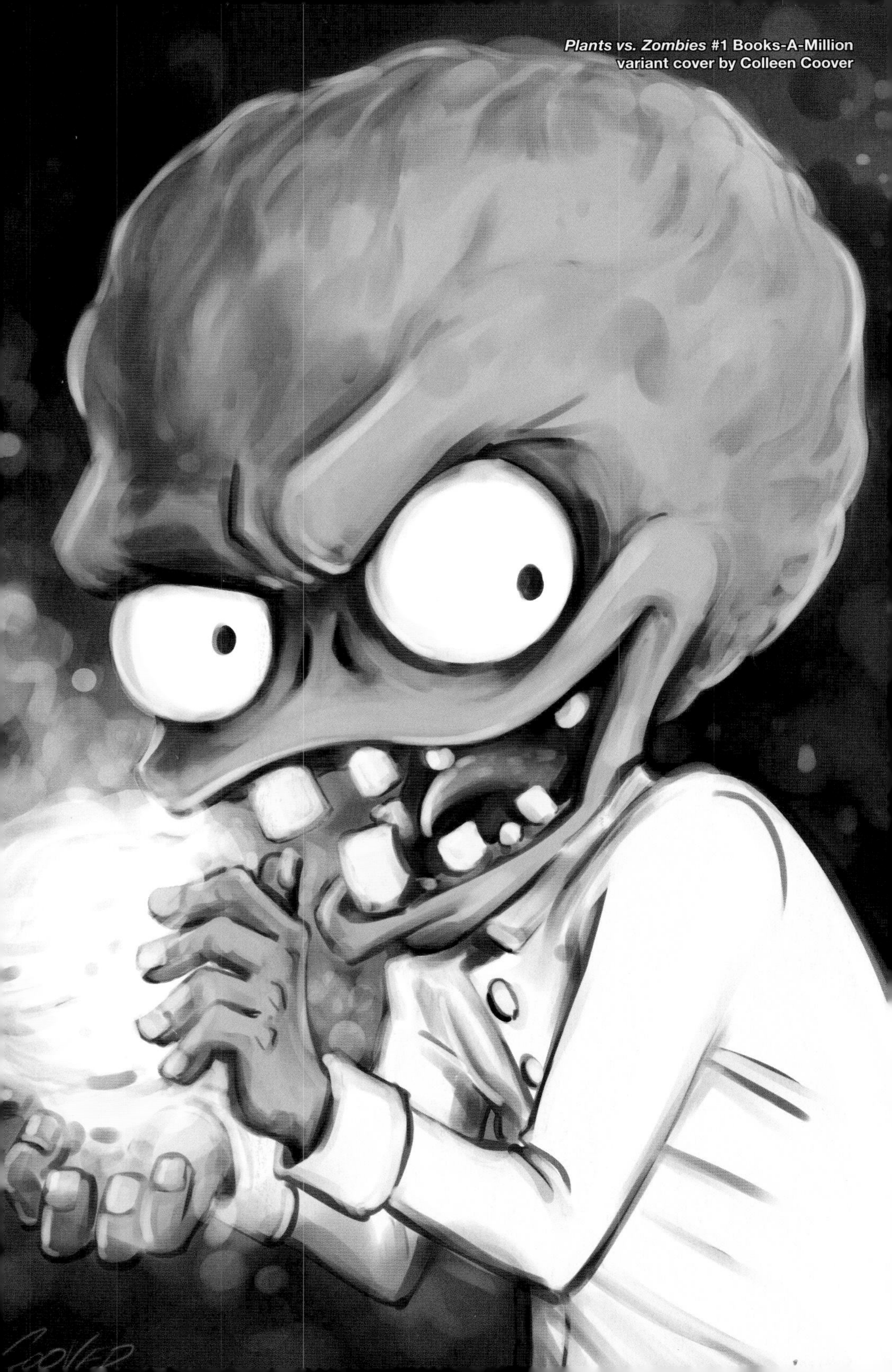
COOVER

Plants vs. Zombies #1 Books-A-Million
variant cover by Colleen Coover

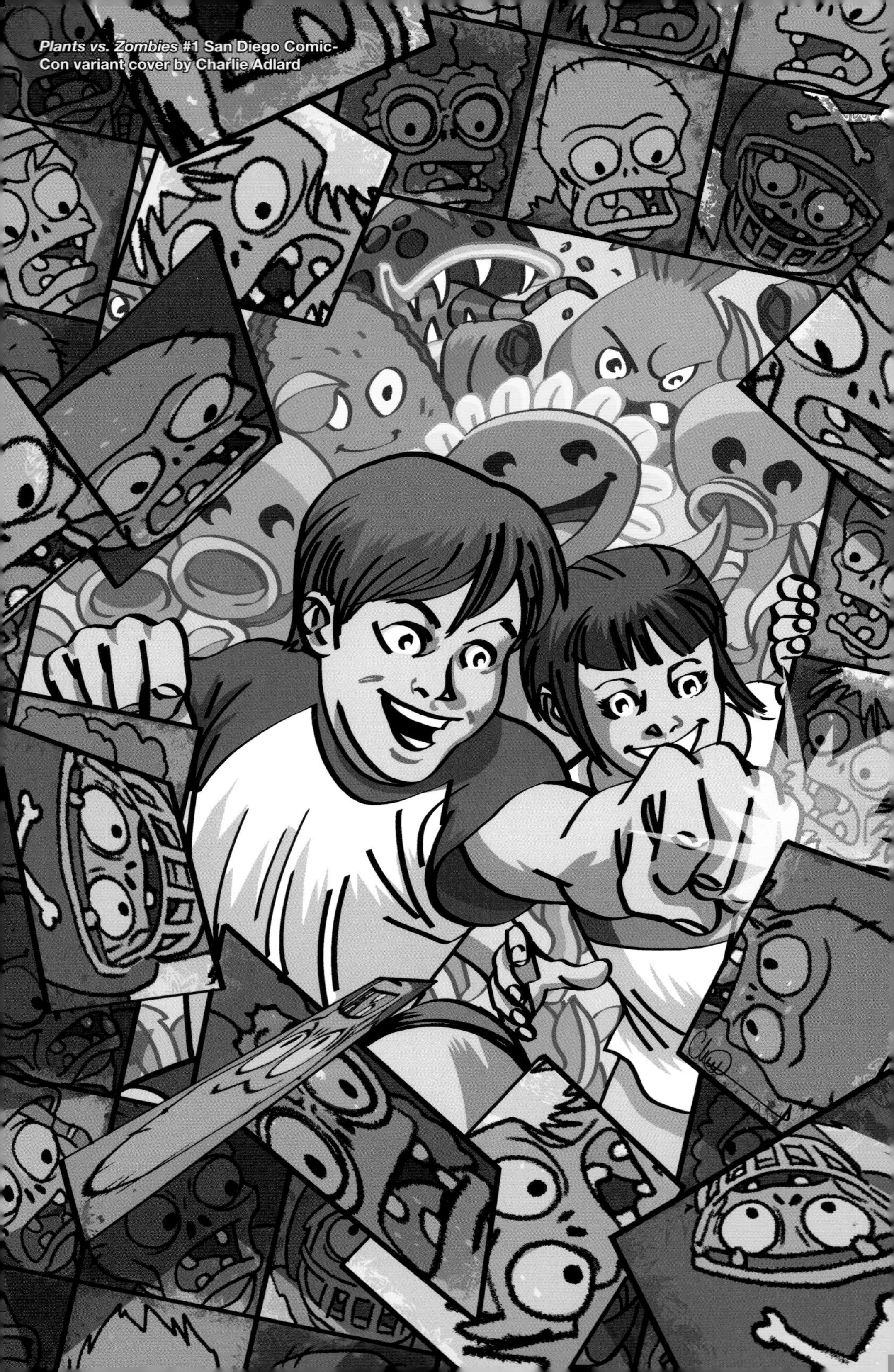

Plants vs. Zombies #1 San Diego Comic-Con variant cover by Charlie Adlard

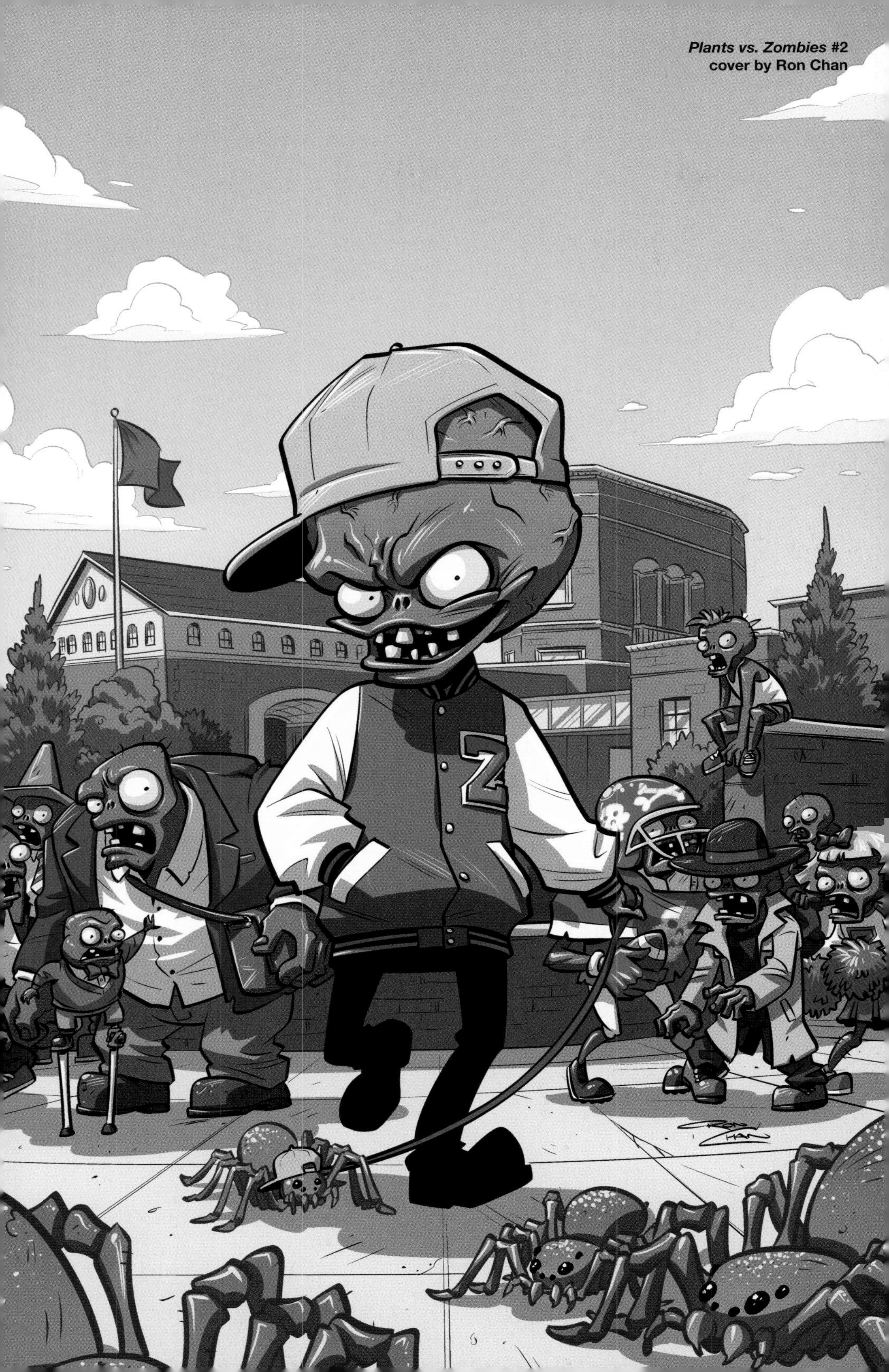
Z

Plants vs. Zombies #2
cover by Ron Chan

Plants vs. Zombies #3
cover by Ron Chan

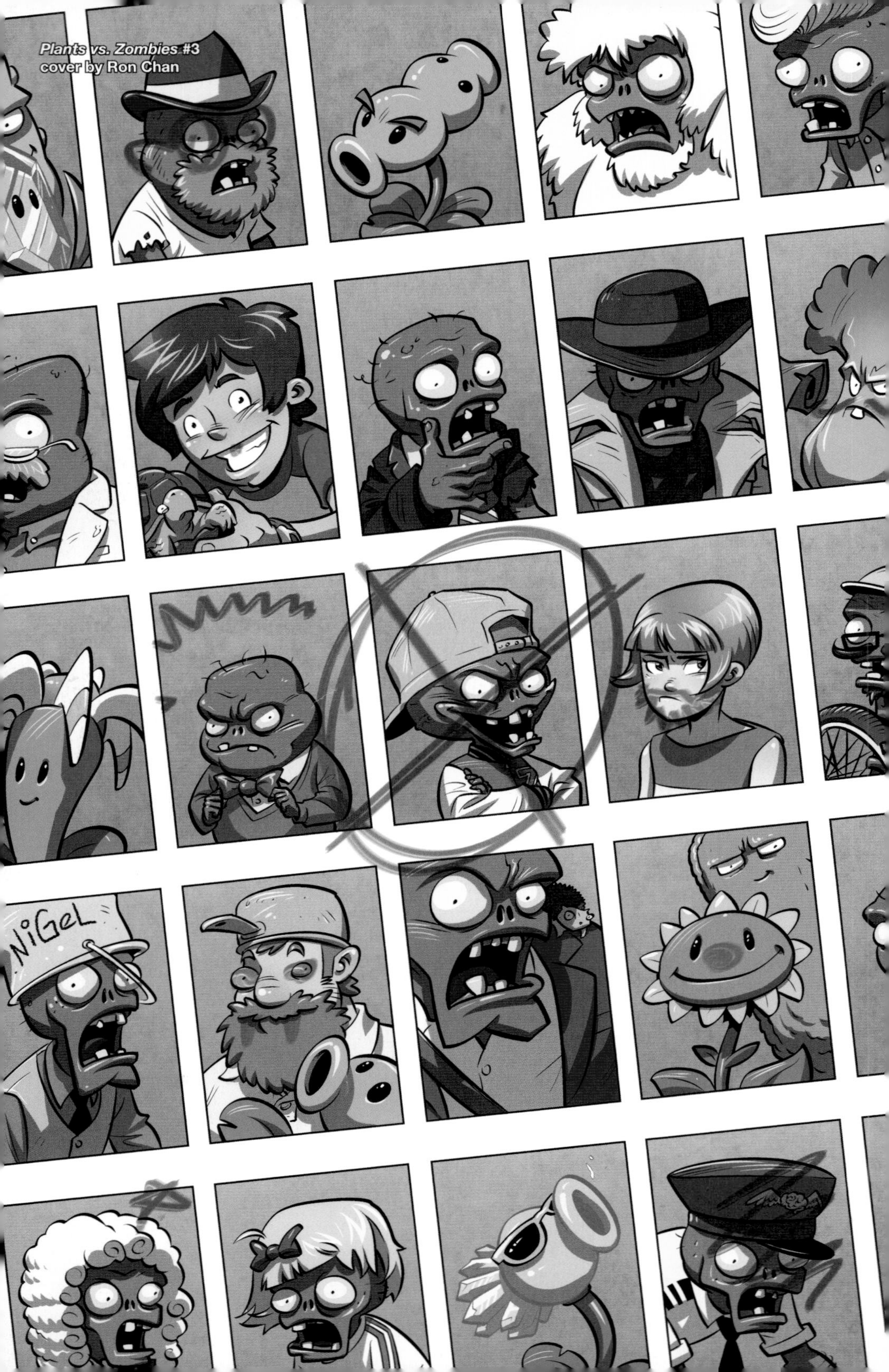
NiGeL

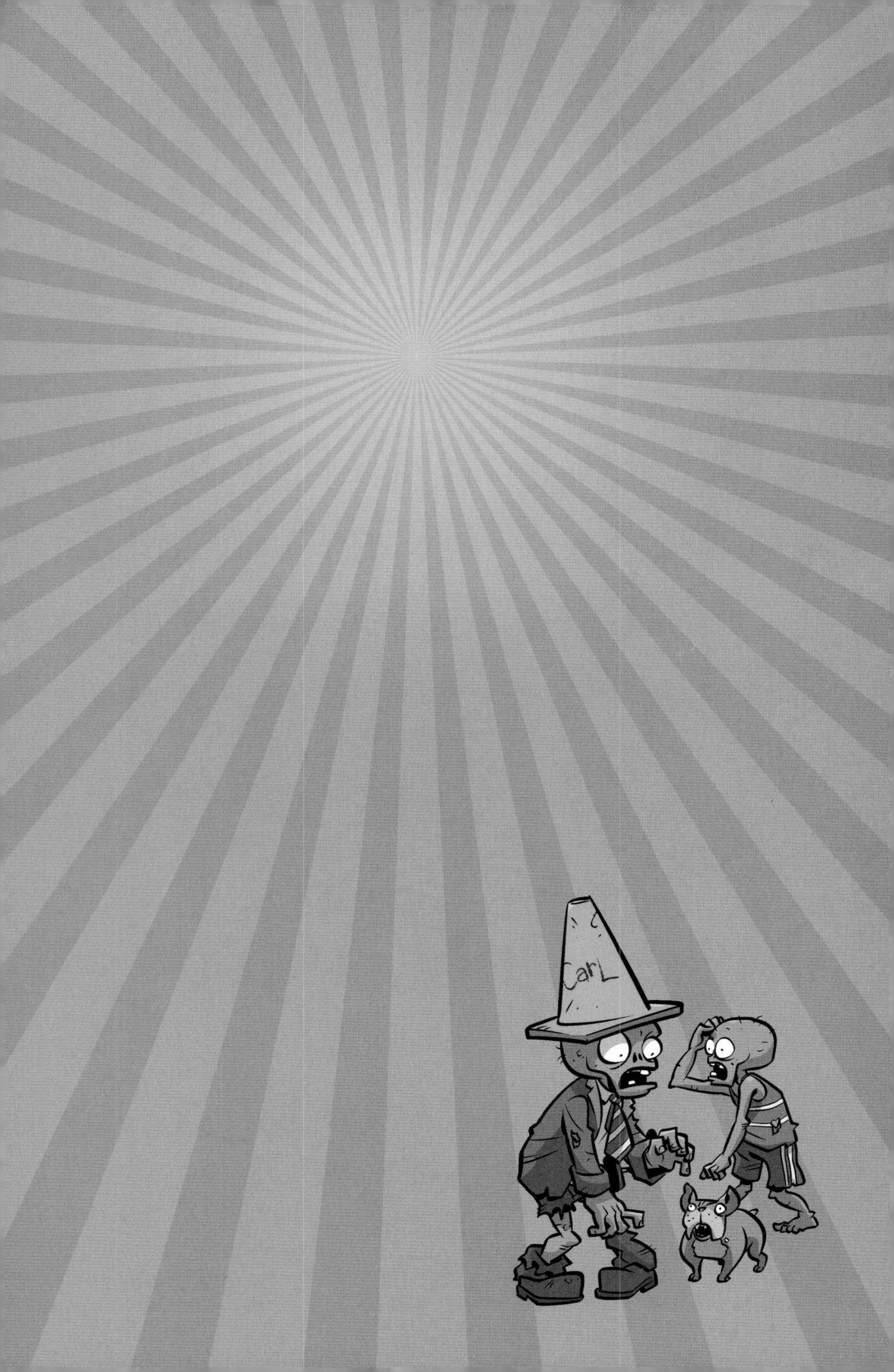
CarL

PLANTS VS. ZOMBIES™

THE CURSE OF THE FLOWER-BOT

Written by **PAUL TOBIN**
Art by **RON CHAN**
Colors by **MATTHEW J. RAINWATER**
Letters by **STEVE DUTRO**

FREE COMIC BOOK DAY

The Free Comic Book Day story that introduced Tugboat, Frogpants, and Nigel Blimpbottom!

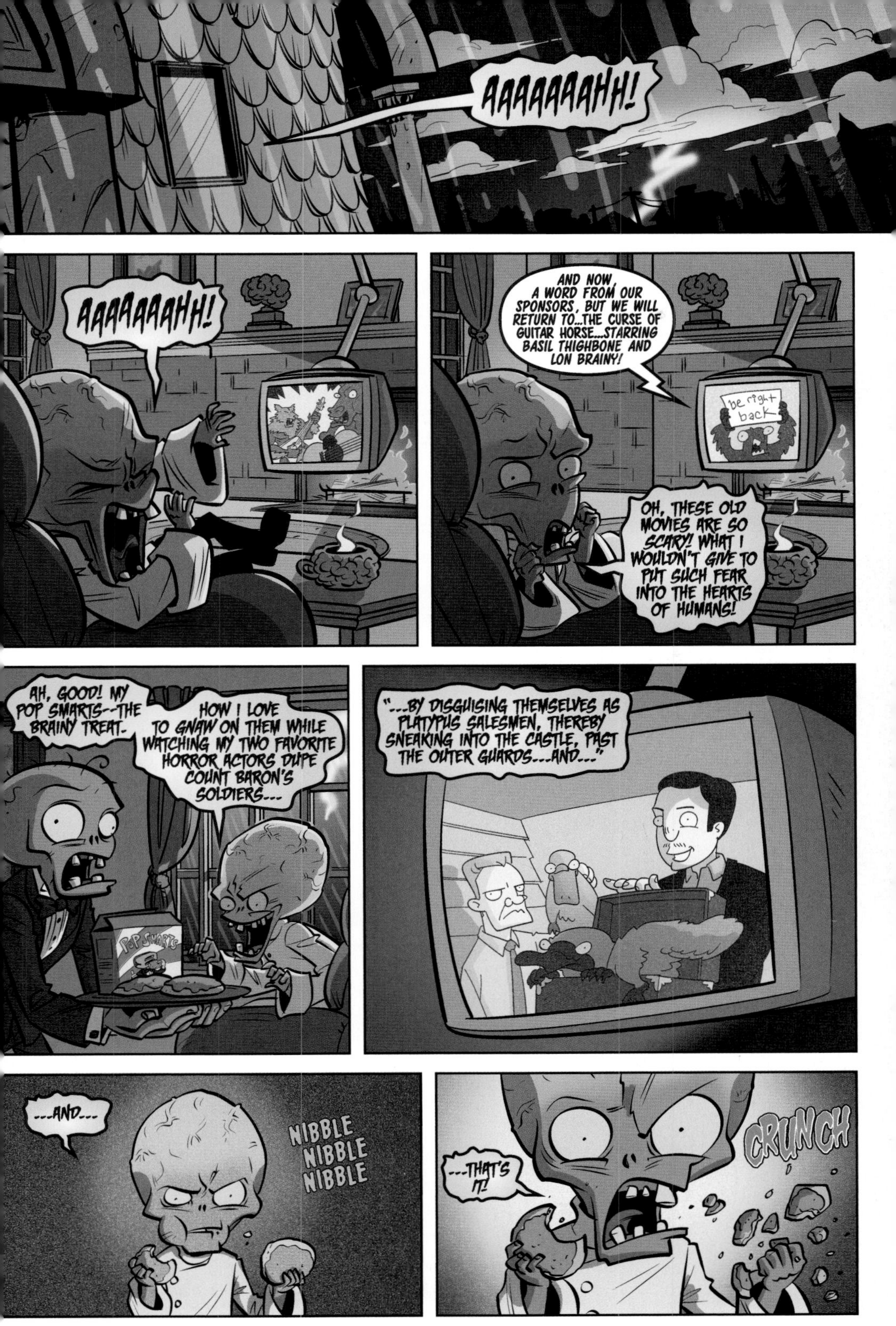
AAAAAAAHH!
AAAAAAAHH!
AND NOW, A WORD FROM OUR SPONSORS, BUT WE WILL RETURN TO...THE CURSE OF GUITAR HORSE...STARRING BASIL THIGHBONE AND LON BRAINY!
be right back
OH, THESE OLD MOVIES ARE SO SCARY! WHAT I WOULDN'T GIVE TO PUT SUCH FEAR INTO THE HEARTS OF HUMANS!
AH, GOOD! MY POP SMARTS--THE BRAINY TREAT.
HOW I LOVE TO GNAW ON THEM WHILE WATCHING MY TWO FAVORITE HORROR ACTORS DUPE COUNT BARON'S SOLDIERS...
POP SMARTS
"...BY DISGUISING THEMSELVES AS PLATYPUS SALESMEN, THEREBY SNEAKING INTO THE CASTLE, PAST THE OUTER GUARDS...AND..."
...AND...
NIBBLE NIBBLE NIBBLE
...THAT'S IT!
CRUNCH

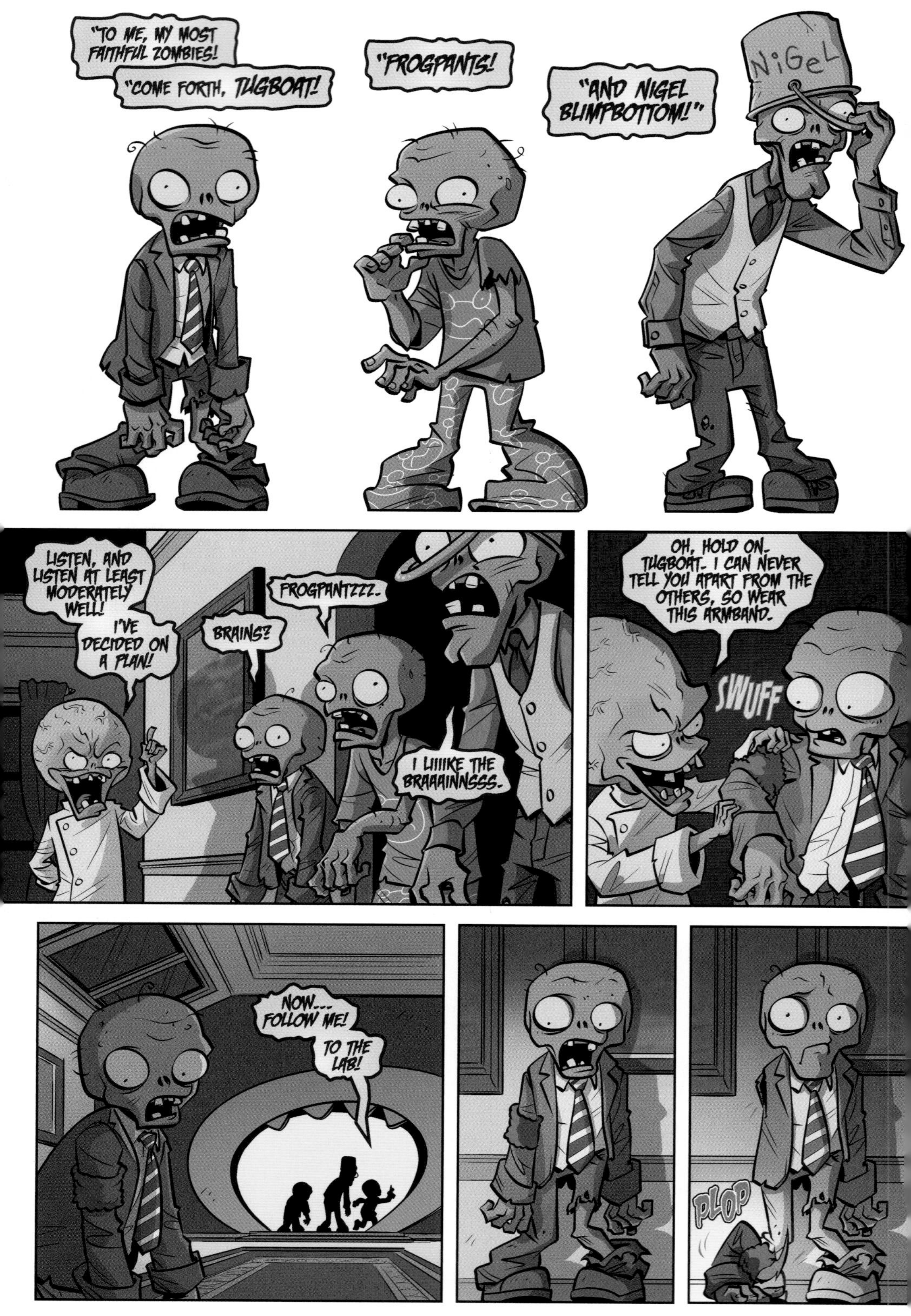
"TO ME, MY MOST FAITHFUL ZOMBIES!
"COME FORTH, TUGBOAT!
"FROGPANTS!
"AND NIGEL BLIMPBOTTOM!"
NiGeL
LISTEN, AND LISTEN AT LEAST MODERATELY WELL!
I'VE DECIDED ON A PLAN!
BRAINS?
FROGPANTZZZ.
I LIIIIKE THE BRAAAINNSSS.
OH, HOLD ON. TUGBOAT. I CAN NEVER TELL YOU APART FROM THE OTHERS, SO WEAR THIS ARMBAND.
SWUFF
NOW... FOLLOW ME!
TO THE LAB!
PLOP

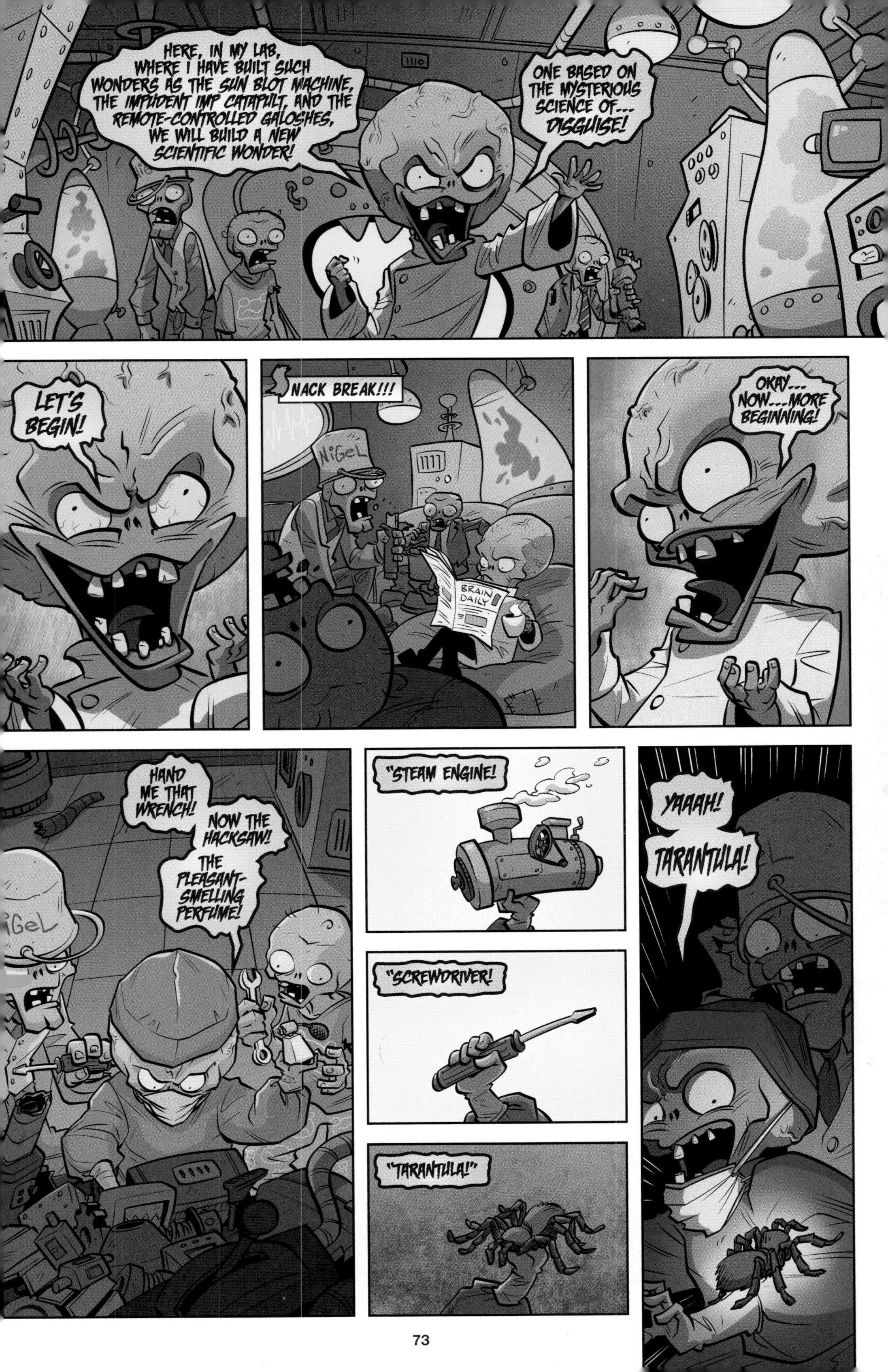

HERE, IN MY LAB, WHERE I HAVE BUILT SUCH WONDERS AS THE SUN BLOT MACHINE, THE IMPUDENT IMP CATAPULT, AND THE REMOTE-CONTROLLED GALOSHES, WE WILL BUILD A NEW SCIENTIFIC WONDER!
ONE BASED ON THE MYSTERIOUS SCIENCE OF... DISGUISE!
LET'S BEGIN!
NACK BREAK!!!
NiGeL
BRAIN DAILY
OKAY... NOW... MORE BEGINNING!
HAND ME THAT WRENCH!
NOW THE HACKSAW!
THE PLEASANT-SMELLING PERFUME!
NiGeL
"STEAM ENGINE!
"SCREWDRIVER!
"TARANTULA!"
YAAAH!
TARANTULA!

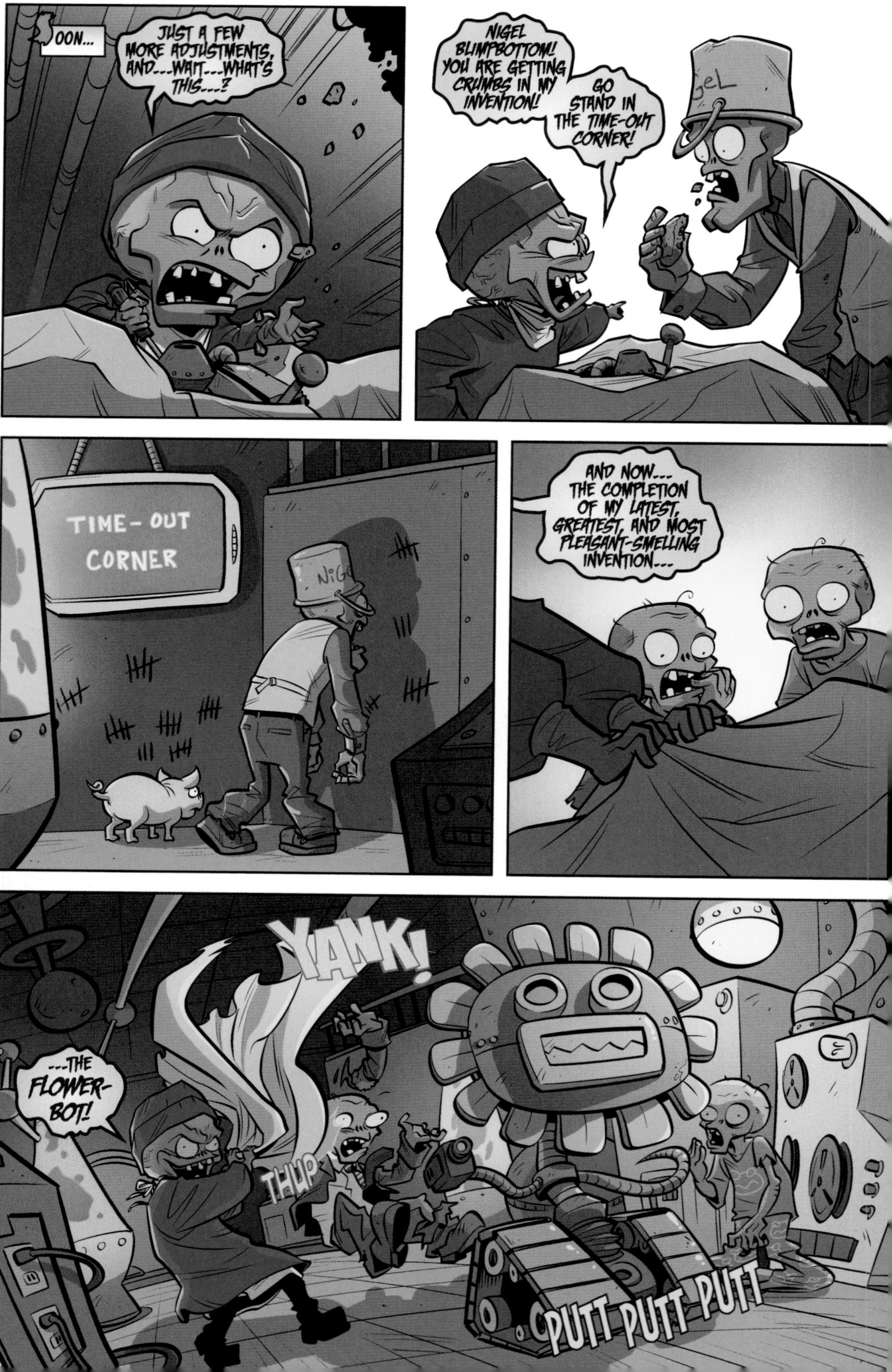
SOON...
JUST A FEW MORE ADJUSTMENTS, AND...WAIT...WHAT'S THIS...?
NIGEL BLIMPBOTTOM! YOU ARE GETTING CRUMBS IN MY INVENTION!
GO STAND IN THE TIME-OUT CORNER!
TIME-OUT CORNER
AND NOW... THE COMPLETION OF MY LATEST, GREATEST, AND MOST PLEASANT-SMELLING INVENTION...
YANK!
...THE FLOWER-BOT!
THUP
PUTT PUTT PUTT

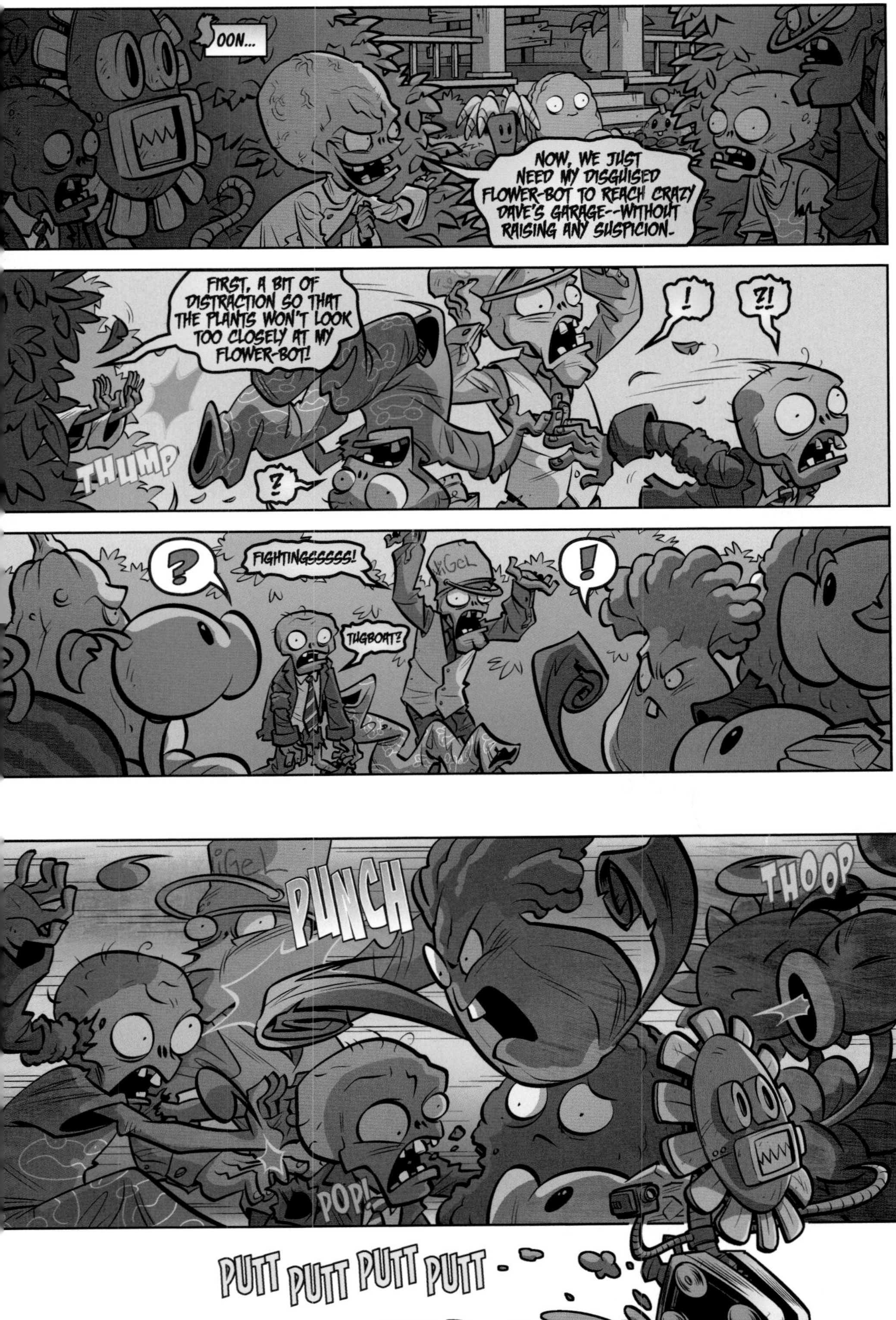
SOON...
NOW, WE JUST NEED MY DISGUISED FLOWER-BOT TO REACH CRAZY DAVE'S GARAGE--WITHOUT RAISING ANY SUSPICION.
FIRST, A BIT OF DISTRACTION SO THAT THE PLANTS WON'T LOOK TOO CLOSELY AT MY FLOWER-BOT!
!
?!
THUMP
?
?
FIGHTINGSSSSS!
!
TUGBOAT?
PUNCH
THOOP
POP!
PUTT PUTT PUTT PUTT

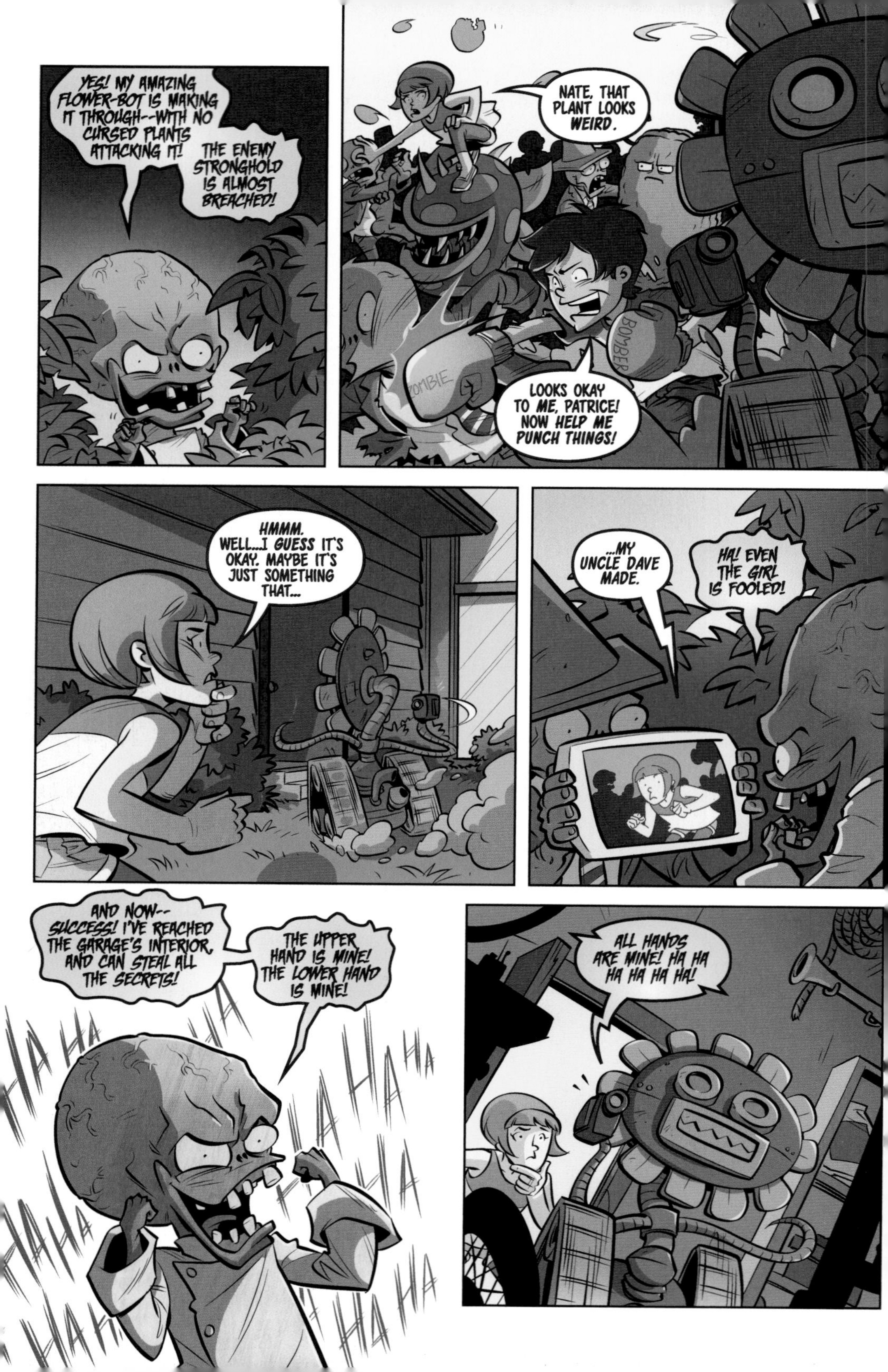
YES! MY AMAZING FLOWER-BOT IS MAKING IT THROUGH--WITH NO CURSED PLANTS ATTACKING IT!
THE ENEMY STRONGHOLD IS ALMOST BREACHED!
NATE, THAT PLANT LOOKS WEIRD.
BOMBER
ZOMBIE
LOOKS OKAY TO ME, PATRICE! NOW HELP ME PUNCH THINGS!
HMMM. WELL...I GUESS IT'S OKAY. MAYBE IT'S JUST SOMETHING THAT...
...MY UNCLE DAVE MADE.
HA! EVEN THE GIRL IS FOOLED!
AND NOW--SUCCESS! I'VE REACHED THE GARAGE'S INTERIOR, AND CAN STEAL ALL THE SECRETS!
THE UPPER HAND IS MINE! THE LOWER HAND IS MINE!
HA HA HA HA HA HA HA HA HA HA HA HA HA
ALL HANDS ARE MINE! HA HA HA HA HA HA!

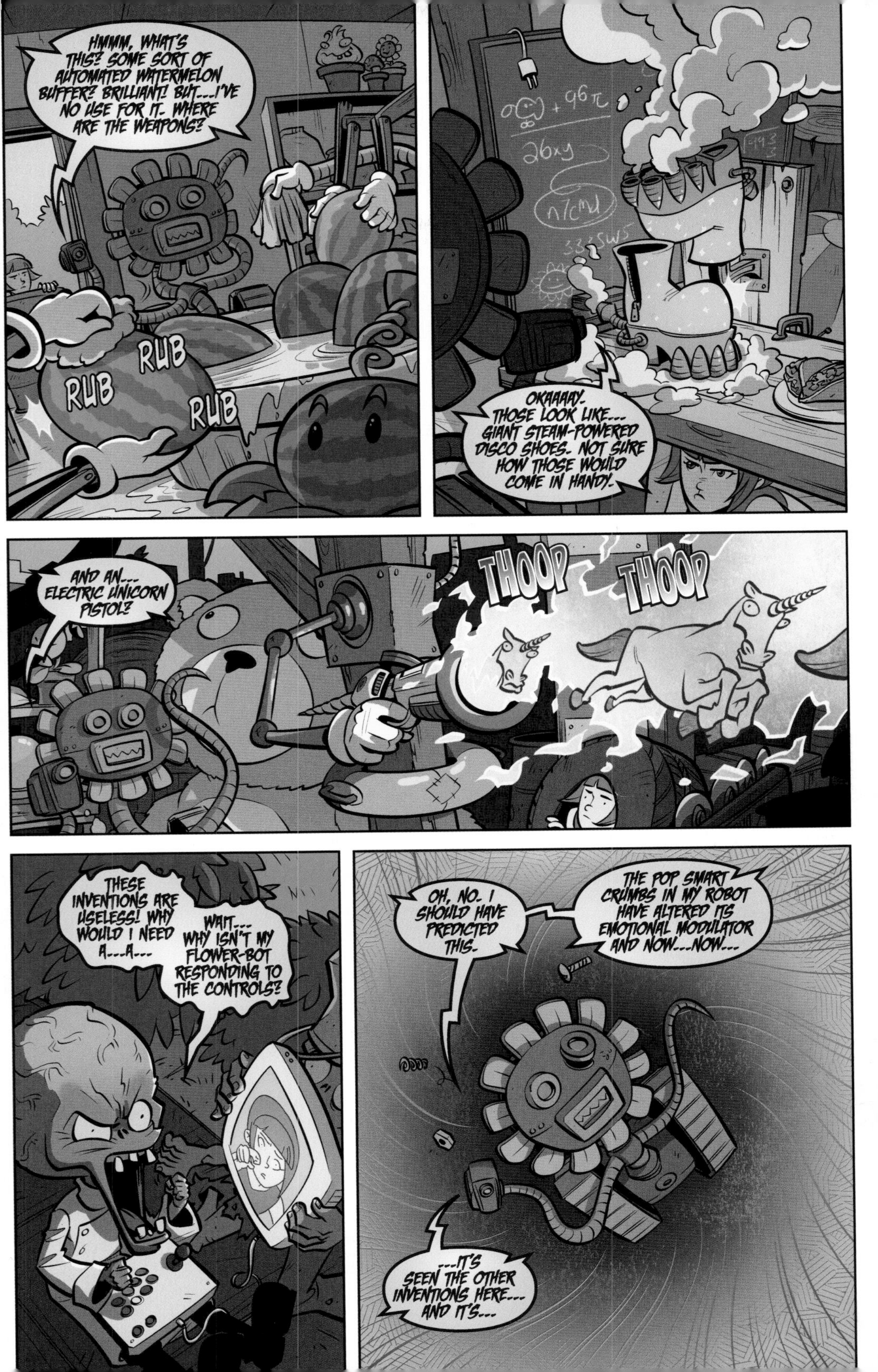
HMMM, WHAT'S THIS? SOME SORT OF AUTOMATED WATERMELON BUFFER? BRILLIANT! BUT...I'VE NO USE FOR IT. WHERE ARE THE WEAPONS?
RUB
RUB
RUB
OKAAAAY. THOSE LOOK LIKE... GIANT STEAM-POWERED DISCO SHOES. NOT SURE HOW THOSE WOULD COME IN HANDY.
AND AN... ELECTRIC UNICORN PISTOL?
THOOP
THOOP
THESE INVENTIONS ARE USELESS! WHY WOULD I NEED A...A...
WAIT... WHY ISN'T MY FLOWER-BOT RESPONDING TO THE CONTROLS?
OH, NO. I SHOULD HAVE PREDICTED THIS.
THE POP SMART CRUMBS IN MY ROBOT HAVE ALTERED ITS EMOTIONAL MODULATOR AND NOW...NOW...
...IT'S SEEN THE OTHER INVENTIONS HERE... AND IT'S...

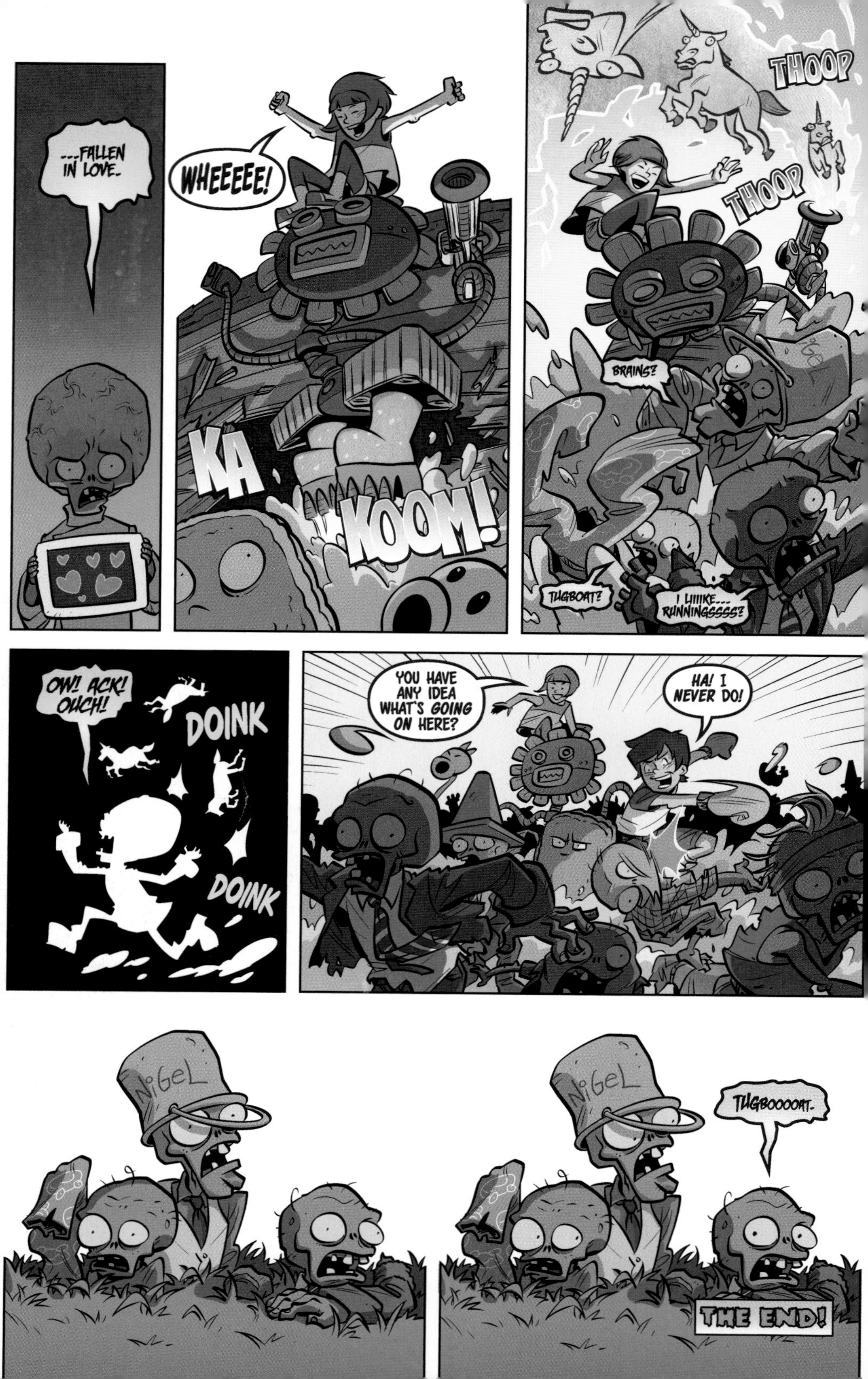
...FALLEN IN LOVE.
WHEEEEE!
KA
KOOM!
THOOP
THOOP
BRAINS?
TUGBOAT?
I LIIIIKE... RUNNINGSSSS?
OW! ACK! OUCH!
DOINK
DOINK
YOU HAVE ANY IDEA WHAT'S GOING ON HERE?
HA! I NEVER DO!
NiGeL
NiGeL
TUGBOOOOAT.
THE END!

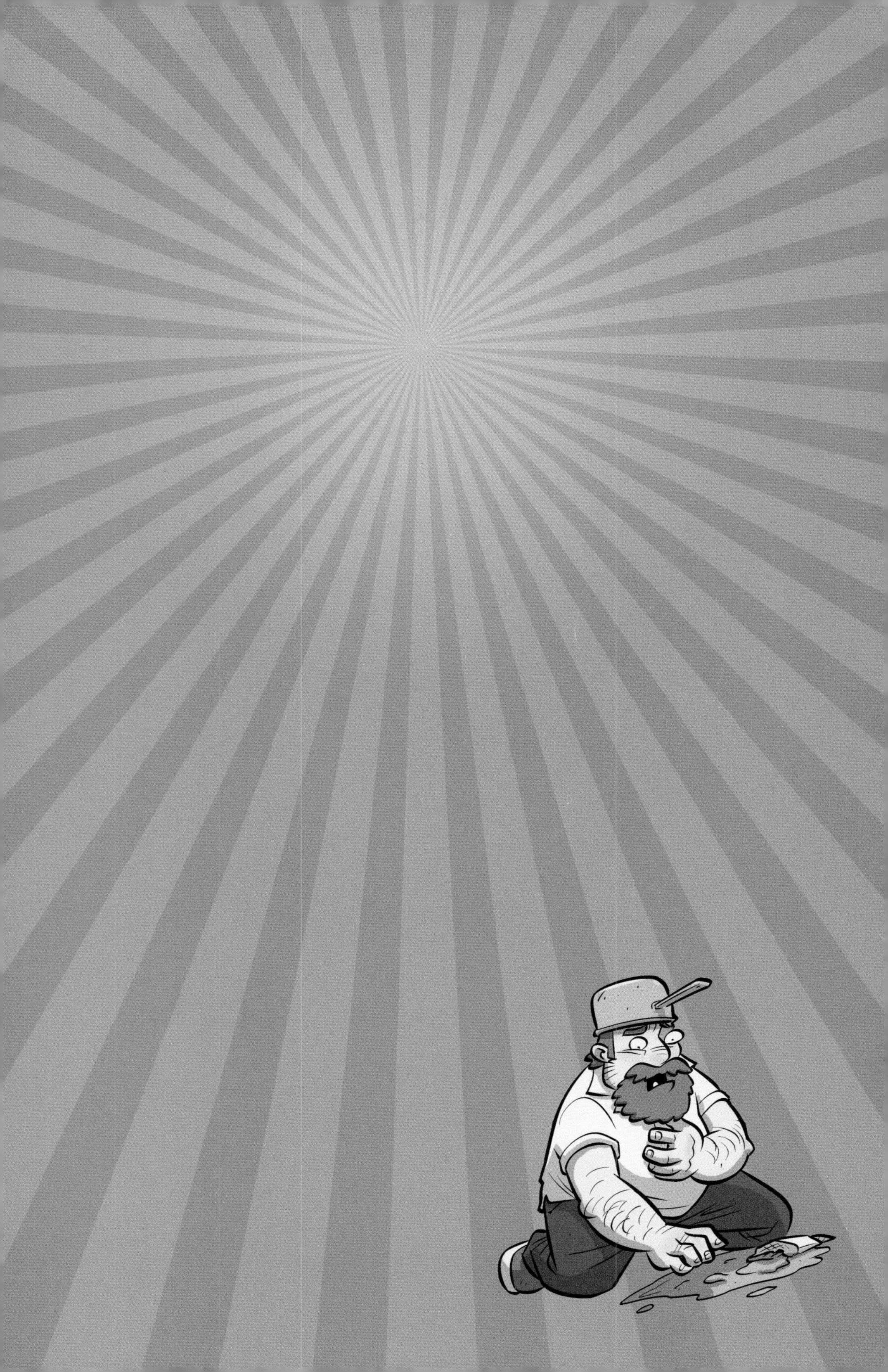

BONUS STORIES

POKEY PIQUENOSE

Written by PAUL TOBIN
Art by DUSTIN NGUYEN
Letters by STEVE DUTRO

BONK CHOY BRO-DOWN!

Written by PAUL TOBIN
Art by DUSTIN NGUYEN
Letters by STEVE DUTRO

BLOWN AWAY

Written by PAUL TOBIN
Art by JENNIFER L. MEYER
Letters by STEVE DUTRO

THE SUNFROWNER

Written by PAUL TOBIN
Art by JENNIFER L. MEYER
Letters by STEVE DUTRO

THE EMPTINESS

Written by PAUL TOBIN
Art and letters by PETER BAGGE

MR. STUBBINS'S ADVENTURES

Written by PAUL TOBIN
Art and letters by PETER BAGGE

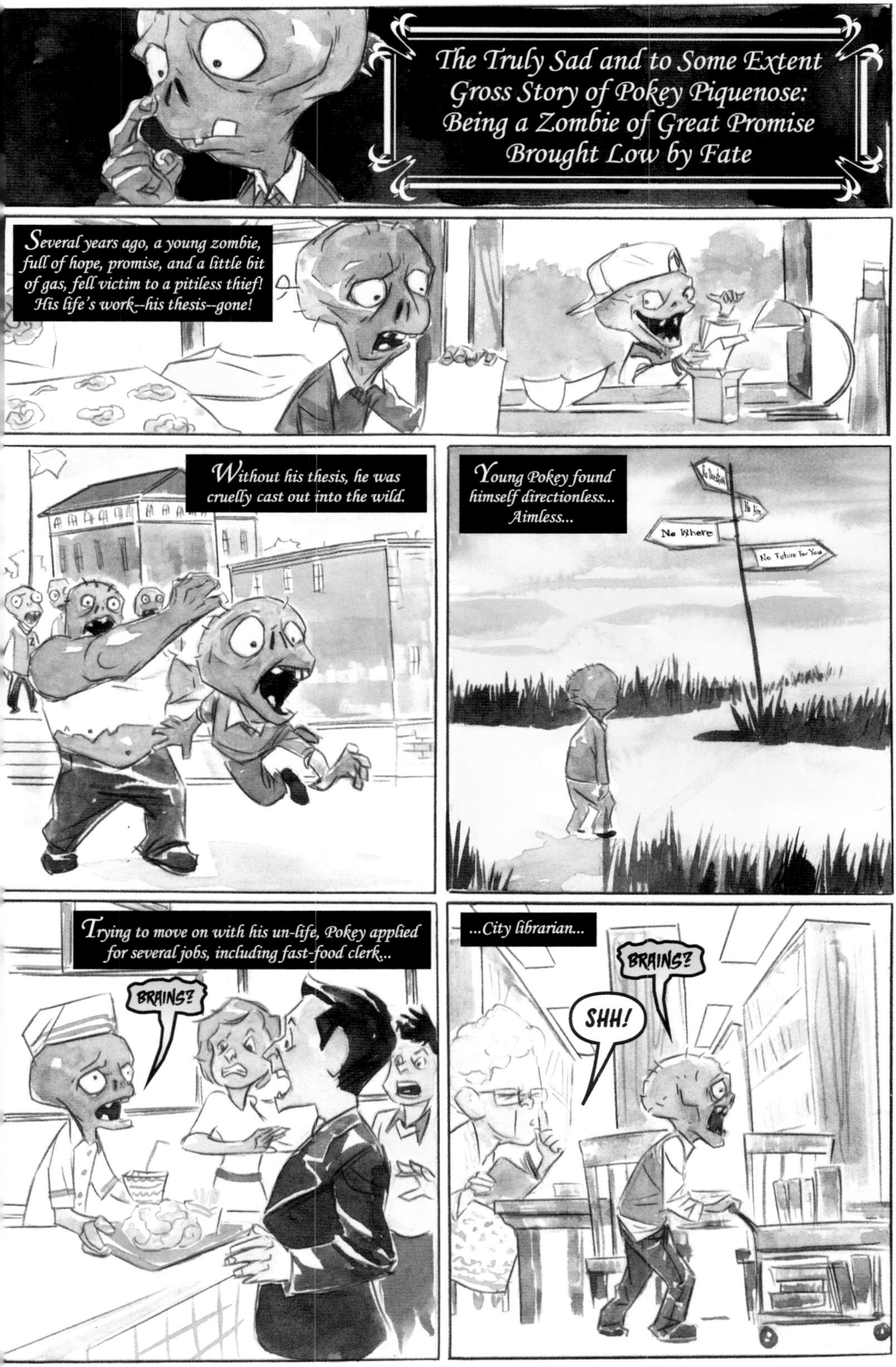
The Truly Sad and to Some Extent Gross Story of Pokey Piquenose: Being a Zombie of Great Promise Brought Low by Fate
Several years ago, a young zombie, full of hope, promise, and a little bit of gas, fell victim to a pitiless thief! His life's work--his thesis--gone!
Without his thesis, he was cruelly cast out into the wild.
Young Pokey found himself directionless... Aimless...
No Where
No Future For You
Trying to move on with his un-life, Pokey applied for several jobs, including fast-food clerk...
BRAINS?
...City librarian...
BRAINS?
SHH!

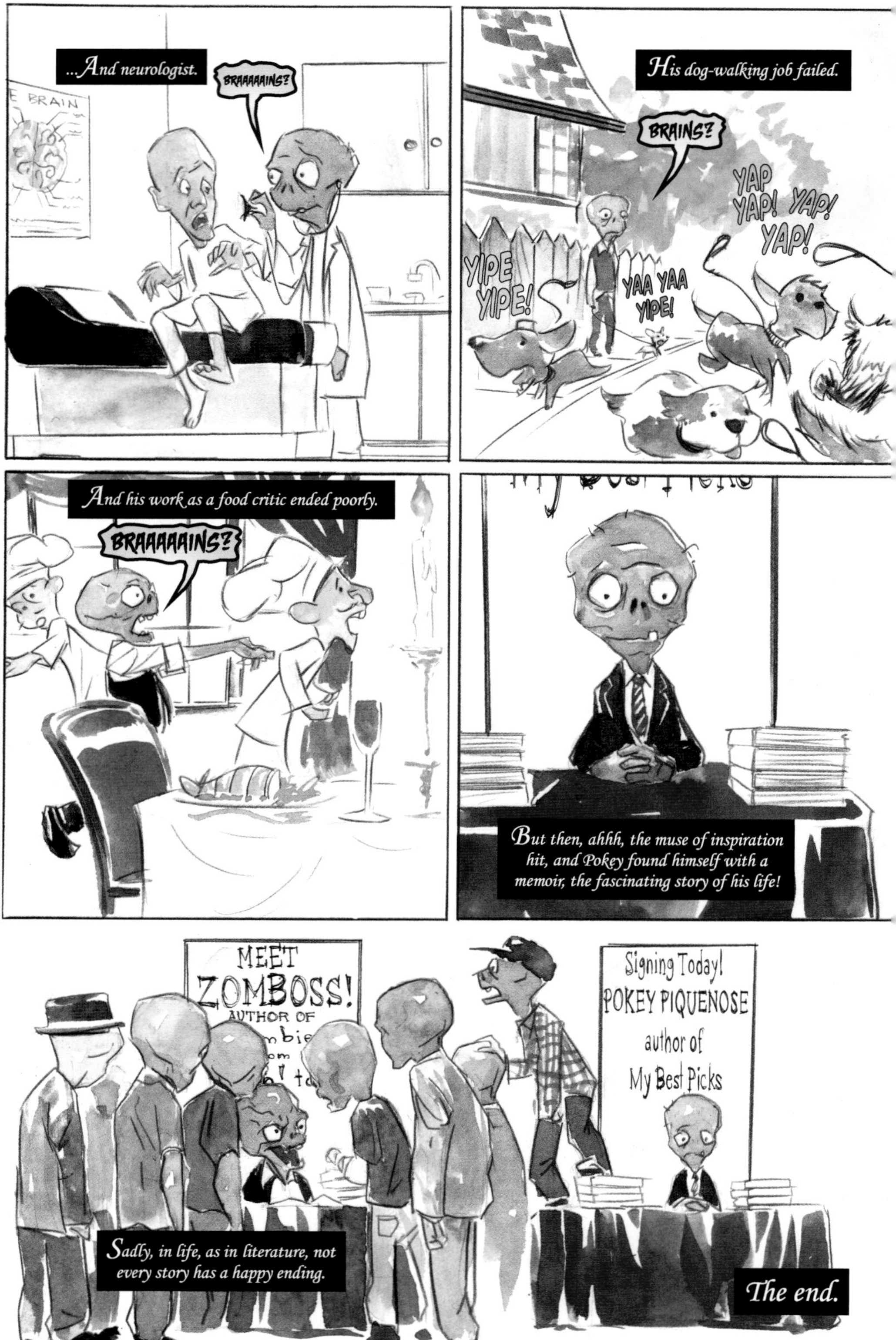
...And neurologist.
BRAAAAAAINS?
His dog-walking job failed.
BRAINS?
YAP YAP! YAP! YAP!
YIPE YIPE!
YAA YAA YIPE!
And his work as a food critic ended poorly.
BRAAAAAAINS?
But then, ahhh, the muse of inspiration hit, and Pokey found himself with a memoir, the fascinating story of his life!
MEET ZOMBOSS! AUTHOR OF
Signing Today! POKEY PIQUENOSE author of My Best Picks
Sadly, in life, as in literature, not every story has a happy ending.
The end.

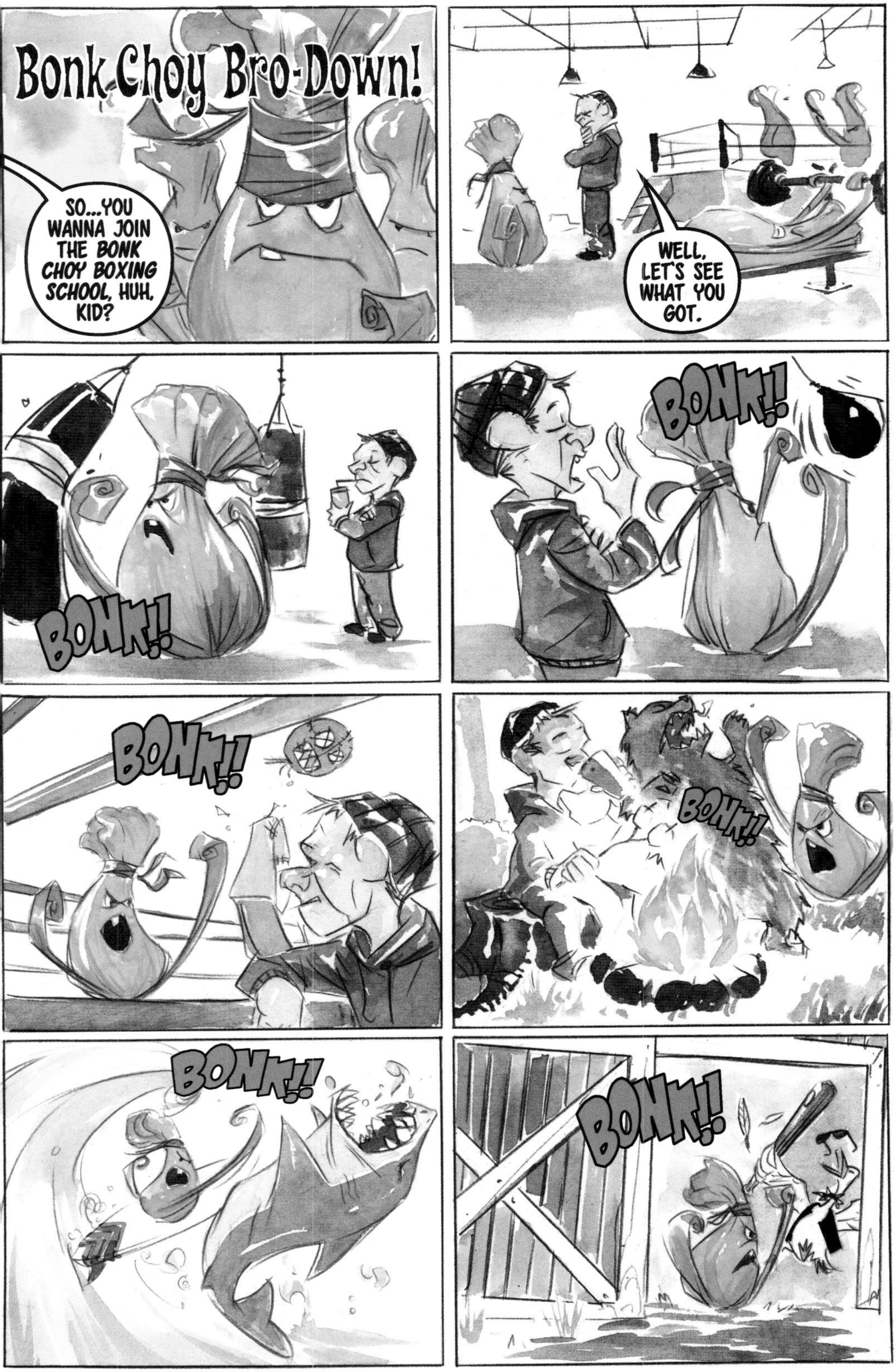
Bonk Choy Bro-Down!
SO...YOU WANNA JOIN THE BONK CHOY BOXING SCHOOL, HUH, KID?
WELL, LET'S SEE WHAT YOU GOT.
BONK!!
BONK!!
BONK!!
BONK!!
BONK!!
BONK!!

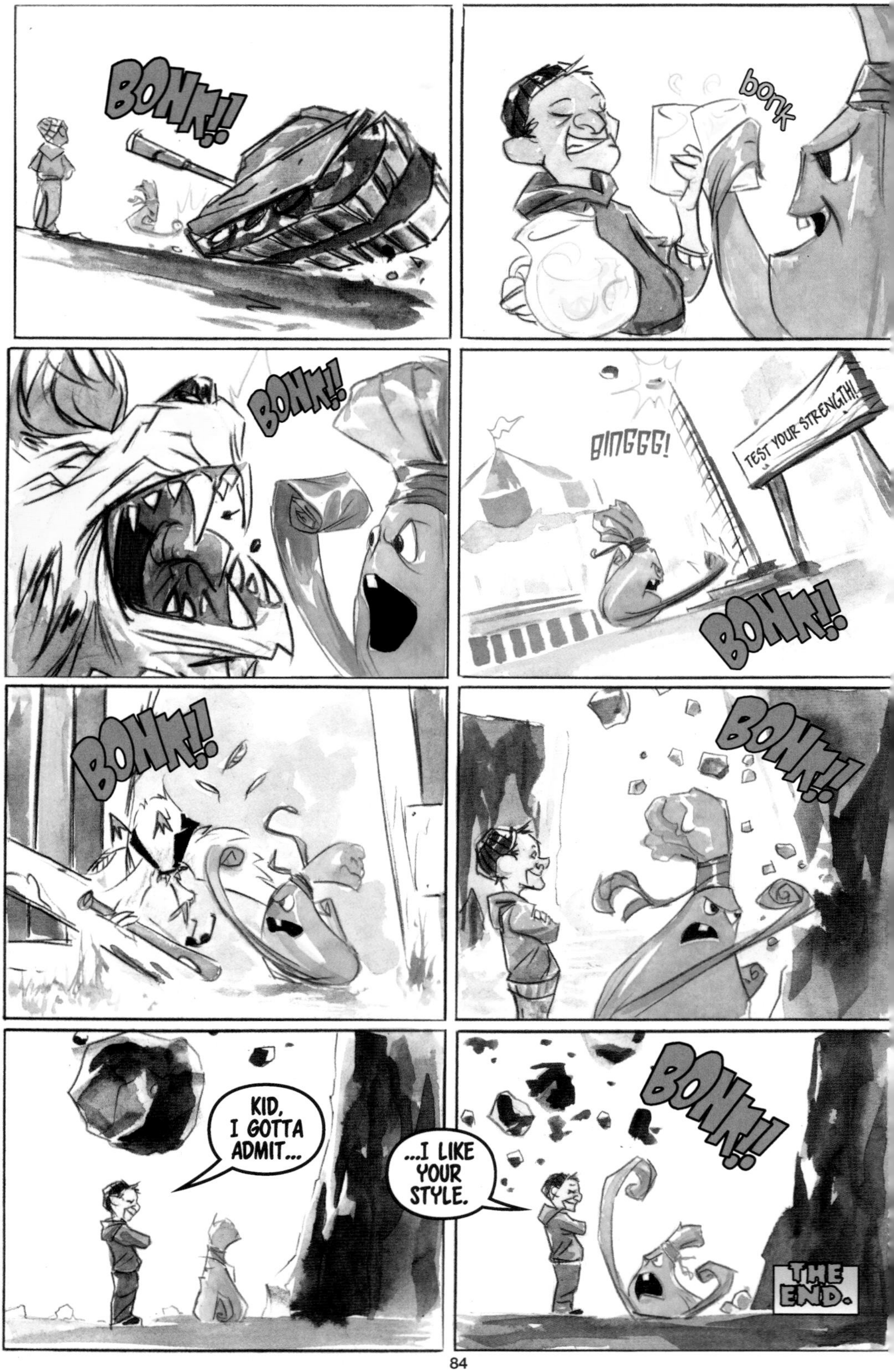
BONK!!
bonk
BONK!!
BINGGG!
TEST YOUR STRENGTH!
BONK!!
BONK!!
BONK!!
KID, I GOTTA ADMIT...
...I LIKE YOUR STYLE.
BONK!!
THE END.

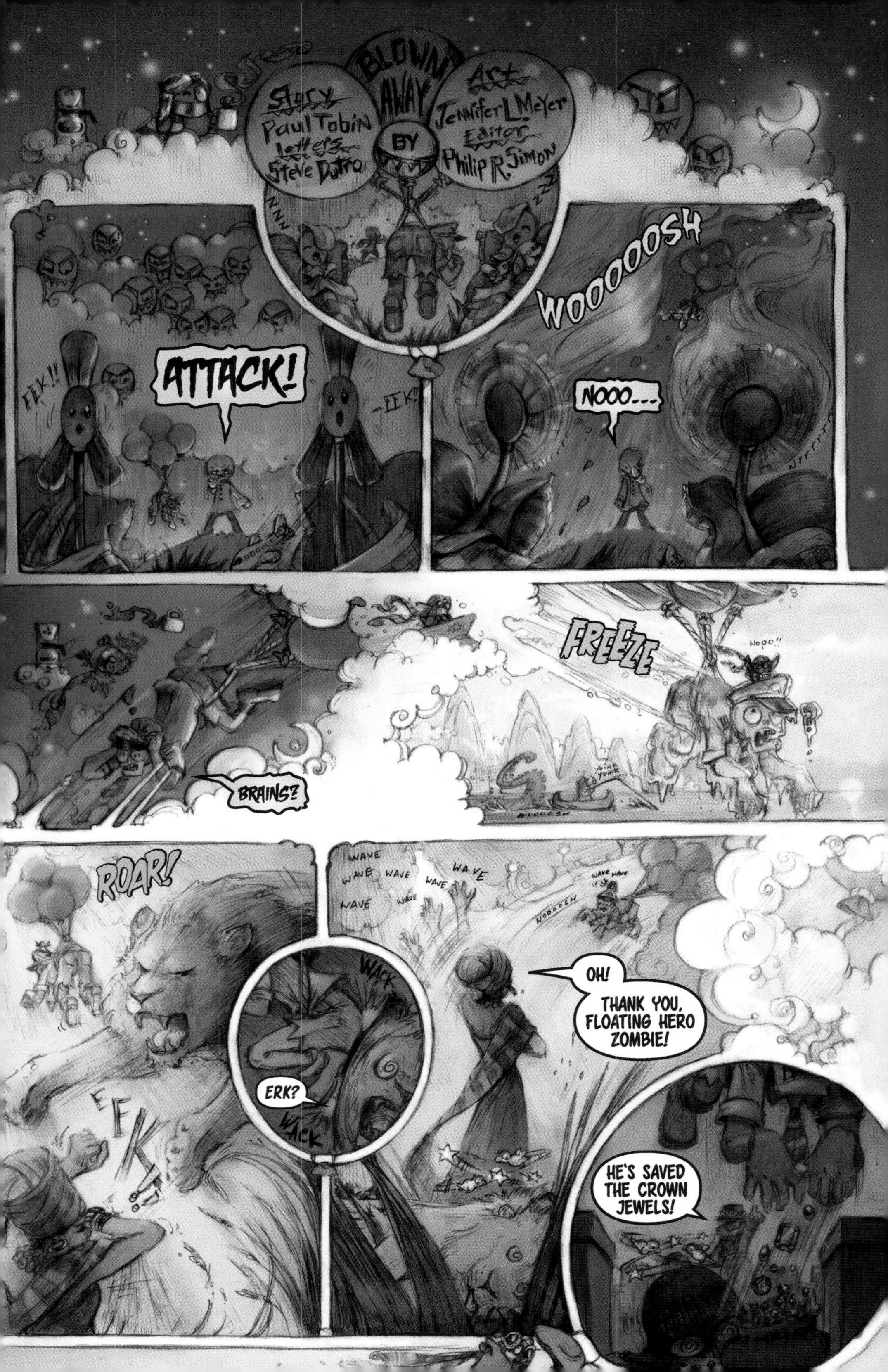

BLOWN AWAY
Story Paul Tobin
Letters Steve Dutro
BY
Art Jennifer L. Meyer
Editor Philip R. Simon
EEK!!
ATTACK!
EEK!!
WOOOOOOSH
NOOO...
FREEZE
WOOO!!
BRAINS?
ROAR!
WACK
ERK?
WACK
EEK
WAVE WAVE WAVE WAVE WAVE WAVE WAVE WAVE
OH!
THANK YOU, FLOATING HERO ZOMBIE!
HE'S SAVED THE CROWN JEWELS!

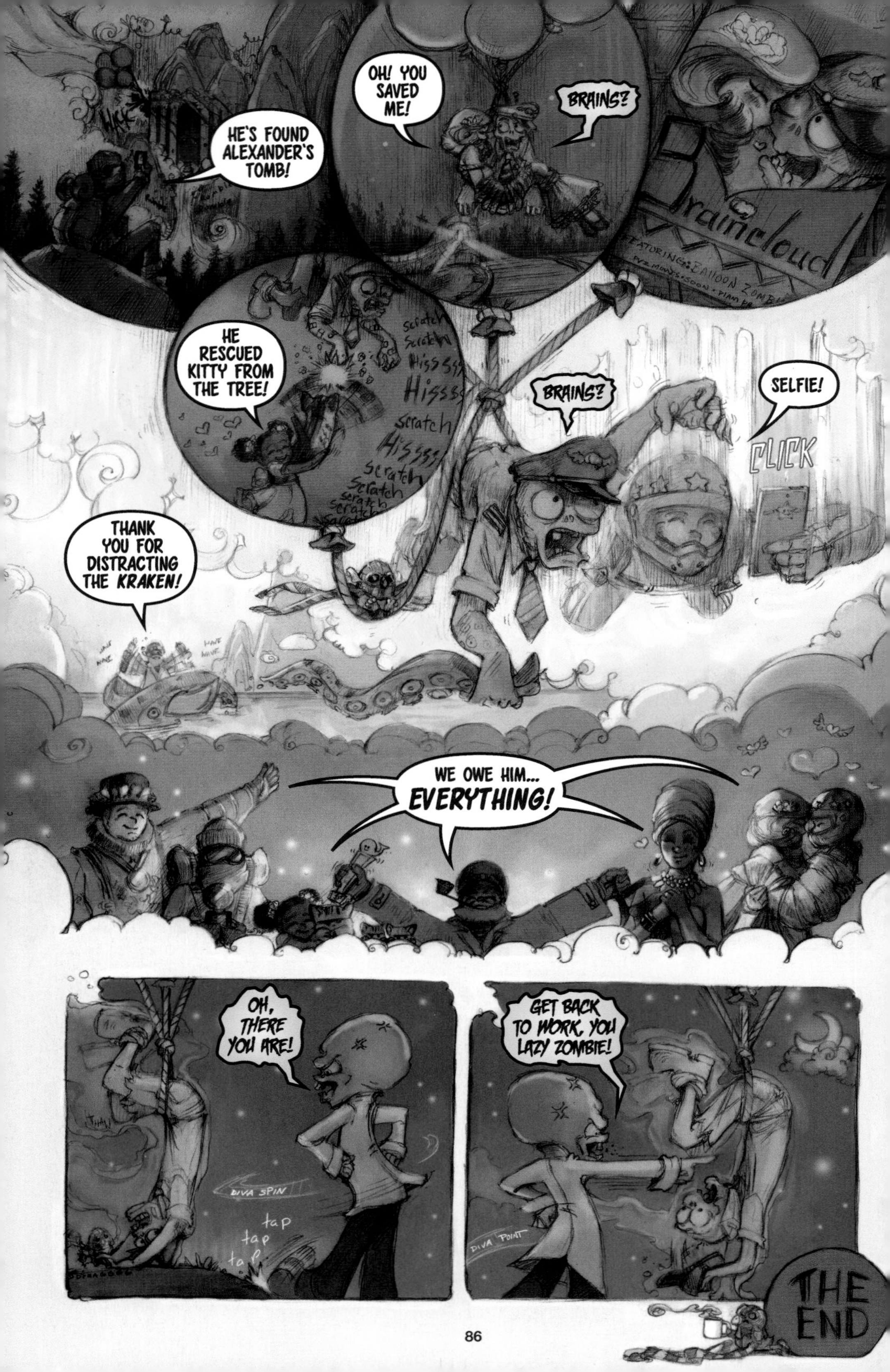
HE'S FOUND ALEXANDER'S TOMB!
OH! YOU SAVED ME!
BRAINS?
Braincloud
FEATURING: BALLOON ZOMBIE
HE RESCUED KITTY FROM THE TREE!
scratch scratch Hissss Hissss scratch Hissss scratch scratch scratch
BRAINS?
SELFIE!
CLICK
THANK YOU FOR DISTRACTING THE *KRAKEN!*
WE OWE HIM... *EVERYTHING!*
OH, THERE YOU ARE!
DIVA SPIN
tap tap tap
GET BACK TO WORK, YOU LAZY ZOMBIE!
DIVA POINT
THE END

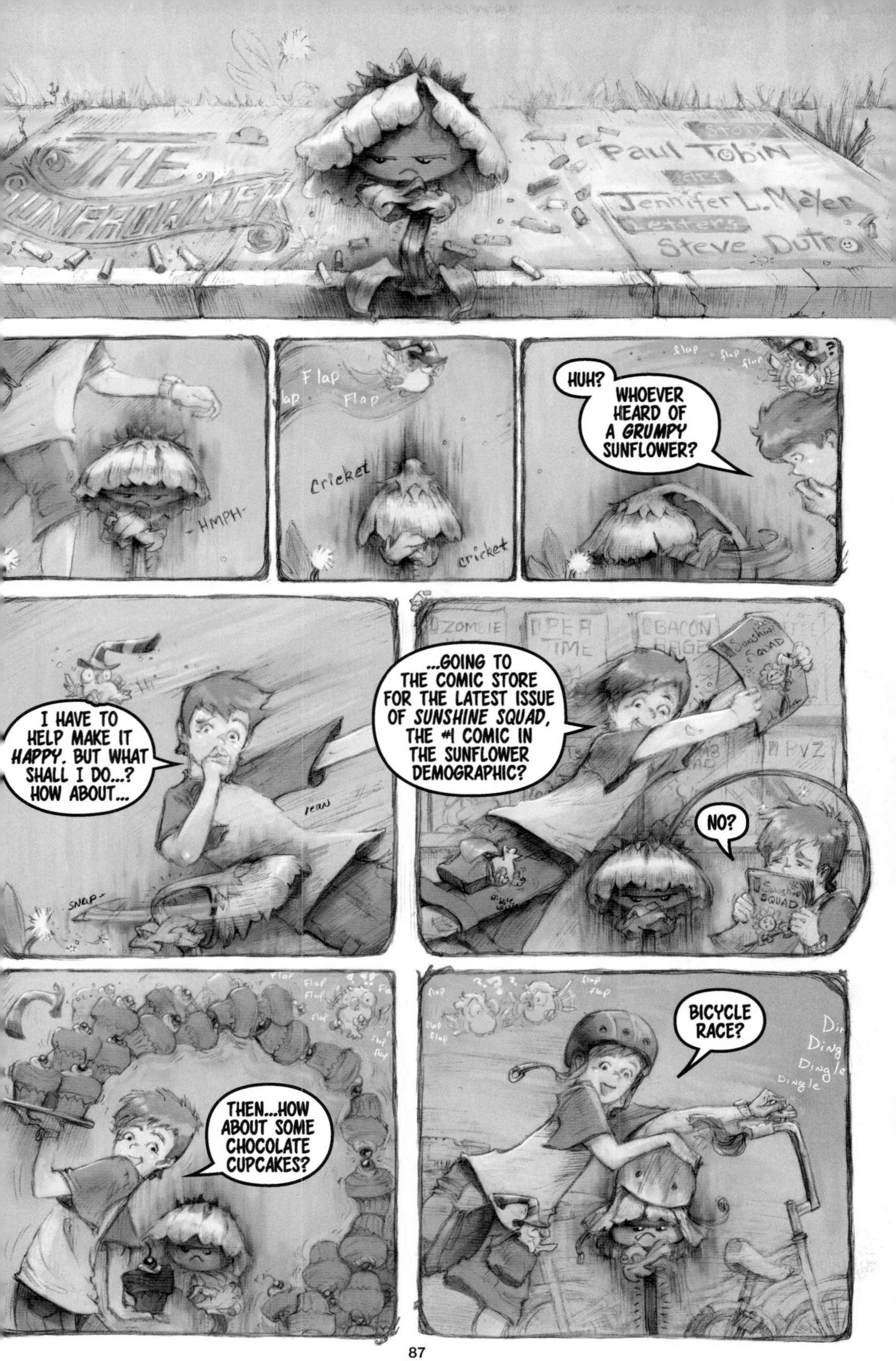
THE UNFROWNER
Story
Paul Tobin
art
Jennifer L. Meyer
Letters
Steve Dutro
-HMPH-
Flap
Flap
cricket
cricket
HUH?
WHOEVER HEARD OF A *GRUMPY* SUNFLOWER?
I HAVE TO HELP MAKE IT *HAPPY*. BUT WHAT SHALL I DO...? HOW ABOUT...
lean
SNAP
...GOING TO THE COMIC STORE FOR THE LATEST ISSUE OF *SUNSHINE SQUAD*, THE #1 COMIC IN THE SUNFLOWER DEMOGRAPHIC?
ZOMBIE
BACON
PvZ
Sunshine Squad
NO?
Sunshine SQUAD
THEN...HOW ABOUT SOME CHOCOLATE CUPCAKES?
BICYCLE RACE?
Ding
Dingle
Dingle

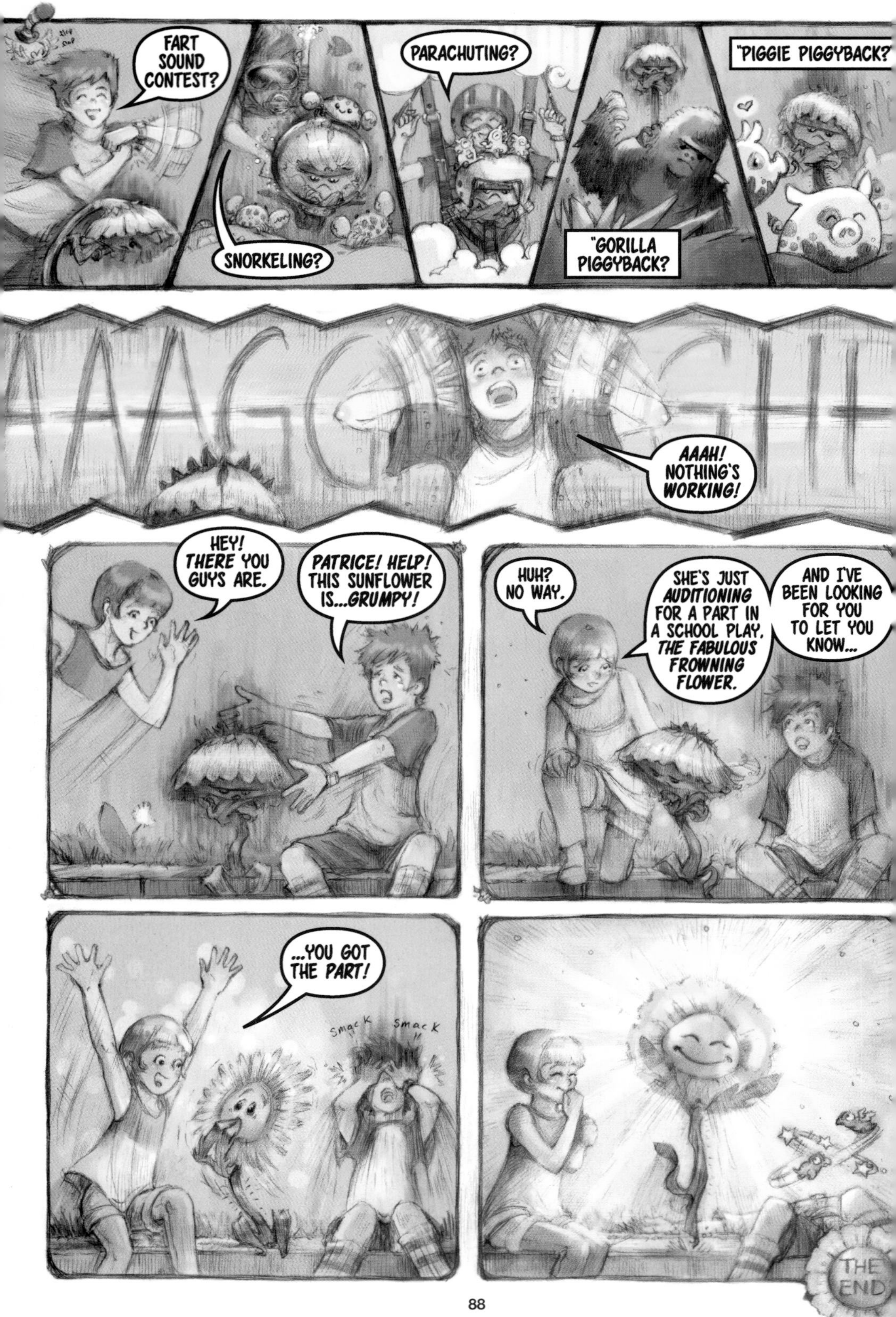
FART SOUND CONTEST?
SNORKELING?
PARACHUTING?
"GORILLA PIGGYBACK?
"PIGGIE PIGGYBACK?"
AAAH! NOTHING'S WORKING!
HEY! THERE YOU GUYS ARE.
PATRICE! HELP! THIS SUNFLOWER IS...GRUMPY!
HUH? NO WAY.
SHE'S JUST AUDITIONING FOR A PART IN A SCHOOL PLAY, THE FABULOUS FROWNING FLOWER.
AND I'VE BEEN LOOKING FOR YOU TO LET YOU KNOW...
...YOU GOT THE PART!
Smack
Smack
THE END

THE EMPTINESS

POP SMARTS

THE BRAIN-FLAVORED TREAT!

NEW ENNUI FLAVOR

?!?

STORY: PAUL TOBIN • ART: PETER BAGGE

OUT OF POP SMARTS?

BUT WHAT WILL I EAT?

MY STOMACH... EMPTY...

SO EMPTY...

=SHAKE= =SHAKE= =SHAKE=

=GRUMBLE= =GRUMBLE= =GRUMBLE=

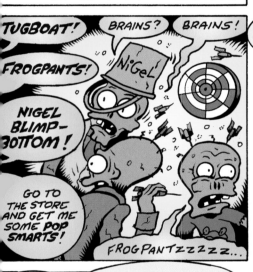

TUGBOAT!

FROGPANTS!

NIGEL BLIMP-BOTTOM!

GO TO THE STORE AND GET ME SOME POP SMARTS!

BRAINS?

BRAINS!

NiGeL

FROGPANTZZZZZ...

I WANT TWO BOXES CHERRY FLAVOR...

ONE BOX APRICOT SUNDAE...

AND FIVE BOXES EINSTEIN FLAVOR!

FROGPANTZZZ...

AND GO IN DISGUISE!

WE CAN'T HAVE YOU DRAWING ATTENTION TO YOURSELVES.

FROGPANTZZ?

SOON...

YAP! YAP! YAP!

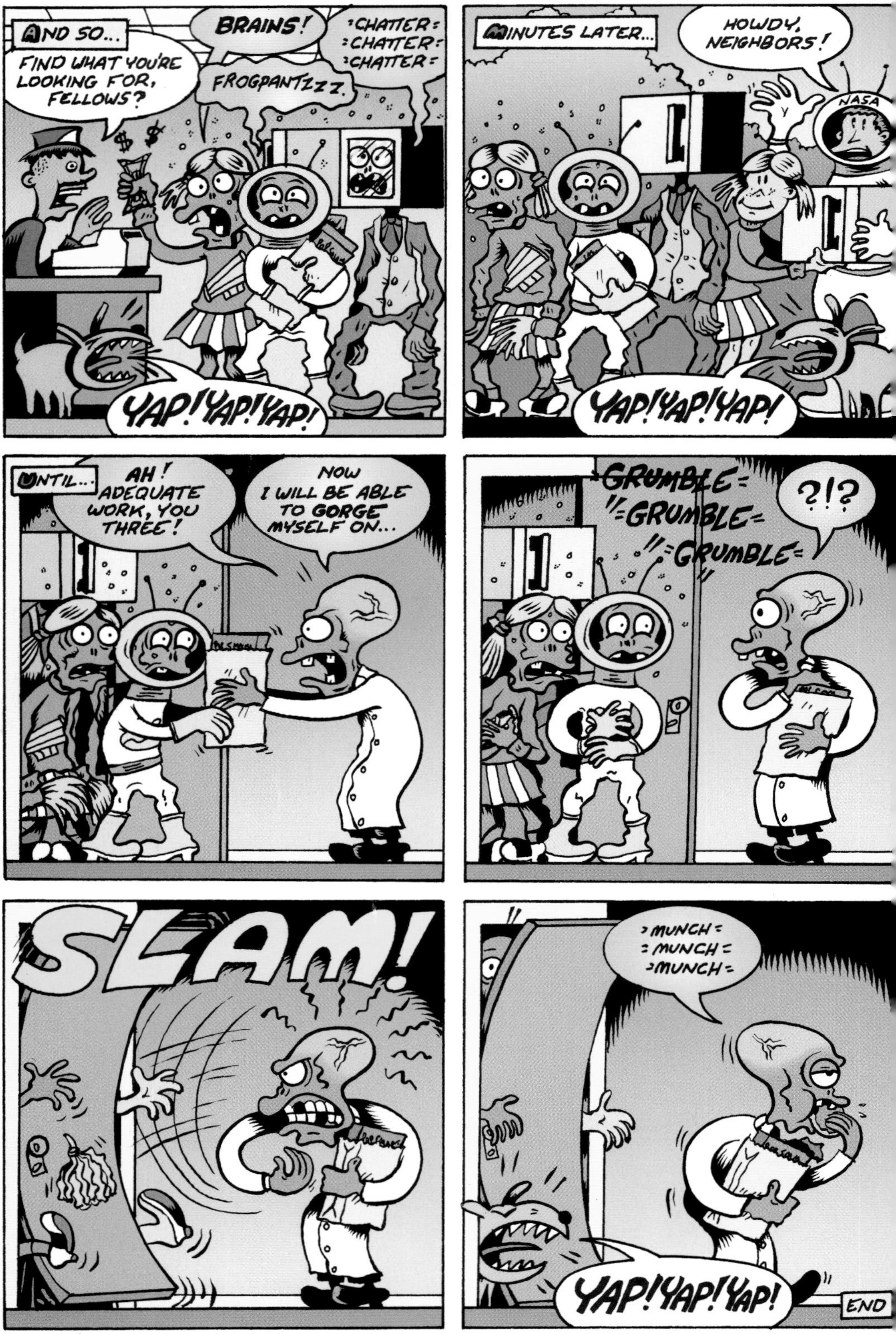
AND SO...
FIND WHAT YOU'RE LOOKING FOR, FELLOWS?
BRAINS!
FROGPANTZzzz.
:CHATTER: :CHATTER: :CHATTER:
YAP! YAP! YAP!
MINUTES LATER...
HOWDY, NEIGHBORS!
NASA
YAP! YAP! YAP!
UNTIL...
AH! ADEQUATE WORK, YOU THREE!
NOW I WILL BE ABLE TO GORGE MYSELF ON...
GRUMBLE GRUMBLE GRUMBLE
?!?
SLAM!
:MUNCH: :MUNCH: :MUNCH:
YAP! YAP! YAP!
END

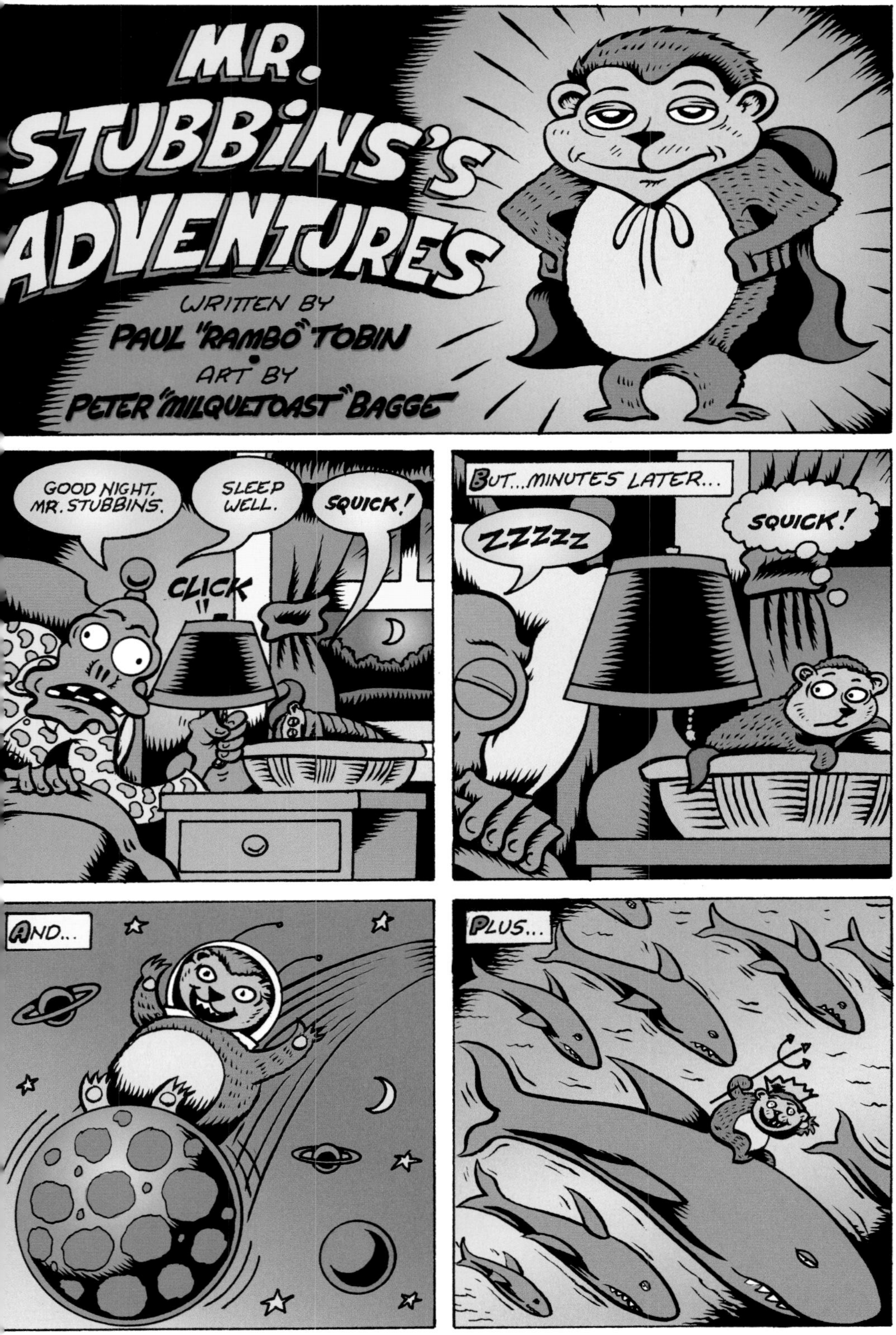
MR. STUBBINS'S ADVENTURES
WRITTEN BY
PAUL "RAMBO" TOBIN
ART BY
PETER "MILQUETOAST" BAGGE
GOOD NIGHT, MR. STUBBINS.
SLEEP WELL.
SQUICK!
CLICK
BUT...MINUTES LATER...
ZZZZZ
SQUICK!
AND...
PLUS...

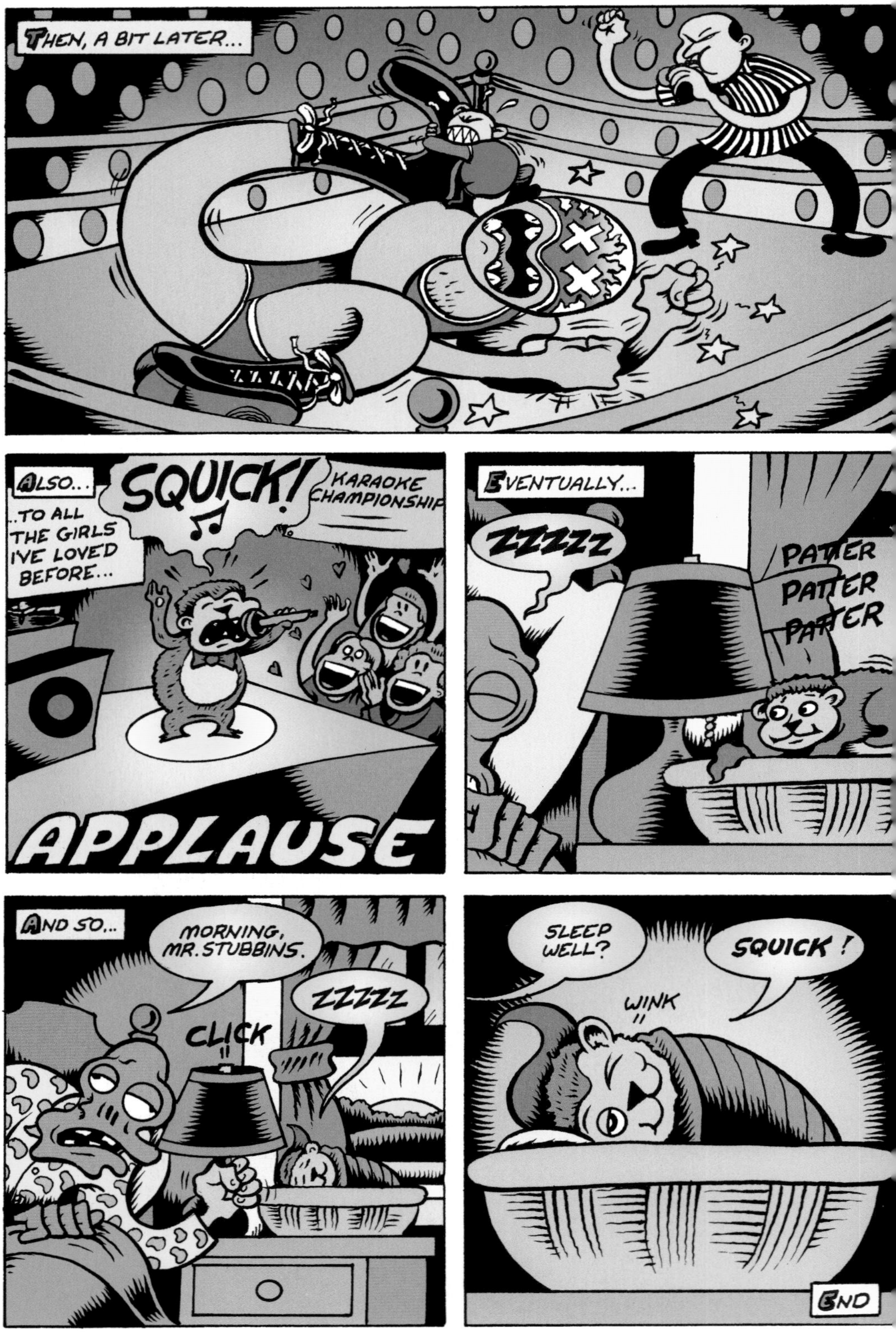
THEN, A BIT LATER...
ALSO...
..TO ALL THE GIRLS I'VE LOVED BEFORE...
SQUICK!
KARAOKE CHAMPIONSHIP
APPLAUSE
EVENTUALLY...
ZZZZZ
PATTER PATTER PATTER
AND SO...
MORNING, MR. STUBBINS.
CLICK
ZZZZZ
SLEEP WELL?
SQUICK!
WINK
END

CREATOR BIOS

Paul Tobin

Ron Chan

Matthew J. Rainwater

Steve Dutro

PAUL TOBIN is a critically acclaimed freckled person who has a detailed plan for any actual zombie invasion, based on creating a vast perfume and cologne empire—both of which would be vitally important in a zombie-infested world. Paul was once informed he "walks funny, like, seriously," but has recovered from this childhood trauma to write hundreds of comics for Marvel, DC, Dark Horse, and many others, including such creator-owned titles as *Colder* and *Bandette*, as well as *Prepare to Die!*—his debut novel. His *Genius Factor* series of novels about a fifth-grade genius and his war against the Red Death Tea Society begins in March of 2016 from Bloomsbury Publishing. Despite his many writing accomplishments, Paul's greatest claim to fame is his ability to win water levels in *Plants vs. Zombies* without using any water plants.

RON CHAN is a comic book and storyboard artist, video game fan, and occasional jujitsu practitioner. He was born and raised in Portland, Oregon, where he still lives and works as a member of the local artist collective Periscope Studio. His comics work has been published by Dark Horse, Marvel, and Image Comics, and his storyboarding work includes boards for 3-D animation, gaming, user-experience design,

and advertising for clients such as Microsoft, Amazon Kindle, Nike, and Sega. He really likes drawing Bonk Choys. (He also enjoys eating actual bok choy in real life.)

Residing in the cool, damp forests of Portland, Oregon, **MATTHEW J. RAINWATER** is a freelance illustrator whose work has been featured in advertising, web design, and independent video games. On top of this, he also self-publishes several comic books, including *Trailer Park Warlock*, *Garage Raja*, and *The Feeling Is Multiplied*—all of which can be found at MattJRainwater.com. His favorite zombie-bashing strategy utilizes a line of Bonk Choys with a Wall-nut front guard and Threepeater covering fire.

STEVE DUTRO is a comic book letterer from northern California who can also drive a tractor. He graduated from the Kubert School and has been in the comics industry for decades, working for Dark Horse (*The Fifth Beatle*, *The Evil Dead*, *Eden*), Viz, Marvel, and DC. Steve's last encounter with zombies was playing zombie paintball in a walnut orchard on Halloween. He tried to play the *Plants vs. Zombies* video game once but experienced a full-on panic attack and resolved to stick with calmer games . . . like *Gears of War*.

ALSO AVAILABLE FROM DARK HORSE!

THE HIT VIDEO GAME CONTINUES ITS COMIC BOOK INVASION!

PLANTS VS. ZOMBIES: LAWNMAGEDDON
Crazy Dave—the babbling-yet-brilliant inventor and top-notch neighborhood defender—helps young adventurer Nate fend off a zombie invasion that threatens to overrun the peaceful town of Neighborville in *Plants vs. Zombies: Lawnmageddon*! Their only hope is a brave army of chomping, squashing, and pea-shooting plants! A wacky adventure for zombie zappers young and old!
ISBN 978-1-61655-192-6 | $10.99

THE ART OF PLANTS VS. ZOMBIES
Part zombie memoir, part celebration of zombie triumphs, and part anti-plant screed, *The Art of Plants vs. Zombies* is a treasure trove of never-before-seen concept art, character sketches, and surprises from PopCap's popular *Plants vs. Zombies* games!
ISBN 978-1-61655-331-9 | $9.99

PLANTS VS. ZOMBIES: TIMEPOCALYPSE
Crazy Dave helps Patrice and Nate Timely fend off Zomboss' latest attack in *Plants vs. Zombies: Timepocalypse*! This new standalone tale will tickle your funny bones and thrill your brains through any timeline!
ISBN 978-1-61655-621-1 | $9.99

PLANTS VS. ZOMBIES: BULLY FOR YOU
Patrice and Nate are ready to investigate a strange college campus to keep the streets safe from zombies!
ISBN 978-1-61655-889-5 | $10.99

PLANTS VS. ZOMBIES: GARDEN WARFARE VOLUME 1
Based on the hit video game, this comic tells the story leading up to the events in *Plants vs. Zombies: Garden Warfare 2*!
ISBN 978-1-61655-946-5 | $10.99

VOLUME 2
ISBN 978-1-50670-548-4 | $9.99

VOLUME 3
ISBN 978-1-50670-837-9 | $9.99

PLANTS VS. ZOMBIES: GROWN SWEET HOME
With newfound knowledge of humanity, Dr. Zomboss strikes at the heart of Neighborville . . . sparking a series of plant-versus-zombie brawls!
ISBN 978-1-61655-971-7 | $10.99

PLANTS VS. ZOMBIES: PETAL TO THE METAL
Crazy Dave takes on the tough *Don't Blink* video game—and challenges Dr. Zomboss to a race to determine the future of Neighborville!
ISBN 978-1-61655-999-1 | $9.99

PLANTS VS. ZOMBIES: BOOM BOOM MUSHROOM
The gang discover Zomboss' secret plan for swallowing the city of Neighborville whole! A rare mushroom must be found in order to save the humans aboveground!
ISBN 978-1-50670-037-3 | $10.99

PLANTS VS. ZOMBIES: BATTLE EXTRAVAGONZO
Zomboss is back, hoping to buy the same factory that Crazy Dave is eyeing! Will Crazy Dave and his intelligent plants beat Zomboss and his zombie army to the punch?
ISBN 978-1-50670-189-9 | $9.99

PLANTS VS. ZOMBIES: LAWN OF DOOM
With Zomboss filling everyone's yards with traps and speci soldiers, will he and his zombie army turn Halloween into the zanier Lawn of Doom celebration?!
ISBN 978-1-50670-204-9 | $10.99

PLANTS VS. ZOMBIES: THE GREATEST SHOW UNEARTHED
Dr. Zomboss believes that all humans hold a secret desire run away and join the circus, so he aims to use his "Big Z Adequately Amazing Flytrap Circus" to lure Neighborville citizens to their doom!
ISBN 978-1-50670-298-8 | $9.99

PLANTS VS. ZOMBIES: RUMBLE AT LAKE GUMBO
The battle for clean water begins! Nate, Patrice, and Crazy Da spot trouble and grab all the Tangle Kelp and Party Crabs th can to quell another zombie attack!
ISBN 978-1-50670-497-5 | $10.99

PLANTS VS. ZOMBIES: WAR AND PEAS
When Dr. Zomboss and Crazy Dave find themselves membe of the same book club, a literary war is inevitable! The positic of leader of the book club opens up and Zomboss and Cra Dave compete for the top spot in a scholarly scuffle for the age
ISBN 978-1-50670-677-1 | $9.99

PLANTS VS. ZOMBIES: DINO-MIGHT
Dr. Zomboss sets his sights on destroying the yards in tow and rendering the plants homeless—and his plans include dog cats, rabbits, hammock sloths, and, somehow, dinosaurs . .
ISBN 978-1-50670-838-6 | $9.99

PLANTS VS. ZOMBIES: SNOW THANKS
Dr. Zomboss invents a Cold Crystal capable of freezin Neighborville, burying the town in snow and ice! It's up to th humans and the fieriest plants to save Neighborville—with th help of pirates!
ISBN 978-1-50670-839-3 | $10.99

PLANTS VS. ZOMBIES: A LITTLE PROBLEM
Will an invasion of teeny-tiny miniature zombies mean the par for Crazy Dave's two-hundred-year-old pants gets canceled
ISBN 978-1-50670-840-9 | $10.99

PLANTS VS. ZOMBIES: BETTER HOMES AND GUARDENS
Nate and Patrice try thwarting zombie attacks by puttin defending "Guardens" plants *inside* homes as well as in yard But as soon as Dr. Zomboss finds out, he's determined circumvent this plan with an epically evil one of his own . . .
ISBN 978-1-50671-305-2 | $9.99

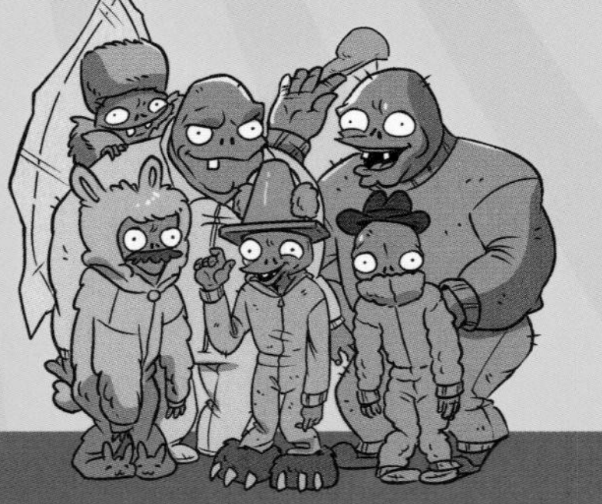

AVAILABLE AT YOUR LOCAL COMICS SHOP OR BOOKSTORE
To find a comics shop in your area, visit comicshoplocator.com. For more information or to order direct, visit **DarkHorse.com**

MORE DARK HORSE ALL-AGES TITLES

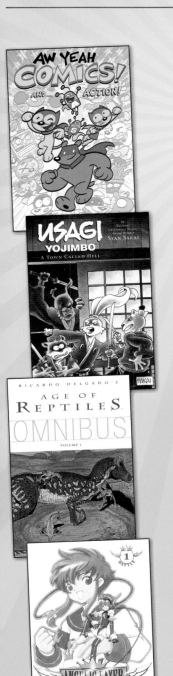

AW YEAH
COMICS!
AND... ACTION!

AW YEAH COMICS! AND . . . ACTION!

Cornelius and Alowicious are just your average comic book store employees, but when trouble strikes, they are . . . Action Cat and Adventure Bug! Join their epic all-ages adventures as they face off—with the help of Adorable Cat and Shelly Bug—against their archnemesis, Evil Cat, and his fiendish friends!

ISBN 978-1-61655-558-0 | $12.99

USAGI
YOJIMBO
A TOWN CALLED HELL
STAN SAKAI
SAKAI

USAGI YOJIMBO

In his latest adventure, the rabbit *ronin* Usagi finds himself caught between competing gang lords fighting for control of a town called Hell, confronting a *nukekubi*—a flying cannibal head—and crossing paths with the demon Jei!

Volume 25: Fox Hunt
ISBN 978-1-59582-726-5 | $16.99

***Volume 26: Traitors of the Earth* | $16.99**
ISBN 978-1-59582-910-8

***Volume 27: A Town Called Hell* | $16.99**
ISBN 978-1-59582-970-2

RICARDO DELGADO'S
AGE OF
REPTILES
OMNIBUS
VOLUME 1

AGE OF REPTILES OMNIBUS

When Ricardo Delgado first set his sights on creating comics, he crafted an epic tale about the most unlikely cast of characters: dinosaurs. Since that first Eisner-winning foray into the world of sequential art he has returned to his critically acclaimed *Age of Reptiles* again and again, each time crafting a captivating saga about his saurian subjects.

ISBN 978-1-59582-683-1 | $24.99

1
BATTLE
ANGELIC LAYER
Story and Art by
CLAMP

ANGELIC LAYER BOOK 1

Junior-high student Misaki Suzuhara just arrived in Tokyo to live with her TV-star aunt and attend the prestigious Eriol Academy. But what excites Misaki most is Angelic Layer—an arena game where you control a miniature robot fighter with your mind! Can Misaki's enthusiasm and skill take her to the top of the arena?

ISBN 978-1-61655-021-9 | $19.99

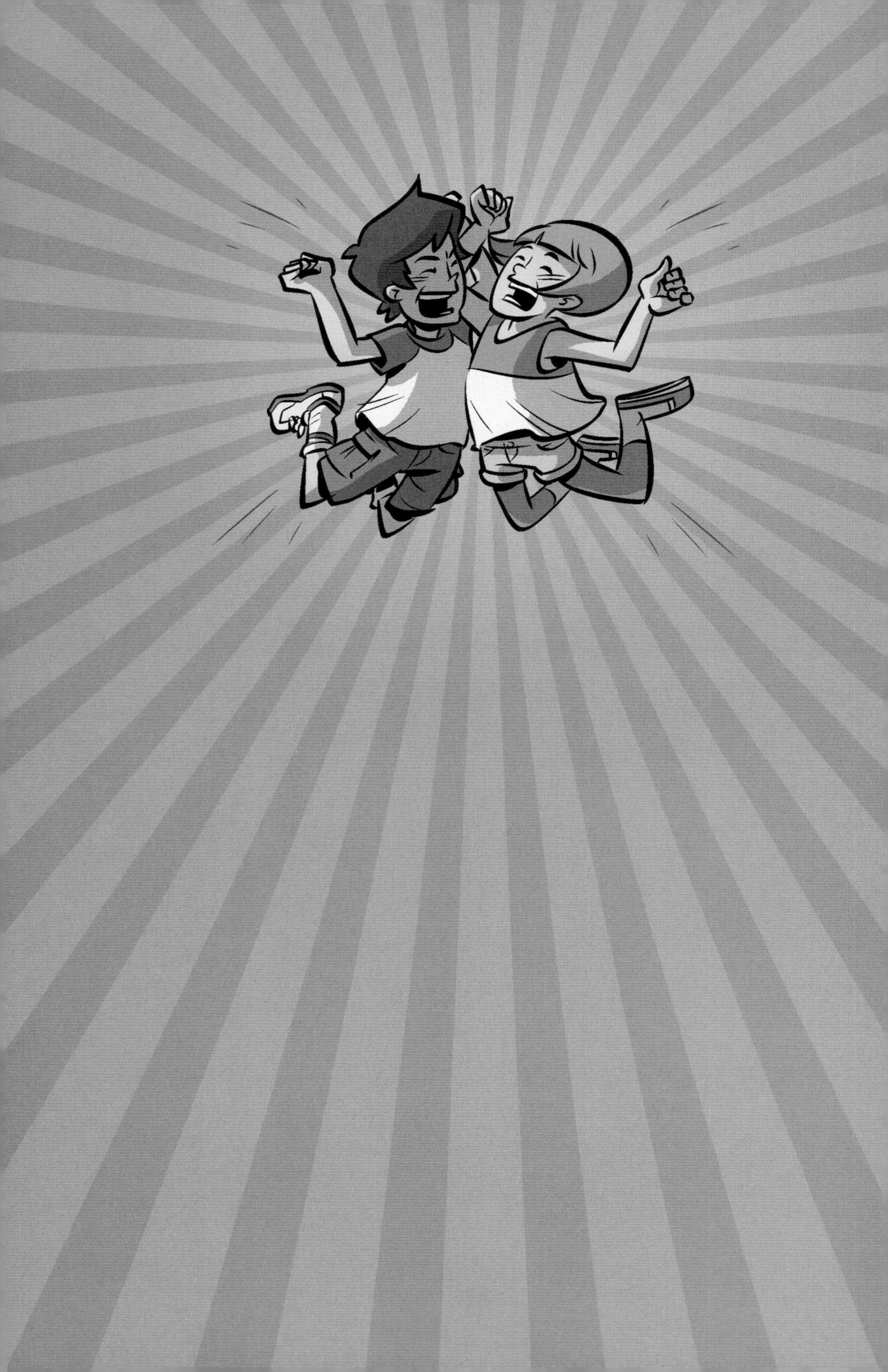

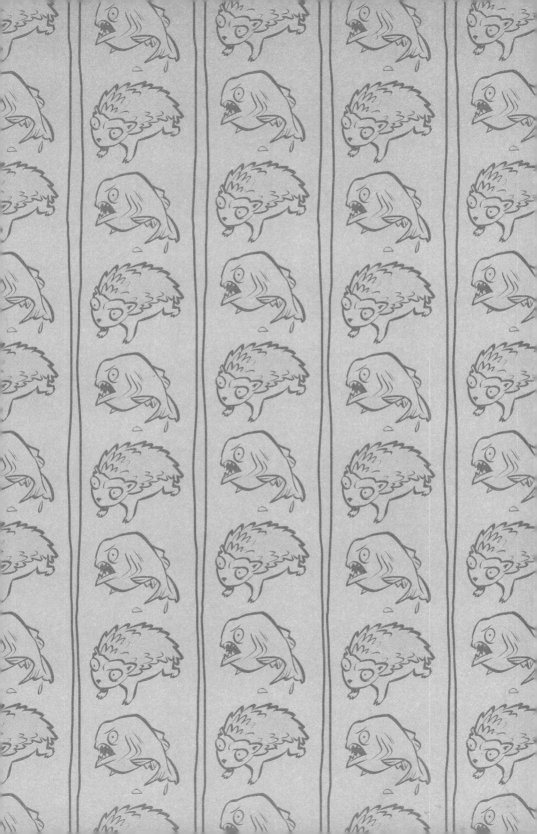